# Sculpted With Steel

## Crafting Humanity
### Book Four

*For Kathleen, Margaret and Maryclare*

# Prologue
# Re-Creation

Just sleep!

Riley pulled the pillow onto her face with force, attempting to use the feather pressure as a remedy to another sleepless night.

Her nose pressed against the stretched fabric suffocating her as  her elbows dug deep into the old mattress. She forced thoughts from her mind, willing herself to a state of complete nothingness until she felt a fluttering of her eyelids.

She relaxed for a second. Maybe this was it, she thought, hoping her brain would turn off. She let go of the pillow and replaced it under her ponytail. Darkness swirled in her vision and the thoughts flying through her brain shut off.

Beep beep beep

Riley grabbed the pillow and whipped it at the wall.

"Goddamnit!" she snarled as she slammed a hand down on her alarm.

She swung out of bed cursing whoever had decided to mess with her team's scheduling. Sending them from one side of the country to the other every other week had thrown off her internal clock.. She trounced down the stairs, avoiding the step nearest the first floor that shifted with anyone's weight.

Useless step, she thought jumping to the main floor.

She walked to the kitchen where her HOLO emitter waited, sleeping. Her unprompted scowl at the apparatus only reinforced what she knew, she hated her career.

With the coffee pot in hand she poured a cup of the steaming liquid. Light had not even begun to peek through outside and Riley thought about the days she had left on this project.

21 to go, too long. She sat in front of her emitter and waved her hand over the sleeping device, eliciting a response. The transparent glass-like surface sprang up in front of her, analyzed her biometrics, and let her inside its system.

She scanned messages, overnight work from her development team, robotic process developments, status dashboards, and the insane list of to-dos. The schedule pinned to the left side of her monitor looked like a mosaic in an old church. Peppered with greens, yellows, blues, and reds each representing a different meeting, location, or deadline. Travel plans hung at the bottom of each day's square in purple.

"Goddamnit," Riley muttered. Twenty base visits in the next twenty one days. That was going to be miserable. She brushed her future sleepless nights away from her mind and turned her focus to reviewing the robot's progress developing the controls for the latest installation. The dashboard popped up with a series of graphs and charts delivering real time analysis of the project's completeness

Riley took a sip of coffee and squinted at the screen checking on a progress report for a code deployment when her HOLO flipped off. She caught herself staring into blank air for a moment, too tired to realize her eyes were no longer focusing on anything. The power cord normally hooked up to her HOLO was not there and she searched the area racking her brain as to where she could have put it when she noticed the half empty glass of water next to the sink.

She knew who to blame. "Dad." Riley grumbled.

Sleeplessness drained her emotions and pulled at her eyelids as she made her way upstairs to her father's office. The door, per usual, sat ajar and the soft glow of a green shaded lamp emptied into the hallway. She peeked around the corner, knowing she would find an empty office, then pushed the door and stepped into her father's primary residence within the house.

Her eyes roamed the room with precision as she searched for the cord. The space held a desk, a chair, and locked file cabinets. The walls were barren except for a small colonial-era flag hanging on the wall. Grey drapes framed the chipping, white painted windows, open at the bottom, her father's aversion to air conditioning always on display.

"Even in New Orleans," Riley muttered, shaking her head at her father's stubbornness. Over a hundred degrees and seventy percent humidity could not stop him from proving his point. Beige walls ensconced the drab interior, unmistakably designed by a man whose life had been defined by military service.

Riley approached the desk, her eyes searching for the cord. The desk was as sparse as the rest of the room with sheets of paper stacked neatly on one side, a clock embedded in a crystal on the other, and a worn writing surface with a wrist protector built into the middle.
Her fingers pulled at the scratched brass knobs to the single drawer. It slid out with ease when she pulled. If there was one thing she knew about her dad, everything worked as if it were in pristine condition even if it didn't look it.

The contents of the drawer were typical, pens, paperclips, post-its. Coiled in the center of it all was her charging adapter. She dropped it into her pocket, reminding herself to guard her things more closely, especially now that her dad had begun using HOLOs. He had been against them for so long, she'd never needed to worry about sharing. Now that the military had made the plunge though, he was off to the races. He ran so many project plans for operations at once that at night it looked like a Christmas tree show. She had never seen someone take to something so quickly.

She closed the desk, and her eyes faltered for a second., Her heart quickened, more sleep?

Through her sleepy haze she pushed up from the flat leather seat and saw something she did not recognize. A flat cylindrical object floated just above the desk next to the clock.

"You're new…" Riley said. She picked it up and dropped it in the center of the desk. There were no indications or markings about how to work it. Riley chewed over ideas in her mind.

She prodded the device with her finger and was greeted by the rubberlike plastic used for most HOLO devices. There was no response. Not giving up, she tapped it, flicked it, and even tried dropping it from a short distance above the table. Nothing. Stumped and becoming frustrated she stared begrudgingly at the device. She had poured enough potential sleep time into the object when she remembered the latest update to the HOLO tech. She waved a hand over the flat black circle.

A blue light flickered to life and a fully interactive HOLO screen hovered before her eyes. She had never seen such a complex, complete, and well built piece of HOLO tech. The screen looked like the old glass displays that this new invention replaced. Her fingers brushed against the surface, surprised at the intensity of the tactical feedback. A menu with icons next to purposefully hidden words appeared. Unsure of what to do next and certain her father would not be a fan of her snooping, she clicked an icon at the bottom of the list, intending to turn off the device. Instead, the screen spread wide, melting into the background and a new room took shape around her. Six people sat behind desks, only their torsos visible.

"It's that easy Phil!" A young, slender man with wild grey eyes spoke animatedly.

"Oh is it?" said an unidentified voice.

"Yes. Believe me. We can reshape the entire Tibetan region within weeks. Imagine the possibilities, preventing earthquakes, stopping the effects of climate change, altering currents to aid areas experiencing drought. All it takes is a simple swipe and sweep of the electromagnetic nets then poof," the man's eyes twinkled as he spoke, and the intensity of his voice and facial expression took Riley back. There was something about the man she could not quite determine to be good or bad, but whatever it was felt like a lot. As if a kind of influence ran through the man's blood effortlessly.

"Thank you, Edgar, we're glad to hear the terraforming is going well."

"Much better than well," Edgar replied sitting back in his chair, "World changing."

"I believe it." The same disembodied voice spoke, and Riley looked around trying to figure out its source when she realized it was her father speaking. He must be in the seat where I am. Now tracking two of the people in the room, she turned back to the conversation.

"Marissa, when can we expect the prototypes to be ready?"

One woman in the room answered, "Going according to plan. The initial groups were very responsive to our tests, so we have complete control over them. Their handlers are still figuring out the nuances to commanding such unique machines, but every day is progress." Her black hair and manicured appearance eluded power, emphasized by the crisp, controlled delivery of each word she spoke.

"Thank you, Marissa. This is all great to hear. Who would have thought we'd be here today?" Her father's tone was one of true disbelief, a sentiment he did not offer lightly.

"What are the applications looking like in your mountains Philip?" Edgar asked. His eyes fixed trancelike on the screen. As she watched her hand slipped from its poised spot hovering above the device. The screen shifted and she found herself sitting next to Edgar looking at her father from across the room.

The shock of seeing a younger version of her father threw her. His eyes were the same flint steel , but his jawline sloped at a less severe angle and the grey covering his temples did not exist. The biggest difference was the edges of his mouth appeared as if they still knew how to smile. Riley liked the look.

"Pretty cool gotta say Edgar," her father said. His voice took on a renewed timbre and his face lit up with excitement, "I've got close to 6,000 acres of forest meshing with about every kind of ecosystem on the planet. Jungles from the equator, their vines freezing and thawing without loss it's…"

"Magical," Edgar said spreading his hands in a rainbow motion and eliciting another rare grin from her father.

"Sure."

"Building a world in the human image. So many possibilities."

"Can't get too carried away though," The older man in the room, quiet until now, spoke up. Everyone except Marissa nodded. Riley glanced at the man, and although it took a moment, realized it was the president who had led them through the Joining. His face was still vibrant, even youthful. Full of the vigor that had not only won him elections but carried him through the most tumultuous period the world had ever experienced. Riley eyed him with wonder and sorrow, already knowing what the next few decades had in store for him.

Whatever you say Marcus," Marissa said dismissively. Croyton jumped in, stopping any confrontation before the side-eye from the future president could turn into a more aggressive conversation.

"Secretary Tawles, at this point we're only testing the HOLO's ability to run the terraformers. Nothing more. Once we have the initial testing done, we can start looking at civilian applications."

"He's right Marcus. Apologies for any slight. I'm tired of…doubting the future."

Marcus raised his hands in understanding, "I get it. I do. I can't stress guard rails enough though. We know the ramifications of this kind of technology. I mean, one second we're reshaping the world, the next we're-."

"Reshaping minds?" Edgar interrupted and the room became completely silent.. Edgar smiled, but the undercurrent of sadism lurked behind his straight, white teeth. "Is that what we're worried about? Reshaping humanity's thoughts? Why?"

"Edgar…" uttered the other woman in the room in warning. Her grey streaked hair gave her the air of respected seniority, but Edgar did not seem  bothered by her words.

Something isn't right here, Riley thought, examining the faces exhibiting a shared disquiet, until she settled on her father's. His face had regained its stoic militarism and his stare forced everyone's attention back to Edgar.

"We've talked about this. It's not something we should mess with. It's a step too far."

"It's the next step in our evolution Philip. How else do we reach the pinnacle of society other than orchestrating its growth from the top? We have no hope of reaching our true heights as a species unless we can legitimately control the outcome. Weee are an experiment. That's all." Edgar's smile had changed from its disarming manipulation into a malevolent glare causing everyone in the room to look back and forth between her father and the man threatening something Riley did not understand.

"Raspin, that is a line we will not cross. Not now, not ever."

"Why? What's so wrong about it? Come on Captain."

"General now," Tawles spoke up from the side of the room, but his words were deftly ignored by the two men locked in their private battle.

"We're not meant to be the masters of people. You cannot force evolution."

"That's what you think." Edgar responded, and with his words her father's eyes became slits. He glowered at the overconfident younger man seated across the room.

"What are you talking about Edgar? What have you done?"

"Nothing as far as you're concerned. But let me ask you this, how will you keep up when the future arrives?"

"What the hell are you talking about Raspin?" Marcus broke in with frustration. "Marissa, what is going on? I thoug-"

"Don't worry about it Mr. Secretary," Edgar broke his gaze from Croyton who continued to stare, anger pouring from his eyes, "We have another meeting we're late for. I'm glad to hear the initial tests are going well," he said, readdressing Croyton with a smirk on his lips.

"Goodbye Edgar. Keep in touch," Her father said, ignoring the taunt.

Just before the screen disappeared, Edgar's smile was replaced by a mask of pure malice and Riley found herself staring at the very real face of her father watching from the doorway with his arms across his chest.

"Taking a look at the past I see?" he said walking towards the desk, taking the object, and dropping it into his pocket.

"What was that?" Riley asked.

In the blink of an eye his expression changed from that of a hardened military leader who had just been reprimanded by a subordinate to her father. Riley knew he could never treat her as one of the people under his command and, unlike anyone else in the world, she held nothing back when speaking with him. She hoped he would respond as he always did.

"That was the last time I saw the man responsible for the Melt and the architect of the BlankZone's creation."

Riley's mind spun and she counted back the decades since that meeting must have taken place. Terraforming, HOLO tech nearly 20 years ago, something about advancing society. It doesn't make sense.

"What are you talking about? What did he mean about the experiments you were running?"

Her father's face softened and he looked at the ground in thought before he spoke, "That was the beginning of the end Riley. That man, Edgar Raspin, took a technology we spent decades developing together and turned it into something reprehensible. As much as I want to, there are pieces of this I cannot discuss with you, but when the time comes, all I ask is you trust me." Her father looked at her with pleading eyes and Riley nodded. The earnest expression on her father's face could not be faked.

"I will."

"Good, now try to sleep. I cleared your calendar for a bit. You're sticking around here. I've got a new squad coming through that I want you to work with."

"What?" Riley asked, surprised, relieved, and already feeling the guilt of leaving her coworkers in the lurch, "But I have to hit twenty bases in the next month. How…?"

The General waved his hand in the air and turned to the door, "Not anymore. I need someone like you here with me. Grab a drink, relax tomorrow. We've got a lot of work to do."

The lights flipped off in the room and her father's footsteps grew softer until his bedroom door shut with the crack associated with sticky paint. The young woman stared out the window.  Her mind swirled questions mounting on top of one another until her vision blurred and her eyelids fluttered.

"I'll continue this tomorrow," she said, shaking her head and standing. Walking towards the door she braced her hand on the table, already thinking about where she'd grab her Hurricane the next day.

# PART I

# Chapter One

*CRACK! BOOM! CRACK!*

Thunderclaps grew louder with each roar. Wind buffeted James's face as noise bounced through the atmosphere pulsing the air around him as a series of flutters.

"Hold the line!" an unknown voice shouted in his earpiece. James grabbed the coil of steel rope, clenching the coarse material. Thick gloves protected his hands from the peeling metal wire, and he ducked under the taut rope to better position himself on the other side of the line.

"Ready!" he shouted into his headset, hoping the team could hear him.

He held the deck's bar with every fiber of his being as lightning illuminated the scene. Windswept water rushed in torrents against the ship. Whitecaps covered the foaming sea's surface, and dark troughs highlighted the depth of the waves on which the *Kaleidoscope* sailed. Her bow cut sharply through the ocean, rising and falling in the daunting elements.

"Flip the main!" Deck's voice fought through the storm, and James pulled the lever beneath his hand.

As he did, vents on the deck opened and a torrent of cold water rushed James's ankles.

"Main's open!" He alerted the rest of his team and crouched back under the wire, clipping himself onto one of the safety wires strung along the deck.

He held tight to the cord as wind cut into his body, pushing him into the ship's steel walls. He tongued the mouthguard of his breathing piece, always ready for the worst to happen. He glanced at the sea. Mountains of water grew by the second, their unnatural velocity intensified by the thunder and lightning bathing the world in shadows. Columns of water had started to mount higher and higher into the air, creating shadows of their own against the frothy white seawater. A massive spiral of gray liquid rose and fell, crashing back to the surface, creating more waves on impact.

*Time to get back in there*. James picked up his pace, grasping the safety cord tighter as he moved. Twenty feet later he palmed the rivets to the door.

"Outside!" he shouted, preparing to unclip.

"Come on in," Heather's voice came over the line, and light poured from the opening to the ship.

Two pairs of hands grabbed him and pulled him inside. The sound of locks securing the door gave James his first chance to relax.

The silence was the first thing he always noticed. Everything made noise in the BZ's version of the ocean-faring world.

"All good out there?" Janus stood over him holding his hand out, which James accepted, hoisting himself to his feet.

"Aye, aye, Cap," James replied. He shook water from his hair and tried to knock out the water lodged in his ear. "Nothing's going to flood this ship."

"Let's hope not." The tall, bearded captain strode away, his thick corded hair swinging down his lean back. "Should be out of this in a few hours."

"We're around if you need anything else."

Janus waved a hand over his head and disappeared through a doorway—no doubt headed back to the bridge, his near permanent home.

"Such a quiet guy," Deck said as he removed the harness from James's back. "Seafaring folk man. Strange creatures."

"Quiet isn't bad, Deck. Take a page out of his book."

"You kidding me? The amount of medication I need to walk around this goddamn death trap! It's a miracle I'm not drooling half the time, buddy."

"That's a good point," James replied, nodding. Deck's debilitating motion sickness had Bob prescribing a medley of cocktails that would make most junkies envious. But with precise measurements Bob had somehow pulled off the impossible, and their scout could function as usual. So long as he kept up with his meds. Without them, he was a mess.

"Rough out there, huh?" Heather pecked him on the cheek and threw a towel over his head.

"Those waves are something else right now."

"Next time, it's my turn," Heather said with a competitive edge in her voice.

"Next time, beat me at rock paper scissors and it's all yours." James grinned from under the towel, getting a smirk in response.

"Here, I'll help with those," Heather said, ignoring the friendly competition for a second to help peel off the top of his suit. Salt stung his skin as rivulets of water ran down his chest and abdomen.

"Cold?" Liam asked, ducking into the cramped quarters.

"A little bit actually. Thought these suits were supposed to be magic or something," James replied, inspecting the suit for tears.

"It's artificially chilled ocean air, James. No suit is ready to take on something like that," Rhia chimed in, joining the group of bodies packed into the entrance of the ship.

"Good point. Either way, I'd like to stay warm."

"And I'd like to get the hell off this goddamn ship. If wishes were horses, I'd drown one to get to shore." Teresa entered the overcrowded room. She carried James's gear to the hooks in the room on the far side of the hallway, relieving the inhabitants of her presence.

James glanced at Liam who shook his head. Teresa had been impatient to get off the ship and was not silent about her dislike of the long voyage. Janus and his crew were quiet professionals, but their tolerance was being tested.

"We'll get there, T. Don't you fear," Deck spoke cheerfully, gathering James's tank from the ground and connecting it to one of the air compressors stationed at each doorway. James handed his mask to the smiling scout who hung it dutifully next to the tank.

"Thanks, bud," James said. "And he's right, T. We're not far off."

"I'll believe it when I hear it from someone who knows what the hell they're talking about," Teresa replied. She straightened the other suits hanging from their compartments.

James shrugged at Liam who brushed away the help. *She'll be fine on dry land*, James thought as he pulled the waterproof socks off his feet.

"Anything to eat downstairs?" James asked, suddenly hungry.

"Same as yesterday." Bob's somber voice floated behind him as the medic leaned against the doorway. "We could really use Kev."

James nodded. "We certainly could."

"Come on, let's get you some food," Heather said. She grabbed James's bicep and pulled him down the hallway.

Pipes and metal planks girded the ship's walkway. Emergency masks were stationed every twenty-five to fifty feet, and alarm boxes sat poised next to them. Their glass structures gleamed in the halogen lights shining along the tight corridor.

Heather led the way with the rest of the group in tow. James followed her, winding through the maze of hallways deep into the ship. They finally came to the door with *MESS* stamped in bold block letters across the top. Heather pushed the door open, and James clambered inside after her.

Metal walls intensified the sounds of their cafeteria—voices, shouts, rustling, walking, tapping, boiling, laughing. The combination of everything in the space created a dense fog of noise. To further the confusion, rolling seas disoriented James's internal balance, making the room into a roller coaster without seatbelts.

"I'll get a tray for us," Heather said. Before James could attempt to be the gentleman, Heather disappeared into the crowd and stood in line waiting for a helping from a steaming pot of chili.

James sniffed the air, trying to distinguish between the food and the cramped bodies, but seawater and sweat were all he could detect. *Could be worse*, he thought, noticing Liam who waved at a pair of seats across the room.

"It don't matter, man. We've done this trip dozens of times now. Comms won't work out here. End of story."

"Hmmph," Rhia retorted, staring at her HOLO while her fingers moved asynchronously with the rest of her body. "That's why I'm me and you're you, Wally."

Wally waved her off. "I'm telling you, not worth it. But go ahead, waste your time. James, you look lovely right now, mate. Have a seat." Wally scooted over, making space on the bench.

James sat next to the sailor, running a hand through his hair to squeeze out the remaining liquid. "That obvious?"

"Blotchy skin, soaking wet hair, out of breath. You're either coming off a bender or were on deck releasing the flood guards." Wally grinned at James who nodded in return.

"Janus asked for some help."

"Need to learn when to scamper off to the mess. No way we're staying above water tonight."

"That's what I said," Deck interrupted, sitting across the table and muscling Rhia out of his way. "James, right? Didn't I say that?"

James rolled his eyes. Deck's infatuation with Janus's crew presented itself through constant adoration and an incessant need to be accepted by the seafaring people.

"No bother though, we can dive with them open."

James bobbed his head, unable to continue talking as hunger gnawed at his stomach.

"How much longer, Wally?" Teresa asked, flopping in a seat on the other side of Deck. Liam followed her, standing on the other side of the table and chewing his lip in annoyance.

"Teresa, my dear, as long as we make it through the Roll, we'll be fine. Two days after that, we arrive." Wally answered her without making eye contact, shoving food into his mouth and talking between bites. "Have to break the Wall first though."

"When's that happen?" Teresa asked, her eyes boring unnoticed holes in Wally's face.

The lanky sailor responded with a shrug. "No telling. Navigation out here isn't straightforward. The BZ throws magnetic waves at us knocking out any traditional instrument, and those looms produce so much goddamn moisture we don't have a way to check the stars for our course. That's why Janus lives in his bridge. Never know when you might catch a break. At the end of the day, crossing is a dangerous game of red rover."

James turned and caught a glimpse of Heather next in line with their trays. *Thank God,* James thought, turning back to the conversation, his empty stomach aching in anticipation.

"How do you do this so often?" Deck asked, the glimmer in his eyes giving away his love of the sailor's experience.

"We deal with it the same as you do on the lines, I guess. Plan for the worst, hope for the best."

"No goddamn timeline though. We keep those," Teresa grumbled, staring at the tin cup of water in her hand.

"Cheer up, T. It'll come sooner than you know. Then you'll hate it. I'm gonna grab some more grub." Wally picked up his plate and scooted off the bench, making his way to the back of the line.

"This trip sucks," Teresa reiterated, taking a sip from her water.

"Like he said, there in no time. Gotta hold on a little longer." Liam soothed his wife, rubbing her shoulders.

"Yeah, cheer up, T. Sooner than you know!" Deck quipped, oblivious to the death stare Teresa shot at him across the table.

James understood Teresa's frustration with the length of the trip. They had been at sea for more than six weeks, getting pushed, pulled, dropped, flipped, and thrown by the BZ's loom interference with the ocean. The looms, normally used to curate lands and terraform structures for the BZ military, were also used as defensive barriers for their continent. James had no idea how many looms were spread up and down the coast, but their impact was devastating. By harnessing their power, the BZ generated a tidal wave of energy compounded across half the ocean. Mass storms permanently ran at full tilt making for near-impossible crossings. The lightning, thunder, wind, waves, and currents combined to create a world of mayhem on top of the ocean. While the *Kaleidoscope* was submersible, the state of the world under the water was not a safe haven by any means. Strong tides brought on by the swirling mess above the surface drove the water underneath to act in odd ways. Underwater funnels sucked the energy from anything nearby, sending even the strongest ships to the ocean floor. On top of that, the constant waves caused a motion under the water, disrupting instruments and essentially blinding the ship when it submerged.

However, the incessant talk on the ship was about the Wall and the Roll. Wally, Kady, and other members of Janus's crew had explained both to James on countless occasions, but he was still fuzzy on the details. From what he garnered, the looms created their own tidal energy, pitching the sea into a sort of horizontal whirlpool that ran the length of the entrance to the Mediterranean. The vortex churned at a constant rate, stopping only when one of the motherships exited or entered the BZ's waters. On top of it all, they had built some sort of self-sustaining tidal wave—referred to as the Wall. The *Kaleidoscope* would need to punch through both of these to access the BZ's landmass.

When Teresa questioned the reason for not going farther north and entering the BZ over land, Wally shared an image of the former Iberian coastline. Charred earth and an endless line of Sentinels guarding the land border was all that remained. In his words, it was "certain death over land versus the probable one crossing the ocean." Time and time again James heard it was one of the most dangerous operations ever attempted in history. Whenever he heard that, James bit his tongue. None of those missions went on to destroy one of the BZ's ships from inside their borders *after* breaking through the Wall. They could not dream of the dangers he did.

"Eat up!" A tray clattered in front of him, and James's hunger exploded in a rush of energy as his brain recognized food.

He shoved a spoonful from the mound of rusty brown chili into his mouth, biting into elastic pepper skin as another quickly followed.

"Don't choke," Heather said hesitantly.

James looked at her and gave her a thumbs-up.

Heather shook her head and grinned, spooning a moderate amount of the warm stew past her lips. "Pig."

James didn't care, pushing food into his face until the pain in his gut subsided. He took a breath and turned to Heather. "I was trying to say thank you."

"I know. Still a pig." She grinned as James pushed her into Bob who was nudging the quivering mass of food around his plate.

"What's wrong, Bob?" Heather asked.

James poked her ribs, and she shot him a look, but it was too late.

"I miss Kevin's food is all."

"We'll be back soon enough," Heather replied, realizing her mistake and trying to stave off another of their medic's lament sessions.

"It's no use. Oatmeal, beans, chili—it's useless. They don't have…it. You know?" Bob asked, pleading with Heather to understand his anguish.

"We get it, Bob. You're hungry."

"It's so much more than that," Bob mumbled, dejected as he spooned a helping of chili, only to let it slide back onto the plate.

James hid his grin, but he did understand where Bob was coming from. James missed their friends himself. He would have loved Stacie on board. She would have been a nightmare for Janus and the crew with her demands, questions, and suggestions, but James believed her presence would have been valuable to their success and the ongoing success of the ship. Missing Kevin was obvious, and Kyle's simple, relaxed nature coupled with his ability to ease any situation was sorely missed. Jon's general bad attitude was happily absent, but his ability to manipulate tech and his insane level of competition with Rhia could have pushed the two of them to create a communications line that would break through the staunchest of BZ interrupters. Aside from their unique personalities and capabilities though, James missed his friends. Laughter and easy conversation were still in abundant supply, but it was different than being with the people you had lived with for over a decade.

Clint bounded up to the table. "What's happening, everyone? Bob, you still crying in your soup about Kev not being here?" His hands were covered in grease, and the sweat dotting his brow showed some serious exertion.

"You don't get it."

"Yeah, I'm sure, pal. If you're not going to…" Clint did not wait for the medic to respond before scooping his plate out from under him and taking the spoon from Bob's hand.

"Take it. I'm too sad to eat," Bob said, lying his head on the table.

"Suck it up, bud. I think we're almost there."

James's ears perked up. "You hear something from Janus?"

Clint shook his head. "Nah, but Kady and I've been going over the engines all day now. He had Stefi toss extra fuel in the engine block too. Can't be long."

A surge of adrenaline ran through James's stomach. He was as ready as everyone else to get off the boat, but he couldn't show it, not liking the message it would send.

"Thanks for the intel," James said demurely, hiding his building excitement.

"Hell yes, get off this fucking boat," Teresa exclaimed, slapping the table. "About ti—"

"ALL HANDS, ALL HANDS, ALL HANDS! WALL APPROACHING! REPEAT: ALL HANDS! WALL APPROACHING."

"Guess it's time." Clint winked and tipped Bob's bowl back into his mouth. The bulky mechanic scooped the rest of the chili down with grease-stained hands and ran out the door.

"Time for the show." Wally's voice accompanied a pair of rough hands grabbing James's shoulders.

As James rose to his feet, the lights in the room turned red, and a bell sounded in the background. Everything morphed into a single point, and James headed to the door. His thoughts focused on his next steps, but the moment they

had been waiting for had finally arrived. They were at the
Wall.

# Chapter Two

Red light clung to the dull metal walls of the ship's interior.

A pulse of energy radiated in the air. Janus's crew walked with deliberate footsteps. Each had a role in the organized chaos growing with every passing second.

Adrenaline coursed through James's veins as he followed Wally through the tight corridors. At every turn a new group of sailors passed them. James noted the innate movements of the men and women aboard the ship. At each doorway Wally stopped with perfect timing, dancing in choreographed steps leading to a cataclysmic moment of unsurmountable danger.

As they raced up the final staircase to the deck, James saw their captain don one of the many breathing devices hanging throughout the corridor. Noticing the group charging up the steps, he tossed two at Wally who deftly snatched them and passed them back to Heather.

"Listen to instructions out there. We're about to hit the Roll, and if things aren't timed exactly right, there's nothing we can do to help you, got it?" Janus's calm delivery was unchanged, but his somber tone underscored the danger of the moment.

"Yessir," James said, yanking a breathing device from the wall and pulling his suit up from around his waist.

"Where do you want us?" Heather asked, zipping her suit and turning to help Deck with his.

"Stay with Wally. Keep to the lines and don't unclip. We need to catch the wind and dive. Wally?"

"Yes, Captain?" Wally replied.

"Make sure they get inside once the wings are done."

"Aye, Captain."

Janus nodded at his crew member and disappeared. James watched the tall figure make his way back up to his perch on the bridge. *How many times has he done this?* James wondered as he slipped the foam rubber mask over his mouth and nose. He cinched the corded wire behind his head and looked around the room. Wally, hands planted on his hips, waited for everyone to finish. His calm demeanor impressed James, and he made a note to stick close to the lanky crewmember.

When Bob finished securing his mask, he gave a thumbs-up to Wally who turned to address his crew.

"Alright, so as you might have assumed, we've hit the Roll. We need to get up to the highest speed possible to get under it. To do that we're going to pop the wings, retract them before we hit the deck, gun our engines as we enter the water, barrel through the whirlpool, and finally break through to breach the Wall on the other side. Easy stuff.

"Our job is to get those wings open. They'll give us the lift we need off the water. Then, we close the wings and go below. Then we hit the Roll. When you get back inside, strap in or grab hold of something for dear fuckin' life. We're going to be tossed like you'd never believe. Any questions?"

"How'll we know if we made it?" Liam asked.

"You'll be alive. Anything else?"

Quiet tension met his question.

"Listen to instructions. Everyone on this ship has a job to do. We do ours so that everyone else lives through this. See you on the other side." Wally winked at the team as he turned the lever to the exit hatch.

A scream of wind tore through the steel room as Wally stepped through the opening into the storm.

"See you back here." Heather winked at James pulling her torso through the opening.

James took a deep breath and followed Heather's tight braid. The wind ripped into his suit. Its strength created a semi-parachute with the skintight material, and James clipped onto the safety line. Once secure, he looked over the side of the ship, stunned at what he saw.

Although hail and rain slammed into his face with unparalleled speed, it was impossible to miss the churning water raging hundreds of yards below.

The ship perched on the crest of a wave, and a sideways vortex of water swallowed the sea, sucking every bit of the surface into its fury before crashing back into itself. James was blown away by the sheer force of nature.

He imagined the crushing power generated by the constantly swirling water, feeding from a self-sustained source.

"James! You good?" Deck's voice crackled over his earpiece and a hand tapped his shoulder.

"Yeah, I'm on it," James said, snapping out of his momentary lapse in concentration.

"Good, thought you had a stroke. Or peed yourself. No one likes to walk in pee-pants."

James continued in Heather's footsteps trying to dislodge the uncomfortable thought of urine-soaked pants from his mind.

Wally stopped and turned to face the group.

"Space out five feet apart up and down these railings. You've all seen the wings automatically come out, but the winds are too strong up here for our engines to pull double duty both pushing us forward and operating the wings. We're the engine. The crew who followed us are out on the tips as stabilizers and guides. Do everything I say and we'll get back inside safe and dry. Ready?"

James glanced at the trio of crew members standing by each wing release. He couldn't see their faces through the elements, but he knew he'd find the stoic masks of Janus's crew. Blank faced and prepared.

"Heather, get to port, and James, you set up behind me. The rest of you fan out to either side. I'll lead the starboard side."

James did as he was told and gripped the railing. Janus had turned the ship into a precarious position, riding the top of the wave at a precise speed, balancing on top of the world. As the rest of the team took their places James glanced at the gaping maw of the sea below and watched as it churned into a wrath of foaming water.

He looked back and saw Bob give a thumbs-up, signaling his place at the back of the line.

"Starboard ready!" Wally shouted, eyeing Heather's line. "Port ready!"

Wally stood tall as the wing guides formed parallel lines between them. The six black-clad figures stood poised, waiting their turn. James noticed their feet remained in place

as the ship bucked and kicked against the heavy surf under
the ship.

"Heather, James, grab the lines," Wally said over the
intercom. James watched Heather pick up the steel-
reinforced rope threaded down the bow of the ship as Wally
fed an identical cord to him to pass behind to Rhia who
handed it back to Bob.

James stood tense with the heavy rope in his arms as
rain pelted his face with renewed ferocity. The saltwater
stung his eyes, filling the sockets and creating fuzzy
apparitions of the people around him, but he knew his job.
Pull.

"Engines ready?" Janus's voice crackled over
James's earpiece.

"Aye, Captain," Kady's voice replied over the radio.

"Release the wings."

"Release the wings!" Wally cried and tugged at the
rope. James followed suit, seizing on the cord as hard as he
could to keep up with the experienced sailor leading their
team.

"Heave! Heave! Heave! Heave!" Wally called out
with each pull, keeping the team in rhythm. After twenty full
pulls of the cord Janus's voice returned. "We're a third out.
Wing stabilizers begin descent."

The first crew member in each line stepped nimbly
onto the steel railing and without hesitation stepped off and
plunged from view. Aghast, James gritted his teeth to keep
his jaw from dropping.

After fifteen more pulls, Janus's voice came back.
"Second team, you're up."

The next two followed over the railing, dropping
from sight, leaving in their place a torrent of wind and rain
blowing against the dark black sky.

"Turning into the Roll. Teams, prepare to hold the
wings."

"Five more, mates!" Wally shouted, ripping the cord
into James's hands with renewed vigor.

"Final stabilizers off." Janus's instructions sent the
last of the black-clad crew members over the railing.

Simultaneously Wally turned to them. "Clip in and hold on. We'll pull them back in on the captain's command."

James nodded, knowing his gesture was unseen. He sensed a change in position as the bow of the ship turned perpendicular into the crest of the wave and the earth shifted vertically.

His stomach floated into his chest and his heart took up residence in his throat as the ship tipped into the mountainous face of the wave. James gripped the railing and looked over the side. There on the wing, spread out in twenty-foot intervals, hung the crew members, holding the structure in place and thereby directing the ship's only source of protection and keeping it from flying away into the water and leaving no chance of surviving the descent.

"Keep close to the rails for the next round, team," Wally said over the earpieces. They had just finished pulling over three hundred feet of steel rope, but the seasoned sailor wasn't the slightest bit winded. James's arms and lungs burned as he pushed the limits of his breathing tubes.

From his new position James could see the rest of the process, and he steadied himself while catching his breath for the next round.

As they skated farther and farther down the mountain of water, their speed picked up. James guessed they were three hundred yards from the surface of the Roll, and gnawing angst clawed at his stomach when Janus's calm voice returned.

"Flip the levers.

A *clunk* and a *thud* sounded under James's feet as the pulley system reversed course.

"Retract."

"Pull!" Wally's voice spurred James to action, and he gripped the cord with everything he had.

As he heaved on the rope, the wing tips folded back into the ship. In the meantime, new crew members dropped from farther down the ship to the wings. They attached themselves to the backs of the human stabilizers nearest the ship and waited until they were within feet of the steel walls, winching away at the last possible second to avoid a bone crushing death.

As the wings disappeared inside the ship, their speed picked up, unimpeded by their drag.

"Engines fire." Janus ordered, and a hum erupted underfoot.

Now the wind that tore at James's face was caused by the ship's speed as much as from the storm, and James witnessed the success of the second daring rescue.

"Ten to go!" Wally's voice gave a final plea to the team and James ignored the burn in his forearms that had already turned his shoulders to rubber. They needed to finish.

James glanced out at the wing tip where the last stabilizer held onto the dense, metallic fabric. The pressure from the wind tore at the sailor with a ferocity James could only imagine.

As James became certain the final stabilizer would be torn from the post, a new figure appeared and latched on. James breathed a sigh of relief as the two rose swiftly when suddenly a rogue wave clipped the edge of the wing. The instability sent the two bodies slamming into the side of the hull. The shadow figures bounced like rag dolls from the hit and fell into the teeth of storm.

"Two down in the rescue. Wings inside," Wally reported coolly over the radio. He dropped his cord and turned to the team. "Inside! Move!"

There was no time to wonder or hope the crew members were alive. The decision had been made, and James turned to the hatch. A light erupted in the inky black, and within seconds he stumbled inside nearly running over Rhia.

James fumbled in the red light, tugging at the straps of his mask and wiping the salt, sweat, and rain from his forehead.

"Grab hold of something!" Wally shouted, his voice bouncing off the metal walls, while he bent his tall frame over to pull up one of James's friends, clipping into one of the breathing device holds. "Hook up wherever you can and make sure you have something to grab onto. Get ready for the ride."

Mimicking their guide, James looped his cord around a pipe and attached his carabiner, securing himself as

Janus's voice came over the intercom. "Ship, ready for dive."

A palpable sense of apprehension filled the room as they prepared for what came next. Although outwardly ready, a ball of muscle in Wally's jawline heightened James's concern.

James waited, counting heartbeats and watching his team. The imminent peril Wally had warned of didn't seem to be occurring

"Ummm, did we miss it?" Deck asked, eyeing their seasoned guide, expressing the confusion shown on James's and the rest of the team's faces. "I mean, I kind of expect—"

*WHAM!*

James's back hit the ceiling, and the cinch he was holding tore at his wrist and cut open the back of his hand. In the next second, the ship flipped again and a roar of twisting metal sounded as James rolled over smacking his face into the side of a pipe.

Blood filled his mouth, and James suspended in midair while the ship rocked back and forth.

James's brain spun in his skull as another jolt of movement tore its way through the steel encased room, slamming his legs into the piping on the ceiling. The pain in his shins stung as if shards of broken glass had embedded into his bones.

"Exiting Roll," Janus announced interrupting the violence of the moment and James braced for another impact.

Tasting iron on his tongue, he gritted his teeth and clenched his fists around the steel pipes with all his strength.

"Hold on!" Wally's voice broke through the roar of the ocean battering the walls of the ship. Hardly believing he could hear their crew guide, but without hesitation, James clung for dear life.

Glancing across the room, he saw Heather doing the same, and catching his eye with a grin, gave him a much needed sense hope as the ship emitted a mind-numbing shudder, landing in a state of uncontrolled gravity.

"Prepare for Wall breach." Janus's voice returned over the speakers. Wally moved swiftly across the empty space. James unclipped from the pipe and followed unsteadily wiping blood from his mouth with his shirt and holding the open wound on his wrist. He felt a hard object in his mouth and spit on the ground.

*Ping*

A piece of James's tooth bounced on the ground and ran into the wall. He gummed the spot at the back of his mouth and winced upon feeling the exposed nerve ending.

"Are you spitting on the ground now?" Deck asked, a layer of disgust coating his words, "Revolting."

"It was my tooth," James said, pulling out his cheek and revealing the shattered molar.

"A gentleman swallows his blood, James," Deck said with an air of self-righteousness showing his own bloodied lips. "I think I'm going to need stitches actually. Hey, Bob!"

"One second, Deck." Bob's voice came from the huddle of bodies near the door.

Concerned, James and Deck approached the group. Teresa lay on the ground, her eyes lolling to the side. A thin dribble of blood ran down her forehead and a small pool of the crimson liquid dripped from her ear.

"Minor hit on the head at first but then looks like she got a few raps during the second breakthrough." Wally said with confident experience.

"Will she be alright?" Liam asked with a steady voice, concern plaguing his face.

"She'll be fine. A little woozy and concussed, but okay," Bob said, pulling her into a sitting position, "Wally, what can we expect with the dive?"

"Not a dive. It's a climb. Then, the breach."

"Breach?" Heather asked from behind James. "Like, through?"

"See for yourself," Wally said, pointing at the porthole. "You ever wonder why we have guns on this sucker?" Wally simulated shooting a gun at his hand using the other. "If we hit the wave right, we break through and come down the other side. There's no way to top the wall. Not enough energy in the fucking world to climb that beast, especially after the Roll. We'll get about halfway up, whip the ship around, fire a shot in front of us, and power through into a dive on the other side."

"Excuse me, what was that, Wally old pal?" Deck asked, his face colorless from the description and Wally clapped him on the shoulder.

"You're gonna love it, mate."

Speechless, James gawked at the crew member. *Why didn't I ask how this worked?* James wondered, embarrassed at his lack of preparation and again wishing for Stacie's questioning presence.

"How the hell are we supposed to pull that off?" Deck asked, panic entering his tone.

Wally snorted. "*We*." He shook his head, "Janus isn't a genius for nothing. You all strap in up front and get a good view. It'll be a coup—"

"Ready for breach. Engines fire."

Wally winked at the team with a grin on his face. "It'll be a couple of seconds. I'll get her up there. You should see this."

# Chapter Three

Heather took the space on James's right side with Rhia occupying his left. The slender tech's fists were balled in the empty area between their seats. Her knuckles were white, but her face remained unperturbed.

"Initiating climb in ninety seconds."

Janus's calm intonation had not changed since they began the process of entering the Roll. James was becoming concerned for their captain's mental health. To experience something like this on a regular basis couldn't be healthy. *They're built different*, James reasoned intoning Deck's words.

"All strapped in?" Wally asked walking past with Teresa slung over his shoulder in a fireman's carry. He placed her in one of the seats, her head lolling against her chest as he secured her torso.

James gave a thumbs-up. "Ready."

"Good stuff. Heather, would you and Liam make sure T keeps her neck steady during the ride?" Wally asked, trying unsuccessfully to keep her chin from drooping.

"You got it," Heather replied. She secured her friend's head back, pointing her chin at the ceiling while Liam finished getting prepped.

"We're locked in here, Captain," Wally spoke into his earpiece.

"Twenty seconds to climb," Janus responded, not acknowledging the message, laser focused on the job ahead.

James looked at Deck sitting next to Rhia. The medically induced glow normally present on the chipper scout's face had changed to a greenish hue.

"You alright, Deck?" James asked apprehensively.

"Honestly, I've been better, James. Any more of my cocktail, Bob?"

"Sorry, man, it's in the bunks."

"Huh. Well, that is unfortunate." Deck said, clawing his legs in a tight pincer grip.

"Starting climb."

"It'll be okay, Deck. Focus on the horizon."

"What horizon?"

As if on cue, the steel blinds opened displaying another awe-inspiring sight.

A two-hundred-foot high tidal wave with an incomprehensible power and shape towered above them. *How the hell does the BZ keep doing this?* James wondered.

"Ah, *that* horizon. I do not think that will help," Deck quipped.

"Engines, half power."

"Aye, Captain," Kady replied, and the ship lurched forward, pressing into the vertical unknown.

"Deck, close your mouth and swallow. If anything comes up, I swear to God…" Rhia said through clenched teeth.

"I'll do my best," Deck replied weakly.

"Three-quarter power."

"Aye, Captain."

Another jump forward confirmed the increased speed. The combination of gravity and the ship's thrust driving them upward forced James back into the cushions.

"Prepare cannons."

"Cannons ready," an unknown crew member replied.

"Reverse engines."

"Reversing engines."

At the change in direction, James momentarily became suspended in space with the seat straps holding him in place.

"Turning ship in five, four, three, two, one."

Another shudder rippled through the ship, and upon turning 180 degrees James's vision of the dark gray sky centered on the base of the tidal wave. His shoulders strained against his companions as the restraints once again brought him back to center.

A gurgle escaped from Deck's lips as they finished the turn, and James hoped his friend could hold on a few moments longer.

"Fire cannons." Janus's now familiar calm during the tumultuous situation brought on by the intensity of the swinging ship gave James a sense of unexpected serenity.

"Firing."

*BOOM! BOOM! BOOM!*

The erupting charges shook the ship, and James followed Rhia's lead, gripping the seat. Vibrations from the explosives traveled up his arms, and Heather grasped his hand, staring intensely out the window while still supporting her friend's chin with her other hand.

The missiles penetrated the wave-created vacuum, forming a watery abyss.

"Engines full speed."

"Engines full speed."

"Ready for dive and turn."

As they approached the empty surface of the wave, James clenched his teeth. The newly created hole grew smaller by the second. *How are we going to make this?*

The ship slid farther down the mountain of water, speeding towards the breach in the wave. James held his breath, watching the diminishing target until Janus's calm once again broke into the calamity.

"Diving."

Suddenly they barreled into the empty chasm. James found himself suspended upside down inside the wave, hurtling towards the bottom of the ocean.

"Flipping in three, two, one. Fire engine boost."

"Firing!" Kady yelled, fully engrossed in the final moment of their ocean crossing.

With a decisive twist, the engines drove them forward while the rudder flipped the ship upright and straight through the wave a mere fifty feet under the ocean's surface and into the calm waters marking the entrance to the Mediterranean.

"How's everyone doing?" Wally asked, interrupting the momentary silence that had settled over the group.

Trying to comprehend what transpired, James looked at Heather who was taking deep breaths. He slipped his hand into hers, addressing Wally. "All good, I think. T is still out."

"I'll get her downstairs. Bob can take a better look at her. You okay, Deck?" Wally asked nervously.

"Hmmm." Deck nodded staring ahead. He glanced around the room with deliberate calm, refusing to answer.

"You sure, buddy?" James asked, noticing the odd behavior and getting flashbacks of their trips through the Southern Federation's mountain ranges.

"Hmmm," Deck replied, standing, his movements becoming more frantic as he walked around the tight space.

"Deck, come on, let's get—" Bob tried to intervene, but it was too late. Deck ran to a corner, opened his mouth, and let out a torrent of vomit. A rush of rank odor swept through the confined space.

"Oh, Christ, Deck," Rhia said, holding the crook of her arm over her nose.

Leaning against the wall with his head hanging, Deck turned back to Rhia, and said "You told me to keep my mouth shut, right?"

"Thank you?" Rhia said, holding back her own dry heaves.

"You're welcome. Now, everyone, leave me here. James, my friend?"

"Yeah, Deck?"

"I'm going to stay here and throw up a bit more. Could you bring me a bucket when you get a chance?"

"My pleasure," James replied.

"Good man."

# Chapter Four

For more than a month, James had endured one of the most tumultuous travel experiences of his life. Constant waves, intense storms, dives, drops, and short flights down cascading mountains of water. However, the extremes of that world compared to the serenity of the Mediterranean made James wonder if they were on the same planet.

He stood at the bridge with Kady and Clint, looking at the dark bottom of the sea through reinforced windows. The *Kaleidoscope* traveled stealthily, moving with careful precision. The crew monitored their sensors, watching for patrols lurking in the tranquil waters.

"See now?" Kady pointed at the monitor with a grease-stained finger. "Circling around up there. No clue we're here."

"How? That seems unlike the BZ," James said, leaning closer to the screen. An infrared image of a patrol boat passed overhead, and James's stomach tightened.

"Part sensor depth and part our jamming efforts," Kady said as she fiddled with the dashboard. "I started going on these crossings six years ago, but in the early days it was all trial and error. Janus and the original captains tried everything. Deep crossings were always spotted and higher crossings were detected regardless of the jammers they used. A few ships even tried outrunning the BZ." Kady turned and rolled her eyes and removed a panel to continue her work. "Those years were a complete crapshoot and mostly luck getting ships into the harbor. Soldering iron, please, Clint?"

A bulky forearm handed the implement to his engineer counterpart. "Who figured it out?"

"Janus's wife, Tina. Fucking genius, that one."

"Where's she now?" James asked.

"Lost in the deep. Her ship flipped at the end of the Roll, and they couldn't right themselves in time. Crashed into the Wall."

James's heart stung for Janus's loss. "That's awful."

"Yep, it's why Janus doesn't leave the bridge during the crossing. To him, his wife was the best person to ever captain one of these steel beauties. If he lets up for a second, it's over."

James nodded. He understood the captain's need for control.

"Are we going to go this slow the whole goddamn time? Feel like we'd limit potential exposure if we kicked it up a notch," Clint said, eyeing the speed pilot system Janus could use as an override if the engine order telegraph was unavailable.

"Jammers lose their effectiveness if we do. Slow and steady wins the race. Keeps us from getting blown out of the water by the BZ," Kady replied. Finished with her work, the engineer popped the cover back on the dashboard. She inspected her handiwork and tested the controls before piling gear into her bag. "Besides, we'll be there in no time."

"Be nice to know what *there* is," James said. Since entering the calm waters, he had tried unsuccessfully to get an answer out of Janus, Wally, Kady and every other member of the crew. They were tight-lipped regarding the final destination.

"Sorry, James. Captain's orders. You know how it is."

"I wish I did. Deck tells everything I say to everyone," James replied.

"He does have a boundaries problem," Clint added. He picked up Kady's tool bag and handed it to her. She dropped the soldering iron in and zipped it up. Although she stood an inch over James, her short height, relative to the rest of the crew, made her an ideal engineer for Janus's ship. Tattoos in languages and shapes that would take James years to untangle ran up and down her arms, licking the edges of her collarbone peeking from under her thermal shirt.

"I've noticed," Kady said with a grin. "He still puking everywhere?"

"No. Bob got him back on the meds," Clint replied, following Kady as she walked from the bridge.

"That's good. The smell was something else."

James stopped to look at the stretch of thick glass separating him from the crushing water beyond. Darkness engulfed the ship and James glanced up, imagining the sunlight above.

*Soon enough, man*, James thought, jogging to catch up with Kady and Clint.

The atmosphere on the ship had relaxed since hitting the bottom of the sea. Mess took on the quality of a café rather than the eating quarters of a military vessel and tasks were now pressure-free routines. James appreciated Janus's attitude towards the ship's demeanor when they weren't under immediate threat. His strict adherence to watching for BZ surveillance made James even more at ease and he found himself enjoying the ride.

James tailed Clint's wide shoulders to the rec room where people hung out when they weren't tending to their daily activities. Inside, Heather and Teresa focused on a chess board. Teresa's hand hovered over a bishop shaped like a dolphin. Most of her pawns—or goldfish figurines in this set—were held hostage by Heather who was only a few moves from check with her mermaid queen close to dismantling T's crowned octopus king.

"Come on, T, you're screwed," Heather muttered.

"You'd love for me to give up,"

"Yes! It's been an hour of you running from me on the board. Let me have this one."

"Hmmmm…" T's face scrunched with concentration as she moved her dolphin. When her hand left the piece, Heather moved with speed, knocking the ebony dolphin over with a seahorse.

"Check," Heather said, yawning for effect.

"Stupid bitch," Teresa grumbled under her breath, furrowing her brow.

"What's that?" Heather asked with a cocky smirk. James had been beaten by her enough to know Teresa didn't have a shot, but he secretly rooted for the stocky commander all the same. *Come on, T,* James thought, standing behind his girlfriend on the opposite side of the board.

"Wrapping up?"

"About to," Heather replied. "Want next?" she asked, turning around to him.

"I'll wait until later. Thanks though," James replied. He wanted nothing less than to be demolished in chess.

"She's taking advantage of people with brain injuries, James. Competitive animal," Teresa whined.

"Oh, suck it up."

Teresa, narrowing her eyes in resolve, hovered a hand over the lighthouse that represented a rook. At the last second she changed her mind and shifted her final seahorse knight into one of Heather's bishops, knocking it off the board.

"HA!" Teresa triumphed.

Without skipping a beat, Heather removed Teresa's seahorse from the board with one of her lighthouses.

"Checkmate," she said with mock innocence.

"I hate you," Teresa muttered. She stood and walked from the room, holding a hand to her head. "Giving a concussed woman a headache."

"Good game!" Heather cried gloatingly.

"Fuck you!" came the retort from the hall as Wally and Deck entered the room.

"Heather playing chess, I take it? And ahh yes," Wally said, grinning as he saw Heather breaking down the board.

"You want a round?"

"Not a chance in hell, my dear lass," Wally said, walking past her to Kady. "You fix the dashboards on the bridge?"

"All set," Kady answered, turning to greet her crewmate.

"Any action out there?"

Kady shook her head. "Surface patrol, but nothing underneath."

"What happens if there's something underneath?" Heather asked, rearranging the pieces on the chessboard.

"Ever heard of evasive maneuvers?" Wally asked. He sat across from Heather who stared at him trying to make eye contact for a game.

"Of course," Heather replied, giving up her glare.

"Well, we don't do those," Wally said, leaning back in his chair. "This monstrosity is a bear to move in tight spaces, so if someone comes too close to us, we sit on the bottom of the ocean, turn off the power, and wait."

"That's it?" James asked, surprised by Wally's answer.

"That's it. Other ships used to flee or fight. Waiting them out is safest. It's like those fish that sit with their mouths open waiting for smaller fish to swim in. Difference is, we want the fish to stay the hell away from us."

James nodded and imagined the feeling of terror sitting on the bottom of the sea in a steel coffin, hoping enemy patrols leave you alone. He shook his head to remove the sense of being hunted.

"James! Where the hell have you been?" Deck asked, entering the rec room.

"All over the place, man. Swam up for a peek at the surface with Kady and Clint."

"Not funny. Anyway, Janus is looking for you," Deck said, brushing off James's jab.

"Yeah, yeah, yeah." James waved off the scout. Since they had been on the bottom of the sea, Janus had avoided James, who questioned him about their destination every time they were in the same room. He had finally reasoned that the captain would call him when there was any news.

"No, really. He's at the bridge," Deck said. He sat across from Heather. He picked up a piece and turned it in the air. "How do you play this game?"

"I just came from the bridge. He's there?"

"You've never played?" Heather asked, eyeing her next victim with interest.

"A few times but could use a refresher. Maybe a practice round?"

"Deck!" James said, raising his voice to get the scout's attention. "What did Janus want?"

"Said to meet him there. Now what are these little guys?" Deck asked. He picked up one of the goldfish pawns.

"I think you'll like chess," Heather said. The hunger in her voice was unmistakable, and James knew getting more out of Deck now was pointless.

"I'm gonna go find the captain."

"Have fun," Deck said, waving over Heather's head.

"Yeah, go get 'em, honey," Heather added.

*Supportive group*, James thought, shaking his head as he exited the room.

He made it to the bridge in record time, trying to control his gate to avoid breaking into a run. He did not want to appear in front of Janus in a full sweat. In the glass-walled room, Janus stood in front of the ceiling-high windows, gazing at the watery depths.

Stepping heavily as he entered to get the captain's attention, James was rewarded by the stoic man turning to greet him.

"Thanks for coming," Janus said in his calm tone, pointing to the space next to him.

"Happy to. Thought you might have some news for me."

Janus grinned, a facial expression James had witnessed infrequently on their cross-ocean voyage.

"The general mentioned you were an eager person. Driven. I get it."

"He trained me and chose me."

"That he did." Janus nodded, returning his attention to the outside world. Sounds of the ship's devices echoed in the room. James watched the water with the sailor waiting for him to continue. He was in awe of the fact that they inched along the seafloor hundreds of feet below the surface while crews of BZ sought them with instruments for once incapable of penetrating *their* defenses. It felt good.

"You are about to join a unique group of individuals, James. Very few have left the Federation after the Melt and entered the BZ. Fewer have lived to tell about it."

"That's why I figured it should be me. I don't want to put people at risk without first putting myself on the line."

"Understood and noble, James. But I didn't call you up here to remind you of the dangers of the BlankZone. You know the threats they pose better than anyone in the Federation, and I'm not versed enough to give anyone advice about that."

"Oh, okay. I guess we're almost there?" James was confused. He had expected a lecture about the need to be careful, the same sentiments expounded to him by Stacie, his mother, Croyton, Dolly, and anyone else who felt the need to give an opinion. Although thrown off, the acknowledgement of his prowess as wholly capable was refreshing.

"We are." Janus paused and turned to James. He glanced at the floor, then back up with an intense gaze. "James, not sure if you knew it, but I'm not originally from the Federation. A lot of the people on this ship aren't. Wally and Kady hail from the land down under. Julian's a Southern Federation holdout. Some Kiwis, a few more Aussies—heck, there are six people who escaped from Africa right after the Melt."

He glanced out the window again. "I'm from where all this started. Behind the veil of the BlankZone. I was on a ship serving my country when the attack began. When the Melt happened, we were front line, Tina and me. The end of our country—it was…" Janus's voice trailed off and James bowed his head, reading the heaviness.

After a moment, Janus composed himself and looked back at James, the fierce stare returned in full force. "We're connecting you with the spies in two days. They're all interior BlankZone, having broken out of the confines of their lives through some means or another. No two are the same, but their intentions are pure and simple, and they share a singular purpose. They are on this earth to destroy the BlankZone. Nothing else matters to them."

"Good. We'll get along," James said, nodding.

Janus shook his head. "They are fighting a different war than you. Their mission is the complete annihilation of the BlankZone and all it stands for. Yours is about removing a foreign invader. Their goal is to dismantle a society that replaced theirs. While your objectives align, they may not be the same. Do you understand?"

James was confused, and he shook his head slightly. "We both want the same end. Destroy the BlankZone and everything it stands for."

Janus smile returned, but it was sad this time, layered with a pain of misunderstanding James could not comprehend. "Remember I told you is all. They've been fighting this war longer than you know. Keep that in mind while you embark on your mission. If anyone can do that, I've been told by many, it's you. And after getting to know your team, I believe it too." Janus emphasized his statement with a nod and stuck out his hand.

The captain shook James's hand with a finality and vigor that belied his slender build.

"I'll keep that in mind."

"Good. These are smart people, James. They will be able to help you."

James nodded and grinned, now hiding his thoughts behind a smile as the captain looked back at the depths.

"Get some rest. We'll pull into the channel by this evening. You'll be busy once we get there."

"Thank you, Captain" Janus nodded at James who stopped and turned to face the captain again before walking out of the room, remembering Kady's story from earlier.

"Janus, I'm sorry about your wife," he said.

The captain turned from the window, a pained expression in his eyes. "Thank you."

James nodded again and left the captain staring at the ink black water as they churned onward deep beneath their enemy.

# Chapter Five

"Half ahead."

Janus's calm command guided the ship alongside the stratified cavern walls through which the *Kaleidoscope* swam.

"Where the hell are we?" Deck voiced the question everyone else was thinking as they glided next to the hewn rock walls.

Their trip had changed dramatically. Stationed in the same room where they had watched Janus command the breach of the Wall, the team stood face-to-face with the glass, staring in wonder at another remarkable reveal beneath the water's surface.

The channel was an ancient waterway underneath the BZ landmass that extended the waters of the Mediterranean. Millions of years in the making, its walls were composed of dissolved and eroded rock rendered smooth from the constant rush of water that had filed the edges, creating the monstrosity under the world's surface. As they continued, the water level dropped, and Janus pulled the *Kaleidoscope* to the surface. Their deck lights flooded the cavern, and the team stood for hours on the partially submerged vessel staring at the mineral-rich ceiling reflecting light back at them as if it was the sun.

For the final part of the journey, they gathered in the windowed holding room beneath the bridge watching the bottom of the ocean. James's mind was focused on the mission, but he hoped it would not be the team's last time gazing at the seafloor.

"How doesn't the BZ know about this?" Heather asked, her fingers pressing against the glass as they passed a strip of emerald-colored rock reflecting its green aura back in through their windows. "I mean, this is beautiful but..."

"A security issue," Wally chimed in, nodding, as he finished her thought. "We didn't know it existed until the war started. Janus found it on one of his trips. He was trapped by a few of the BZ's patrol boats and happened upon a cave that never ended. You'd be surprised what risks you'll take exploring if you don't care about coming back."

"Where's it go?" James asked, staring at yellow swirls embedded in a new formation of stratified rock.

"The heart of it all. The center of the entire Resistance movement against the BZ. Janus and the leadership reasoned this would remain safe as long as they needed it to. Thousands of years exploring the seas and no one had found it. Safe bet the BZ wasn't gonna start spelunking, mate."

"Is there another entrance?" James asked, unable to wrap his mind around the mystery.

"Nothing significant. Or at least that we know of. This is the farthest I've gone. Could go on for miles really." Wally shrugged. "I stopped trying to figure it out a long time ago. Like to enjoy it now is all." The sailor sat in his seat and gazed out the window contentedly. James liked the attitude of the seasoned crewmember, still able to appreciate the cavern after dozens of trips through it previously.

*It is that cool*, James reasoned, returning his attention to the undiscovered wonder.

"Quarter engines," Janus's voice instructed.

Kady wordlessly obeyed, and their movement ebbed.

A shudder of steel echoed along the walls as the ship reacted to its engines' command. James gripped his hands into fists, open and closed. The initial phase of their journey was ending, and a new one was about to begin. An odd state of being, stuck between two imperceptible dangers.

Without warning, lights sprouted on the sides of the cave walls. They were long and flat without an obvious power supply. James eyed them suspiciously as the ship floated forward, its exterior lights dimming as the cavern lights took over, illuminating the space.

Other features, more than simple lightbulbs, sprang out of nowhere. Parallel catwalks overhead and a walkway along the side of the wall appeared, each blending in seamlessly with the surroundings. Without the lights, James wouldn't have known they were even present.

The natural cave art had changed again too. The swirls became a deep blue, covering the wall in a single shade rather than the majestic tapestry of intersecting swirls they had seen earlier in their journey.

"Cut engines in thirty seconds."

"Aye, Captain."

James peered ahead, but the lights in front of their vessel had not sparked yet. A hand gripped his, and he enveloped Heather's familiar palm in his own.

As the engines cut, the low hum of the propellers pushing them along stopped. The *Kaleidoscope* glided smoothly, its hefty build sending it forward with its own inertia.

"Engines reverse in five, four, three, two, one. Reverse."

A subtle vibration returned under foot, and James swayed into the glass as the ship pulled backward, halting its forward momentum. The cavern was dark again, the lights had dimmed and now only shone towards the water. What lay beyond was a mystery.

*Someone's hiding out there*, James thought, checking his gut and slowing his heartbeat.

"Cut the engines," ordered Janus. "James, please meet me on the bridge. Crew, begin docking preparation."

James glanced at Heather who nodded at him.

"Guess I'm up," James said, wishing someone else on the team could join him.

"Guess so," Heather said, pecking him on the cheek as he walked towards the door.

Wally nodded at him from his seat next to the exit. "Good luck, mate."

James patted the sailor's shoulder as he went by and heard Deck mutter to the team, "A bit rude to invite only one of us, don't you think?"

James shook his head. *If only Deck knew how quickly I'd change spots*, he thought as he jogged up the stairs to the bridge.

Janus stood in his regular spot as James entered the room. The slender captain greeted him with an indiscernible expression.

"Ready?" he asked.

"Ready."

Without waiting, Janus pulled the lever that released the bridge's hatch to the outside. A low hiss emanated from the room, accompanied by a strong whiff of grease from the porthole's hinges.

"After you." Janus gestured to the unfurled ladder. James took a deep breath as he steadied a foot on the bottom rung and hoisted himself through the hatch onto the top deck of the *Kaleidoscope*.

A stale but pleasant scent greeted James as he exited the ship's recycled air and bypassed the fumes from grease coating the area around the exit. James glanced in awe at the ancient cave hiding their presence from the BZ.

"Remarkable, isn't it?" Looking up, Janus spoke with a tone of wonder—unusual for the seasoned captain. James followed the tall man's gaze toward the ceiling to a place where the two sides of the cavern met. A bright spine of blue marked the convergence along a ridge that ran the length of the formation. "Countless explorers and millions of eons in the making… We're the first to find it." The captain shook his head and grinned. "Guess something good may have come out of the BZ after all."

James smiled at the overt optimism, enjoying the view for a final second before the internal mechanisms of his body reminded him of their mission.

"What's the next move here, Janus?"

"This way," Janus said, nodding in the direction of a ladder leading to the catwalk on the right side of the hull. "Your new friends are waiting for us."

James followed him down the ladder, puzzling over the captain's statement. *How did they know we were coming?* He had not been aware of any communication upon boarding or leaving the ship. Only two people existed on the planet who could pull that off, and he'd been told by one that once on the ship, contact was impossible.

The steel catwalk was embedded in the rock. *My own yellow brick road*, James thought, following Janus along the winding path cut into the cavern walls.

Soft light ahead, barely noticeable at first, turned on as they moved away from the ship. It grew stronger as they approached. After walking in silence for about five minutes,

James turned and looked behind to see that the lights had been extinguished, leaving a chasm of darkness.

"Over here," Janus spoke abruptly. The captain pointed to a break in the rock. James approached hesitantly, following Janus down the tight pathway now only wide enough for two people. Lights turned on overhead, but when James turned to check their progress, he again found they had already dimmed. *They want you to move here*, he thought subconsciously, sticking closer to Janus's long strides.

After another long silent stretch of walking, Janus stopped at a blank stone wall with similar markings of red, blue, and white swirls mingling together across the natural canvas. The lights at the end of the hallway flickered off as others turned on around them, illuminating a space roughly twenty by twenty feet.

Taking a breath, James glanced at the walls as Janus quietly leaned against one of the surfaces inspecting the back of his hand. Mimicking his guide, James nonchalantly studied his new surroundings, searching for clues while all the while maintaining his vigilance as a soldier. The air was different now. Gone was the salt-tinged odor blanketed in clean humidity. Instead, a dusty, earthy aroma gathered in the atmosphere, and although hundreds of feet of bedrock hung between them and the sun, a freshness lingered, giving a hint of the outside.

"Give it a moment," Janus spoke calmly.

"Until what?"

Janus grinned and continued to meticulously inspect his hand.

"Who is he?" A voice sounded somewhere in the chamber.

"Let us in, Fati," Janus replied.

"You know I hate that nickname. Who is he?"

"The general sent him. We have a proposition for you."

"We don't care to hear it."

"You will."

"We won't!" The tone of finality in Fati's statement made James wonder if their crossing had been in vain.

James glanced at his guide who appeared unconcerned. "Come on, Fati. Let us in."

"I told you I *hate* that nickname."

"Alright, alright. Just teasing Fatima. Can we come in?" Janus cooed the last words.

"No."

"Please."

"No, I said—"

"What the hell? Fatima, what are you doing? Who's out there?" A new voice interrupted the first, and puzzled, James looked around the room.

"It's Janus again, and he brought a stranger."

The other voice sighed. "We talked about this, Fatima. The general is sending people back over here to help. He mentioned it before he left, remember?"

"'Course, I do, but he called me Fati!"

"You can't keep them out for messing with your name." Irritation accompanied the new voice's tone. "Go get everyone else. We'll see what's going on, okay?"

"Fine. Goddamn sailors making fun of an old lady stuck in a rock." Fatima's voice faded from the room.

"Lively bunch," Janus said, grinning. James was thrown by the playful attitude of their stoic captain's land-based behavior.

"Seems like it," James replied, waiting for another set of voices to join them. Without warning, the walls to the chamber separated, their breaks emerging from previously invisible seams. A blended world of metal and rock greeted James on the other side, displaying a wide-open room that dissolved into a maze of caves going in all directions.

A tall woman with a dark gray ponytail and a HOLO floating next to her stood in front of James. She looked him up and down, holding out a hand.

"Name's Claudia. Welcome to the Resistance."

James eyed the woman and offered his hand. "James."

Claudia caught Janus's eye. "James, huh? The general's new guy?"

Janus nodded wordlessly.

"I guess so," James replied, showing no emotion. Neutrality was the best defense when encountering an unknown offense. *Keep 'em guessing.*

"Come on in," Claudia said, turning her back, her beige cloak swinging as James followed the captain's lead behind their mysterious host.

They trailed the silent figure into one of the many cave openings. Behind him a rustling woke James's senses, and he turned to watch the walls close off their entrance. *In it now*, he thought ramping up his awareness.

"You make it through okay?" Claudia asked from ahead as lights dimmed into existence upon the trio's approach.

"Lost two during the Roll. Otherwise, it was a smooth trip."

"Sorry for the loss."

"Not your fault."

"It's been an active port since we saw you last. Six months ago?"

"Seven."

"Time flies when there's a war to fight," Claudia said. She shook her head and stopped at the wall, tapping her HOLO keyboard as light swelled in the space.

"This is our HQ," she said, as the room grew into something completely unexpected.

State-of-the-art machinery blended seamlessly with the stone walls. HOLO screen stations and dashboards, weapons caches, camera alcoves, communications machines, and highly advanced computers sprouted across the room. Though most of it was incomprehensible to James, he knew it was a dreamland for the technologically minded, and he shook his head at the sight. A gray apparition floated across the room, and reflexively James's hand flew to the ion knife stuck in his belt.

"Relax, soldier, they're unattached. Harmless servants that we use here to take care of menial tasks. Useful when they're not tools of death." Claudia walked up to the Sentinel and held its shoulder, keeping it in place. "See?"

James's hand cautiously strayed from the hilt of his knife, but he watched the transparent body warily. It was hard to separate this figure from the images of death fighting for the BZ. The holographic humanoid moved away, and James had sudden flashbacks to his training with Croyton.

*I wonder how long they've known about this place,* James thought, filing the question away for later.

"If you say so," he replied.

"There's a lot you have to learn about. And up there, or out there, or whatever, I'll explain it to you in time. How many in your group?" Claudia asked. She sat in front of a set of blank HOLO monitors and waved her palm over a sensor on the table. A keyboard appeared, and the screens showed a composite image of the globe with symbols indicating various sites across its expanse.

"Six, including myself."

"How long will you be sticking around?"

"Depends on how long it takes. Have some work to do."

"Hmmm." Claudia looked away, reached under the desk, and pulled out a dark glass bottle. Opening it she looked back at James.

"Care to elaborate?"

James glanced at Janus whose face remained impassive.

"What do you need to know?"

"Start with everything, and we'll go from there."

James looked at the screen and searched for a key. Not able to find one, he began to analyze the images himself starting from the Northern Federation and moving east. He took his time, counting his heartbeats while he studied the map. The minutes ticked by.

"You're tracking the motherships?" he asked, pointing at the HOLO screen showing the Northern Federation.

"Of course. And more."

"How accurate is that?"

"Very."

"How?"

"My answers first."

James approached the dashboard and pointed to the mothership floating off the coast of the Atlantic. "I left four members of my original team to intercept and destroy this mothership." Trailing his finger across the map, he tapped the icon for their target. "This is the one I'm going to blow up."

He put his hand down and waited. Claudia stared at the screen. She reached under the desk, pulled out another bottle, and handed it to him.

"Have a drink. Let's get your team here. We need to start planning now. In five weeks that ship leaves the station for four years."

James's stomach tightened. He unscrewed his bottle and took a swig—root beer. *Better than desalinated water,* he thought, flashing back to the *Kaleidoscope's* supply.

"That Croyton is one crazy son of a bitch," Claudia said, staring at the monitor and shaking her head.

Leaving the room, James took another sip of his root beer but paused at the mouth of the tunnel and said, "It was my idea."

Claudia glanced at him quizzically and turned back to the HOLO map, "Then you're a crazy son of a bitch too."

# Chapter Six

*Pop hisssss.*

"You're spilling it everywhere, mate!" Deck's voice raised an octave as he hopped from his seat to escape the sugary liquid pooling on the ground.

"It's nowhere near you," Clint replied, rolling his eyes and taking a swig of root beer. "Relax, man. Also, when did you start saying *mate* all the time?"

"I don't say it *all* the time. Only on occasion. It's a friendly, colloquial term, *mate*," Deck emphasized with a swig of root beer, staring at Clint through slitted eyes as he turned in his chair.

James sat across the table from his teammates, ignoring them. He was too distracted by the amount of work to be done in the next few weeks to bother interjecting in a minor squabble.

"When are we getting started?" Liam asked, craning his neck as he glanced around the space, searching the room. "The woman said she'd be back soon. What was her name?" he asked, turning to James.

"Claudia, and thanks for your patience." The Resistance leader's voice echoed as she entered the room through one of the cave openings, followed by her own team who took up seats on the other side of the table.

The domineering leader assumed her position at the head. She looked up and down each side, inspecting the participants one by one, pulling up a small HOLO screen.

While they waited, James took stock of the new people. Across from him and seated next to Liam were the two youngest members of the group, a boy and a girl somewhere in their twenties. Each had jet-black hair and eyes that soaked in the world. So similar were their features that James assumed they were siblings, communicating in unspoken interactions only they could understand. Next to them sat a middle-aged man. His eyes flickered without stopping long enough to absorb anything. His jumpy movements and erratic blinking put James on edge. But catching James's eye, he smiled before his attention pulled in another direction. An older woman with tepid mannerisms sat at the end of the table, inspecting the new group of soldiers. James assumed this was the same woman who had greeted them at the entrance, Fatima. Her gaze settled on him without warming. He smiled in response but received only a suspicious glare. James looked away, feigning interest in something midway between the ceiling and the far wall.

Deck leaned over to him and whispered, "That one's gonna take some time warming up to you."

"Work your charms," James said. If anyone could melt the woman's defenses, it was Deck.

"Already done, mate," he replied, and the woman smiled as Deck gave her a secret wave.

*How the hell does he do that?* James thought, shaking his head as Claudia started to speak.

"Let's keep this brief. Before leaving, the general told us that at some point a team would be coming over to run missions into Centria. Looks like that time has come and expanded into a massive attack on one of the World Order's three primary military assets, the *Odyssey*." As she spoke, the image of the mothership James and the team had been tracking filled the screen.

"We have five weeks."

"Thirty-three days and nineteen hours," the man with the wild eyes corrected her.

"Thank you, Rex. Thirty-three days and nineteen hours until she'll leave port and won't come home for four years. We can't wait."

"No, we can't," Teresa piped in from across the table. "They'll take the entire Federation over the next six months."

"Agreed," Claudia continued. She pointed to the elderly woman. "Fatima used to be high up within the Order's local trade group. She and I will work to get everyone into Centria. Rex can design whatever tech is needed to run the mission and will also be our transport." Facing the twins she said, "Talon and Divan blend in everywhere inside. They'll work with me as your internal guide. Any questions?"

"What can we do?" James asked.

"Move your shit and stay out of the way."

James clenched his jaw without breaking the placid look on his face. "If I'm going in there, I'm part of the planning. I didn't come halfway across the planet to—"

"You came halfway across the planet to blow up a fucking ship in a port that I have been working to break for three goddamn decades. If you think I'm going to let you play anything more than a supportive role in getting your team inside unnoticed, then you are more out of your mind than I already think. Stay out of the way." Claudia glared at James and a reflection of Croyton rushed into James's mind.

Gripping his fists under the table and without emotion James stared back and said, "I've been in active war for a decade. You can do all the planning you want, but seven people in this room have actual battlefield experience with the BZ. None of those include you.

"Rhia and Bob, you work with Rex on the tech side. Liam, Teresa, and Heather, help the twins." James's tone was sharp as he glanced around the table at each team member in turn. Finally, resting his gaze on Claudia, he said, "Deck and I will work with you and Fatima." He stood, waiting for Claudia's response. "We're here to help take this thing down. I'm not going to sit around and let you decide how my team risks their lives."

Claudia's jaw tightened and she nodded. "We'll see."

With that, she walked out as an awkward silence enveloped the room. Rage bubbled in James's gut as he gripped the edge of the table. Heather's hand covered his and squeezed.

"Man, why do I have to be in your group? Everyone's gonna be pissy and upset all the time. This sucks," Deck grumbled, leaning back and crossing his arms. "What kind of food does Claudia like, Fatima? Actually, forget it. It's useless. Kev's not here to bribe her with that."

"She'll get over it. This is…different for her," Fatima spoke quietly. She made eye contact with James and nodded. "You did the right thing. Now though, you really need to move your stuff. It's a mess in here."

"That's fair. Where can we put everything?"

"I'll show you!" the male twin, Talon, sprang to his feet and approached the pile of gear. He looped a few of the heavy supplies over his arms and shoulders and began walking. "It's just back here."

The team loaded their gear and followed Talon through the base's winding maze of tunnels. Etched into the rock formation hundreds of passages wormed throughout the subterranean space. Unique markings adorned each area. Throughout the system, creative forces of the cave produced dazzling pieces of natural artwork displayed as brilliant blues, greens, yellows, and reds running over smooth, bumpy, or ridged walls randomly interrupted by caches of glittering mineral deposits. James walked behind their guide, noting the path with one eye while focusing on the cavern's natural majesty with the other.

"The cave's pretty easy to figure out," Talon said over his shoulder to the group. "We have maps uploaded onto every HOLO. Once you hook in, you'll never get lost."

"Do you run an independent network? Or can we connect to the outside?" Rhia asked.

"I am the wrong person to ask, but Rex can help you. Here's the first set of rooms." Talon stopped outside a short hallway with five entrances covered in cream-colored sheets.

"It's nothing fancy, but Fatima said there were seven of you so we tried to find quarters that would fit everyone comfortably. There are two more rooms down that tunnel." Talon pointed to a dimly lit corridor.

Deck shook his head and poked his face around one of the sheeted entryways. "These are plenty big. Clint, we can room up again! Like the old days, mate." He rushed into the room, leaving a fluttering curtain behind.

"Ahh, the good old days with Deck. At least he's lived with Cristina for a bit. Maybe she's housebroken him." Clint's voice held a hopeful tone.

"That's the spirit," James said, clapping his friend on the shoulder.

"In here." Heather's voice pulled James's eyes to a room on the other side of the hallway. He ducked behind the curtain and into a well-lit cave with a bunk carved into the wall on one side. Cut into another wall was a small wash basin and an apse to hold their gear.

"Not bad, huh?" Heather said, turning the faucet on and testing the water. She took a mouthful of the clear liquid. "Good stuff."

"Has to be better than anything desalinated," James said. The metallic water had left an impression on his tongue he would never be able to scrub off.

"This stuff is gold. Been trickling down here for eons probably," Heather said, holding her hands in a bowl up to James's lips. He took a sip, and after the initial shock from the cold, he was taken by the soft texture and mineral quality of the liquid.

"Good?" Heather asked, still holding her hands to his lips.

"Great," James said. "Privacy too. What is this?" James asked, looking around the room at the swirling silver patterns cut into their walls.

Two hands found the back of his neck, and Heather turned him around with a gentle push on his shoulder.

"Turn that brain off for a little bit. You need to relax." Heather's lips found his moments later. Putting down his defenses, James allowed himself to be swept away by their newfound world under the rock.

After unpacking, James went to find Claudia. Their conversation earlier gnawed at him. He needed her to understand the whole point of their trip. He wanted to start off on the right foot.

Winding and twisting hallways proved confusing as James circled in and out of the labyrinthine Resistance headquarters. He had lost all sense of direction underground and grew more frustrated by the minute, searching for the base leader.

"Goddammit," he growled when he stumbled upon the conference room for the third time, "Stupid underground bases. Make no sense." He mumbled as he pulled up the 3D map Talon had shown him and which he had been avoiding.

"Trouble?" The voice surprised James, and he spun to find Fatima sitting at one of the dashboards. Her eyes focused on the screen in front of her, and she grinned.

"This place is impossible," James said, leaning against a set of HOLO emitters.

"It's very confusing. I've been here for twenty-six years. Still need my map sometimes." The woman took her eyes from the screen and looked at James with the same calming smile she had given Deck earlier that day.

"Well, that makes me feel a little better."

"Happy to help."

"Twenty-six years is a long time," James said as he walked over to her.

"Yes, it is. Worth it though. You've seen the Order, what they're capable of."

"I have. What made you leave?" James asked.

"Hard to explain unless you've seen it up close," Fatima replied. Her fingers moved nimbly over the keyboard and images on the screen shifted in different patterns James did not understand.

"What do you mean?"

"I mean, I was inside, James. I was a part of the Order, a part of the leadership that pulls the strings. You have to see it for yourself to understand why I left," she replied matter-of-factly, continuing to work with her HOLO.

"I see. If it helps, I've been inside a base of the BZ—I mean, the Order," James said, correcting himself, realizing that everyone here was technically a part of the BZ.

"Ransacking a base isn't living in it."

"What about being kept against your will?"

Fatima's fingers stopped moving, and she looked at James with an expression of deep sorrow. "You understand a piece of it already."

James nodded and changed topics. "What've you got up there?"

"Now *this* I can explain *and* show. Pull up a chair."

James grabbed a chair from the conference table, rolled it next to Fatima's, and sat watching as her fingers danced on the light-based keyboard.

"If you want to know the ins and outs of this, talk to Rex. But for basics follow along, okay?"

He nodded hoping his limited understanding of technology would not be too obvious.

"This is where we are," Fatima said. She pointed at a spot on the map and trailed her finger downward through the water. "This is the bottom of the Mediterranean and this"—her finger stopped below the seabed—"this is how we get into the Order's capital city, Centria."

James was confused. *They go down to get into the BZ?*

"Confused? Good. If you got that, you'd be a spy and I'd be forced to kill you. Throughout the world and before the Melt, a series of cables stretched across the seabed. During the breakdown, part of the Order's move was to shut off that mechanism. They blew the cables, and voila, we were cut off from the world. However, they did not properly dismantle the tunnels. Claudia and a group of other early Resistance members dredged the tunnels and created a network to get into Centria. It was a stroke of genius—and luck—when they discovered our cave system. It all clicked together." Fatima looked at the intricate system of interchanging chambers and channels admiring its complexity as James stared, trying to follow her eyes.

"That is impressive, especially before you had all this," he said, gesturing around the cave dwelling. "Where was the Resistance? It must have been a big force to dredge something that deep."

Fatima was silent, and James looked back to see the woman's eyes drooping towards the floor. "The Resistance used to be much larger, much stronger. Unfortunately, it no longer is."

"What happened?" James asked.

"The Order's violence knows no bounds." Fatima spoke with finality, and James did not question further. Instead, he returned his focus to the screen. "So you'll get us in through these tunnels. How the hell do you get from down there up to the surface?"

Fatima smiled. "I'll let Rex give you a tour." The older woman swiped across her keyboard, and after a moment Rex's face popped up on the center HOLO.

"Yes?" Rex spoke with jarring abruptness, and his eyes darted around the room with a rapidity James could not track.

"Are you doing anything right now?"

"Define anything."

"Can you give our guest a tour of the pills?" Fatima asked.

"Sure, how many people?"

Fatima glanced at James. "Who else should join you?"

"Probably Clint, Deck, and Rhia. If we have to keep things light," James said. He knew he'd catch flak from the other members of the group, but transportation, scouting, and technology were key for this kind of trip.

"You got that, Rex?"

"Give me five minutes. I'll come get you all." The video feed shut off and the screen disappeared.

"Rex is an interesting guy," James said. "How will he know who to get? He met them ten minutes ago."

"Like you said, he's an interesting guy. Used to work inside Centria's engineering corp, the group responsible for all tech created and maintained in the Order, from Sentinels to the earth turbines. He had a part in all of it."

"How'd he end up here?"

"Change of heart," Fatima spoke with disinterest. "They don't believe in change much within the Order. Rex is the result of a broken mind at the hands of the Order's leadership. Sadistic fucks."

"I know a bit about it," James said, pushing away memories of his windpipe being repeatedly blocked by the HOLO collar.

"Not like Rex does," Fatima said. She turned to James and looked him in the eye. "You've seen the soldiers. You know how the Order trains their military. How it ensures absolute commitment to the cause. Well, Rex went through that. Subsequently, he had to be pieced back together mentally."

"I see," James said, remembering the soldiers' distant, but intense stares, frenetic movements, and inability to focus. "Raspin mentioned something about that."

Fatima stopped her typing. "I have not heard that name for twenty-six years. There may be more to you than I thought."

"You ready?" Rex interrupted their conversation, and James turned to find the broken engineer surrounded by the requested members of his team looking confused.

"Let's go," James said, walking towards their new guide.

"Have fun. Easy on those corners, Rex," Fatima called to the engineer who gave a thumbs-up as he walked away without a word.

James followed the erratic figure, and Deck sidled up to him. "The hell you doing sending the whacko to get us?"

"He's brilliant," James said. "Just wait."

"I'm sure he is. Doesn't mean he's not nuts."

"Keep up! We nuts walk fast," Rex called from ahead, and Deck's face reddened.

James grinned and broke into a jog to catch up with the engineer, winding his way through the illuminated tunnels that left a trail of halogen marking their path.

Rex's jerky movements kept James and the team on their toes. For someone whose mind had been stitched back together, Rex possessed a powerful memory and navigated the cave pathways without hesitation.

Patterns on the walls shifted as they moved, changing back and forth between brilliant green and dark blue, the colors mingling in a way that gave the appearance of water.

At a break in the pattern James stopped and looked closer. He swore the colors moved, their grooves swimming across each other.

"It's an illusion, but not really," the wild-haired engineer spoke over James's shoulder, startling him.

"What do you mean?" Rhia asked, crowding in on the other side of James, oblivious to her friend's discomfort.

"The colors. When they mash together, it's like they're moving, right?"

"Yeah, I only noticed it here though," James said as Clint and Deck moved in for a closer look.

"It takes a certain kind of light, and it's more obvious between certain colors. But it's not completely an illusion."

"What does that mean—not *completely* an illusion?" Rhia asked. The techie stepped back from the wall and steadied herself, checking the bionic joint connecting her hip.

"The colors are constantly moving. Slowly over time, the walls, caverns, tunnels are getting larger, smaller, skinnier, wider, softer, everything. It's a constantly changing world. The illusion is looking at two colors next to each other and not knowing where one begins and one ends. In reality, the sands of time are represented by colors painting the expansion of the earth's crust as it pushes upward." The frazzled engineer jerked away from the scene and walked away.

"That guy is whacked," Deck said, shaking his head.

"No shit," Clint added.

After another half hour of walking, Rex stopped. James looked around. Most of the room was similar to others they'd seen, but rather than caves, tall rock formations with designs etched into the red clay spread around the empty space. The faint smell of pulverized earth coated the room. James swallowed a gulp of dusty air and inspected the area while Rex talked.

"This is the launch room," Rex said, pointing at nothing in particular, his erratic stare settling on each member of the group in turn. "We'll get to the Centria entrance tunnels, another one thousand meters below. Faster this way."

"Have we been going downhill this whole time?" Rhia asked, looking around the room with wonder.

"I knew it!" Deck exclaimed, "I kicked a rock, and it kept rolling. Quite a thinker."

"Underground Newton," James said, grinning.

"Kind of yes," Deck said, turning his attention back to Rex.

"From here, we have tubes that carry us the rest of the distance. In each tube there are air-pressurized containers called pills. The pills move on their own through the tubes, directed by natural gases repurposed for our needs. Each tube also contains a dangerous mixture of sulfur, methane, $CO_2$, $O_2$, and a bunch of other pent-up air that smells like death, so do not leave one of the tubes open for longer than necessary. It takes forever to air out these places."

James suspected the last part was a joke and attempted a weak laugh. No one joined, and instead he received a series of weird looks, and a pit of self-loathing settled into his stomach. Brushing off his faux pas, he cleared his throat, "Ahem, okay. Well, who wants to lead off?"

"Never heard of 'ladies first'?" Rhia asked.

"Of course, sorry. Rhia, would you care to lead?" James asked, stumbling in his offer.

"I would not," Rhia replied indifferently, checking a HOLO she had whipped out of nowhere.

"My question stands. Clint, Deck? Who's leading us off?"

"If it moves, it's for Clint. I've gotta get my gut right," Deck said, beginning the breathing exercises Bob had taught him to help his nausea when he couldn't get his hands on medication.

"Alright, Clint." James nodded at his friend who stepped forward.

"Strap me in, Rex."

The engineer waved for Clint to follow him deeper into the room and walked around to the other side of the large formation in its center. After a few moments their surroundings changed and a series of dashboards, stations, HOLO emitters, and active monitors appeared from various nooks, crannies, and false rocks in the area. James stared at the seamless integration with the natural world. *Reminds me of the BZ base*, he thought, his mind drifting back to the Sentinel chambers in the Southern Federation.

Rex reappeared and typed on one of the dashboard's interfaces. "And here we go."

Without warning, the face of the center rock formation pulled back revealing four tubes. Within each tube was a man-sized container. James walked closer to inspect the newfound invention hiding behind the rock walls.

Light glinted from the matte metal as he approached. The pills were long hollow ovals with latches inside and out.

"Tight squeeze," Clint said over his shoulder.

*Good thing Kev skipped the trip,* James thought. He imagined their gigantic chef trying to squeeze into one of the gas-propelled devices and chuckled.

"What's so funny? You thinking about Kev in there too?" Deck asked as he walked from the other side of the renovated rock formation.

"How'd you know that?" James asked, shocked again at Deck's uncanny ability to read people.

"I had the same thought," Deck said. He abruptly changed subjects and yelled to their guide busy with his HOLO, "You ready, Rex?"

"Yep. Clint, can you get in the pill on the far left? Once inside, the latches will lock on both the outside and inside. The red handle is your emergency eject mechanism. The tube flies straight down. You'll be there before you know it. When you land, swipe the arrival button on the HOLO dashboard to start the air filters. That will trigger us to send the next person."

"Air filters?" James asked.

"You're 1,700 meters from the surface of the ocean. Two hundred meters of that is beneath the seabed. There's not a ton of readily available oxygen that deep. Air filters keep you alive."

James nodded. *Makes sense,* he thought putting the entire picture together. A brief swell of claustrophobia took over, but disappeared when he heard the clasp of the pill open with a *whoosh*.

"Bare bones in here, Rex," Clint said as he stepped inside.

"You'll love it," Rex spoke without looking at the passenger.

"See you there," Clint said.

"We'll miss you!" Deck cried out as the door clicked shut.

James gave Clint a thumbs-up, and he returned the gesture. A loud sucking noise engulfed the room followed by a *pop*, and the pill disappeared.

"Holy crap," James muttered. He had not even seen the thing move.

"That was fast as hell."

"Give it a minute," Rex said, his eyes focusing on five different HOLOs at once. After what seemed way too long, Rex spoke up again.

"Who's next?"

"Is he down there?"

"Got the signal. Who's next?" Rex asked again, looking between James, Rhia, and Deck.

"I'll go," James said, ready to get it over with.

"Hop in."

James climbed into the metal tube, he had to duck his head and scrunch his shoulders to fit, but after he settled in, the pill felt oddly safe.

"Ready?" Rex asked.

"Ready," James replied.

"Wait for—"

James did not hear the end of Deck's joke as the *pop* from the gas drowned out all noise.

He flew with alarming speed. His body shifted to the top of the pill where, luckily, a foam stopper kept his head from banging into the capsule. The walls outside the small window became a blur, and James wondered how the Resistance had managed to build something so advanced. *This is remarkable.*

Within seconds, the movement slowed and stopped all together. He looked out at the new space below the earth's crust. Clint waited for him with his arms crossed, and James stepped from the pill, examining the room.

A heavy odor of earthy gas overwhelmed his senses, and a damp cold assaulted him. Goosebumps formed on his forearms, which he rubbed to increase blood flow. Musty air filled his mouth and clung to the insides of his nostrils. Dim lights illuminated the area, but it was still too dark to get a good sense of the space.

"It's freezing," James said.

"It sucks here, man. Cold, smells like rotten eggs, and the air is so wet my shirt's already damp."

James glanced at his surroundings with suspicion as the remaining pills entered the space.

Deck exited his pill with a look of disgust on his face. "Where the hell are we?"

Rex approached a HOLO dashboard, ignoring the question, and fiddled around with a few screens, activating more lights and clearing the air. "Something like this should really not exist this deep. Pretty cool though. Let's get moving to the city."

Rhia swiveled her bionic leg on its axis. "Something funny is happening to my joints."

"Probably the moist air. Come on," Rex said abruptly. He picked up a HOLO light and, floating it in front of him, took off without checking on his followers.

"You good, Rhia?" James asked, annoyed at Rex's dismissal of Rhia.

The techie waved it off. "I'll be fine. Bob and I can work out the kinks."

James nodded and followed the engineer as he walked into another tunnel. The space constricted until it was only wide enough for one person at a time.

"Who wants to go first?" Rex asked, stopping suddenly.

James turned to the other three. Seeing the blank, confused, and annoyed expressions glinting in their eyes, James decided to play it safe.

"Why don't you lead us this time, Rex?" James said, blocking him from seeing their faces.

"Suit yourself."

Rex stepped through an unseen opening in the rock face, and James followed.

After ducking through the rocky entryway, he looked up, amazed.

Light filled the glittering underground cavern stretching hundreds of feet into the air. Rocks and minerals sparkled in the eerie underground. James walked dumbfounded behind their guide, staring up at the stone city buried under the earth.

"Welcome to the gates of Centria," Rex said. He gazed straight up and pointed at a circular hole drilled into the ceiling. "That was the first smuggling entrance. Now we've got a few dozen spread across spots all over the city."

James was breathless at the sheer magnitude of the space. "How doesn't the B—*the Order* know this is here?" he asked, walking farther into the room.

Rex shrugged. "No one knew this was here before Claudia found it. If the original Resistance had known"—Rex shook his head—"things would be different."

"Wh—" James started to speak but was cut off by Deck.

"How do you get up there?"

"Steel cables pull the platforms. Up to one thousand pounds of machinery can get carried up and down."

"How the hell do you fit one thousand pounds of anything through that tiny entrance?" Clint asked, looking back and inspecting the fresh scrape on his shoulder.

"You use the bigger entrance." Rex pointed at a wide mouth to the cave a hundred yards from where they stood.

"Why didn't we go through that?" Clint asked, exasperated. He winced when he pulled a piece of sharp rock from his skin and threw it on the ground, a trickle of blood rolling down his shoulder.

"Showmanship," Rex replied with a blank face.

James grinned. "I like it, Rex."

"Good. Let's head back." Rex walked towards the larger entrance.

"Whoa, we're not going up?" James asked. He had spent the last few hours getting down here. He wanted to at least finish the journey with a glimpse of the BZ.

"We need a winch up top. No winch, no way up."

"Winch?" Rhia asked, her eyes glued to the ceiling.

"Someone up top needs to help us out."

"Who's that?" James asked, but Rex ignored the question and instead left the room. Clint followed, grumbling to Rhia about his shoulder on the way.

James and Deck remained rooted to the spot, staring up at the ceiling.

"Would have been nice to see the BZ after coming all this way," Deck said.

"I know. Gotta follow along though."

"Yeah. I hope I'm not scared of heights," Deck said with an edge of unease in his voice.

James grinned. "I've got you, bud."

"You're a good man, James. Can you hold your hands over my eyes when we head up?"

"I'll get you a blindfold."

"I'd prefer the personal touch."

James laughed and shook his head as he followed their peculiar guide back to the Resistance HQ, itching to get their mission started. He was ready.

# Chapter Seven

Six HOLO screens hung across the front of the conference table. Each displaying part of the diagrammed plan Claudia designed to get them inside Centria for their reconnaissance mission. James examined the screens one by one. Time was limited, and spending three days planning their ingress had not been ideal. This would be the only one of these trips. The next would be the real deal.

"When we get to Centria, one team will enter from an empty storefront, the other an empty apartment. Or let's hope they're empty. If not, something's gone horribly wrong," Claudia said. Starting next to the HOLO on the left side of the room, she walked from screen to screen, explaining the diagrams. "Talon and Divan will take you in two groups thirty minutes apart. James, did you create your teams?"

"Yes, ma'am. Gave them to Divan before the meeting," James replied. He and Claudia had haggled about who should travel to the surface for their first trip inside Centria. Her rules: only those with direct impact on the immediate outcome of the trip and no one with bionics. That forced him to leave out Liam and Rhia, and while Bob was a talented medic, he shouldn't be needed for a quick trip in and out.

"Good. Talon and Divan will brief their respective groups on how to behave when arriving. The key will be to act like groups normally seen in the city. Tourists are not a thing in the Order, so there's no blending into a mixed crowd. You either belong or you don't. Fatima, do we have our interceptors set up?"

"Contacted yesterday. Confirmed the first, waiting on the second."

"Tell me when you hear from them," Claudia said. Fatima rolled her eyes at the domineering leader and grinned at James from across the table while Claudia continued her pace.

"Our entrances into Centria are a block apart from one another. From there the groups will take parallel streets

to the harbor, and the teams can install everything needed.
Who's running point on that front?"

"Me and T have it," Heather answered.

"You'll have ten minutes at the harbor. We've
learned that the guards begin tagging people after twenty
minutes, so move fast." Claudia focused on the two women
and turned her attention to the rest of the room. Her intense
eyes landed on each person in the recon party as she
continued. "When ten minutes are up, Talon or Divan will
pull their groups back together and take them to the exfil
points. These are different from the entrances so stick with
your guides. If you get lost, you're on your own. Any
questions?"

"What are our threats at the harbor?" Deck asked.

"Autonomous Sentinels are everywhere in the city,
but it's the Shadow Officers you want to watch for." An
image of a Sentinel disc popped up on the screens. It was
marked by the trident and triangle insignia of the Order.
"They're the same as the ones you saw in the Federation, but
more dangerous."

"*More* dangerous?" Deck asked skeptically.

"Yes." Rex's voice cut in. The group collectively
turned towards the engineer. His eyes darted to each face in
the crowd when he spoke. "Imagine a Sentinel with
unlimited power connected to a source that allowed it to
stretch the limits of its original containment. They can grow
to giants, magic away into a vapor, or move with speed
unseen. They are unprecedented. They are nearly
unbeatable."

"Nearly?" James asked, pushing to see what he
could get.

"Nothing is infallible," Rex said. His eyes drifted
from their stares back to his personal HOLO. "Ionic
weaponry can damage them to the point of breaking, but to
wipe them out completely, their power source has to be
severely limited or destroyed.

"I've knocked out plenty of these things in my time.
Hit 'em in the right spot with a charged ion baton, and zap.
Toast," Teresa spoke up from across the table and leaned

back in her chair. "How do you know they're so different than what we've seen?"

"I designed them." His eyes stared unwavering at Teresa for a full three seconds before breaking away.

The table quieted while they absorbed Rex's new information.

"That explains it, I guess. Steer clear of them," Deck said, breaking the tension.

"Any med supplies Bob can send with us? Stuff we can sneak in?" James asked, hoping they wouldn't need anything but wanted to be prepared in case.

"Only bionic tape. Anything else could tip off the guards if you're searched." Fatima directed her answer at Bob and James. "If a pain blocker is discovered, everyone is screwed."

"Agreed, keep it light. Wear extra cloth to use as binding if needed. I'll try to think of more tricks," Bob said, jotting notes on his HOLO.

"Weapons?" James asked.

"We've got that handled. Divan?"

The black-haired twin walked to the front of the table. She pulled a crescent-shaped hairband from her sleeve and flicked the tight circular object with a *snap*. In the band's place, Divan held a small baton with one pointed edge.

"Each of you will be given one of these. Your personal thumb print will activate the ionic pulse. The pulse is strong enough to take out a few Sentinels, but it's short-lived. Run the second you can." To demonstrate, one of the autonomous HOLOs waiting in the wings walked up to the woman, and she skewered its neck with her band. The figure dissolved in the blink of an eye.

James nodded. *Impressive*, he thought. *Handy little things*

"Anything else?" Claudia asked as Divan took her seat.

Silence greeted her as she inspected the room.

"Great, we leave in half an hour. Meet by the pills."

"Hey, want to get a quick bite to eat?" Heather asked James.

"Let's go," James said, happy for a brief respite prior to the mission.

They walked hand in hand to the kitchen, which doubled as the team's mess hall.

The galley kitchen was embedded in a tight space burrowed into the wall. The electric implements were, like everything else in the base, powered by the same central source from deep under the earth's surface. A long table with two benches—one cut into the stone wall and another made of plastic across from it—sat perpendicular to the kitchen entrance. Two circular tables used for extra countertop space or an easy place for a few people to enjoy a meal floated in the room.

Heather sat at one of the small tables while James bent into one of the fridges. Food in the Resistance HQ was the biggest disappointment. While being underground was ideal for concealment, it lacked the ability to provide flavorful sustenance. Sure, they had done an excellent job growing food especially root vegetables. Potatoes, onions, and carrots were abundant. And using false sunlight for their hydroponic gardens provided a wide variety of vegetables, including lettuce, beans, jalapeños, and tomatoes galore. But the lack of meat was annoying. James knew raising cows was impossible underneath the earth, but wished for it nonetheless. The only meat was a flock of chickens Fatima tended. She rarely killed them, but eggs were in constant supply, and James took his standard three from their container.

"How many do you want?" he asked over his shoulder.

"Two's good," she answered, already aware what was in store for their meal.

James began chopping an onion to sauté with a helping of spinach to serve under the eggs as he chatted with Heather.

"I think this will be good. I do wish we had more medical gear and heavier weapons with us though. Guess that's why I was never fully into the spy game," James said, talking into the air while he cooked. The mission clung to his mind, and now each pane from Claudia's HOLO presentation filtered through his vision on repeat.

"Yeah, I guess." Heather said. She was unusually quiet, but James let it go. Pre-mission jitters maybe. It was not like her, but all of this was new for everyone.

"What do you think it'll be like? I know we've seen pictures of the city and all, but the people… I'm oddly excited. I mean, I wish that you were on my team versus T, but I get it. She'll need someone who can—"

"James," Heather interrupted him, stopping his rambling. Steam from the frying pan hit the back of his head as he turned to her sending a waft of moisture behind his ears.

Heather's face held an uncomfortable grimace, and James's stomach tightened in a way normally reserved for mission danger. Something was off.

"What? What is it? Who is it?" James's mind spun, but he fought to keep his thoughts focused and grounded.

"James… James, I have to tell you something…" Heather glanced uncomfortably at the ground.

The knot in his stomach worsened, and he swallowed. "Tell me."

"We spoke with Claudia and, after some back-and-forth, agreed that leaving behind the bionics and nonessentials was a good idea."

"Okay…What does that have—"

"Hold on," Heather said gently, "She said you had talked about your time in the BZ prison and had mentioned Raspin in a conversation with Fatima a few days ago. James, Raspin's everywhere here. This is *his* home. He knows the territory and can take you or any of us in a second."

She was squirming, but James already knew what was coming. "Heather, just say it."

"James, this is too much of a risk. It's something we've never done. It doesn't mean you can't be part of the final trip—"

"Heather…"

She sighed, "You're not going on the mission."

An acrid smell of burning spinach assaulted his nostrils, momentarily distracting him and he turned back to the pan.

"I'm sorry. It's not my call, James. You know that," Heather continued, part question part statement. James bit his tongue and nodded.

"I get it. I'm a risk."

"Only for this one though. You're also the most experienced operator to escape BZ capture, and Claudia acknowledged that. She thinks you should be there for the final mission, but…"

"Not this one." James cracked the eggs into a separate pan and watched as the yolk covered the dark black material in an opaque yellow.

"This sucks," Heather said.

James was quiet. He was so disappointed and wanted desperately to be angry with someone, but it was the right call. He'd never let someone who'd been captured by the BZ within a mile of this operation. His dignity was hurt, but the mission mattered more. *Shouldn't have fucking said anything*, James thought, recalling his conversations with Fatima and Claudia.

"Nothing we can do about it now," James said, flipping the eggs onto their respective plates and sliding Heather's across the table.

Empathetic eyes met his, and James smiled encouragingly. "Don't worry about me. I'll stay here with the rest of the crew. They'll never want me in the ops room again."

Heather chuckled and took a bite of her meal. "That's the spirit. Plan on being such a pain in the ass they'll beg to send you out."

"Exactly. Who's going instead?" James asked, doing the math in his head and wondering how T would be able to operate without him.

"Bob. They're telling him now, and Liam's walking him through his role."

James nodded. He was happy Bob would be up there. Smartest guy he knew, and a medic was always a plus.

"Good. Who else knew about this?"

"Me, T, Liam, Claudia, and Fatima," Heather said, counting the names on her fingers.

"Deck?"

"God, no. He'd have told you in a second," Heather said, rolling her eyes.

James grinned. He could always count on Deck.

Two hours later, the teams gathered in the entrance chamber to Centria. Suspended a foot off the ground, two circular platforms hung from steel cords that disappeared in the tunnels burrowed into the earth above them. James lost sight of them in the cave's darkness. He was coming to terms with not joining the first big trip into the city. Deck, however, was not.

"This makes no fucking sense. Leave James behind. Moronic," Deck grumbled, attaching his wrist baton.

"Deck, you know he can't go up there. Raspin'd know it in a heartbeat," Clint said, attempting reason with the scout.

"He wouldn't have a freaking clue if James bit him on the ass," Deck replied hotly. "Besides, Bob's barely had time to learn his shit. We're gonna put that kinda pressure on him?"

"I'll be good, Deck," Bob said coolly, walking through his triangulation duties step-by-step on the HOLO's map overlays.

"Of course you will, but it takes time," Deck whined.

"I've performed major surgeries on open battlefields, Deck. This isn't too bad."

"See? He could be doing surgery, and James could be up there leading the charge. Oh, what's the use?" Deck sat on the edge of a platform in a huff, and James patted him on the shoulder.

"Thanks, buddy, but they're right. I'm a risk. I'll be there for the real deal."

Deck waved his hand away and Claudia spoke. "Listen up. Break into your teams and hop onto the platforms. You ascend in four minutes. Pay attention to Talon and Divan. They're your lifeline. Step out of line or move weirdly, and someone in Centria will know. We've got our people up there, but only for emergencies. Set up the sensors. Get back here. Simple as that. Everyone ready?"

The small group looked at each other nodding.

"We're ready," Heather replied for everyone, and Claudia nodded.

"Let's head upstairs."

Heather stepped to the side and kissed James. "See you soon."

"Go quickly," he replied, hugging her before she walked to her spot on the platform next to Deck.

James stepped back to join the remaining Federation people in a line behind Rex and Fatima. All sorts of measures, incomprehensible to James, ran on the HOLO dashboards as the two Resistance member's hands danced over the keyboards. Finally, all went still.

"Send 'em up," Claudia ordered. Her hands clasped behind her back hid her white knuckles while she watched the operation unfold. Her nerves gave James a measure of solace. She took this seriously.

Fatima swiped across her HOLO screen. Each platform shuddered and the riders found their balance as they rose at a steady speed.

The platforms moved at an identical pace, and James's eyes followed, craning his neck. Heather gave a final wave and disappeared into the tunnels hundreds of meters above his head.

"They clear?" Claudia asked looking towards the ceiling.

"In the tunnels. We can't track them until they hit the top."

Claudia turned and walked towards the pill's launch room. "Let me know when we hear from them."

James looked up at the ceiling once again and followed her through the mouth of the cave.

Rhia sat cross legged on the ground and pulled out a HOLO screen. "Now, we wait."

# Chapter Eight

"How much longer?" Rhia asked. The bored techie drew lines in the sand, waiting for the recon team to reappear. "Will we know when they're coming back?"

"It's only been twenty minutes, and yes. They'll send a signal when the platforms are about to descend, and it's about five minutes after that," Fatima replied. She did not lift her eyes from the monitors other than to write in a notebook perched on her knee.

*Five minutes in unlit tunnels*. James grimaced to himself. *Sounds horrible*, he thought.

"What if they signal before that?" Liam asked.

"Not good," Fatima answered, manipulating her HOLO display. James moved closer to get a better look at her work.

A haze of parallel lines spaced an inch apart appeared on the screen and continued in a never-ending column of lines stacked on top of one another. Occasionally, the lines would jump, and Fatima would jot something in her notebook. Curious, James observed the process, unable to discern the notations.

Fatima spoke up, "Care to ask rather than stare?"

"I didn't want to interrupt," James said, embarrassed by his intrusion.

"No problem. Don't block my sight," Fatima said, waving off his apology as she spotted another mutation and noted it.

"So…what are you doing?" James asked, leaning against the dashboard terminal.

Pointing to the screen, she explained, "These lines are energy pulses running into the city. Each one tracks a separate sector of the city, markets, residences, city hall, office buildings, military centers—the works. Each pop in the line, like that little wave, is a charged movement by a Sentinel. Something caused it to expend energy, potentially depleting its resources. I'm establishing a baseline, so we know what everything typically looks like."

"So you'll know if something goes wrong," James said, watching as another bump appeared in a line and she made a notation.

"You got it."

Silently James watched her, following each of the lines and trying to determine what they represented, but it was hard. For one, the key to the various sector indicators was foreign to him, and before they disappeared, he had to match the icons with the corresponding line. As he started to get the hang of it, Fatima let out of *whoosh* of air.

"Glad that's over," she said, rubbing her eyes.

"You're done?" Lines continued to run up the screen, and Fatima nodded, putting drops of a solution into her eyes.

"Twenty minutes of constantly monitoring moving lines. I'd say that's a lot."

"Can I have your notes?" Rex asked, holding out his hand. The older woman passed him her notebook, and he entered the information into a HOLO.

"Why not put them into a HOLO first?" James asked.

"Too much of a risk. I'd make a mistake. Better to do it by hand first and then have Rex hard-code it into our monitors."

"How's it look?" Claudia appeared in the doorway. Her face was expectant.

Fatima gave her a thumbs-up. "We're set."

"Thanks. Take a rest. We've got some time," Claudia said. Her tight expression relaxed a bit upon Fatima's answer, and she returned to the pill room.

"Two-hour mission. Lots to think about," Fatima said with a roll of her yes. She stretched her arms and cracked her neck. "Care to sit?" she asked James as she walked over to the wall.

James followed and sat next to her. The gray-haired woman stared at the ceiling and took a sip from her water bottle. "One thousand seven hundred meters." She shook her head. "All that separates us from *them*," she finished, a layer of disgust palpable in her final word.

"What's it like?" James asked. His disappointment at being left behind stung, but some insight from Fatima would help lessen the blow.

"A nightmare. Nothing is real, James. Everything is planned. Empty, lifeless. Creating a new societal structure is the Order's only goal. One where humanity can take the next step. A forced evolution if you will." She took another sip of water and spat it on the ground, creating a pool of mud in the earth.

"Everyone and everything under tight control. Nothing happens without the Order's permission. It's like a puzzle in which the edges of the pieces have been cut off and forced together. It's not natural."

James nodded. "I can't really imagine it."

"Have you ever been in a city?"

"Of course," he replied.

"Imagine that city in your mind. Picture it. Now, silence the people. Remove the smells, the smoke, the noise, and the underlying roar of civilization. Take away incentives for people to interact. *That* is Centria. A lifeless city existing solely to house people and make them work. Nothing more." Anger edged Fatima's voice, but James dug in.

"What about the Resistance? You have people up there. Why isn't it bigger down here? No offense, of course," James said.

"None taken. You're right. Two old women, a crazed engineer, and twins barely out of their teenage years is hardly a robust Resistance. No. The Resistance used to be something different."

"Different?" James asked casually, hiding his intentions. He took a sip from his water bottle.

"Bigger. With a real hierarchy. Hundreds if not thousands of us worked in bases all over the Order's landmass. We stuck to the coasts, getting on and off the ships traveling between here and the Federation. Growing and making real progress with people infiltrating at the highest levels of government." Fatima stopped and took a swig of her water.

James hid his surprise at the mention of the Federation. Of course his government had been communicating with the Resistance, but to what extent?

"How does something like that vanish?" he asked.

"Raspin. And him." Fatima nodded in Rex's direction. The engineer operated at an uneven pace, diving with abandon between HOLOs and no clear process. Watching him, James wondered how his mind could move so sporadically.

Fatima continued her story. "Raspin pulled him from a group of extremely intelligent engineers who had been working on Sentinel development. Little did he know, but Rex had been feeding us information on their projects for a few months. Little did *we* know Raspin had been feeding false information. Classic counterespionage. When he caught Rex, he broke him, employing the same technique used on their soldiers. Wipe them clean and point. But he changed his methods with Rex. He needed to keep Rex's intelligence alive—the piece he really wanted. At the cost of his sanity, he brought Rex to the edge and forced him to create the Sentinels you see in town. Unlimited power as long as they are close to their energy source. Pure genius."

"So the torture broke him?" James asked. Compassion welled inside James as he looked at the engineer.

"Not exactly." Fatima shook her head. "Raspin pulled his family and tortured them for weeks on end. Three children and his wife. Forced Rex to watch everything." Fatima looked off into the distance. "He never told us specifically what Raspin did, but when we went in for the rescue, they were already dead. Probably better that way."

Compassion morphed to grief and horror as James turned his eyes from the engineer and stared at the ground. His situation had been similar, forced to watch a person he considered a brother tortured mercilessly. He did not realize until now how lucky he had been.

"The fracturing of his mind combined with observing the pain his family endured derailed his brain completely. At the same time, Raspin unleashed the Sentinels on the city, targeting everyone believed to be a part of the

Resistance. He hunted them throughout the Order and went after the bases he discovered buried deep in Rex's consciousness. When he rounded them up, he did not stop the Sentinels from performing their task. Bodies were torn to pieces, unrecognizable. The Resistance all but disbanded after that until Janus found these caves. Now, it's only us and the few people in the city."

"How many are still up there?" James asked, visualizing the carnage that groups of untethered Sentinels could rend on a population.

"A few dozen? Maybe only five? Claudia keeps everything compartmentalized. It's the only way to keep us all safe."

James understood and nodded. He looked at the ceiling towards the city. He had a newfound respect for the members of the Resistance.

"After my cheery story, any other questions?" Fatima asked. She grinned trying to lighten the mood.

James thought for a second. "Why does Janus call you Fati?"

The smile left Fatima's face. "Because that string bean of a sailor thinks he's funny. And just because he married my sister doesn't mean he gets to go around using her nickname for me." Fatima finished her sentence in a *humph*.

"Sister? His wife?"

"Tina was…is my sister."

"I'm sorry for your loss," James said quietly.

"Pain is a part of life. Loss is a part of pain," Fatima replied, looking James in the eye.

*BEEEEP!*

The noise ricocheted off the walls, and Rex whipped his head towards the HOLO on the right. "We've got an alert."

"What's happening?" Claudia appeared at the entrance and walked swiftly to the engineer's chair.

James and Fatima joined her, looking over Rex's shoulder as lines scrolled down the screen.

"Goddammit," Claudia said breathlessly.

James recognized a stark difference between the earlier view and this one. Lines jumped into one another, filling the space between their marks with sharp waves.

"What the hell is going on?" Fatima asked. "I've never seen this."

"No one has. They've released their entire battalion," Rex replied, his fingers flying over the keyboards.

Color drained from Fatima's face and Claudia inhaled. "Rex, what do we do?"

"I'm going to flood their charging lines. It will buy us some time and won't reveal that we're tracking the system. It'll eliminate its use in the future but…" His voice trailed off as he spoke.

"But what?" James asked, waiting for a response.

"They won't come back in pieces," Claudia replied for the engineer.

"I'm going up there," James said. He walked back towards the pills looking for any extra gear he could find.

"Like hell you are. Sit and wait. That's an order."

"You don't know what you're doing," James said, the heat in his voice rising as he spoke. "My people are attached to this, and you're running some sort of glue-and-popsicle-stick operation. Now things have gone to shit." James's chest pounded. Anger caught in the back of his throat, and he was overwhelmed with blinding emotions. Heather, Bob, Deck, Clint… His friends were in the middle of an unprecedented situation in the capital of their enemy. He needed to do something.

"Calm down and sit back," Claudia replied. Her face was crimson, and her knuckles white as she gripped the back of Rex's chair.

"What the fuck do you know about this? Hiding underground for two decades. We've *actually* fought them. Let me in there!" James started to walk towards the console, and Claudia turned to look him in the eye. Venom poured from her glare, and James returned the gaze with equal intensity.

"I said calm the fuck down and sit back." Her voice was razor sharp as a body interjected.

"James, come on. Let's sit." Liam's deep voice interceded as he moved James back from the HOLOs.

Hot air rushed in and out of James's lungs. Rage stuck to every fiber of his being as he watched Rex's fingertips.

A cool hand touched his arm, and James glanced to find Fatima holding his bicep. "We'll get them back." Her voice reassured him, and James breathed deeper to settle his heartbeat.

He couldn't think about the people up top. It was too much, so he concentrated on his breaths.

*One, in, two, out, three, in, four out...* He counted, blocking out the noises and images in his head that did not matter. He focused solely on Rex.

"Omega platform is moving," Rex said suddenly.

*Heather's team*, James thought.

"Any idea who's on it?"

Rex shook his head. "It can't be activated unless it's Talon or one of the team bringing them down."

"Should we prepare for Sentinels?" Claudia asked.

"I would," Rex said.

"Fatima," Claudia yelled over her shoulder, but the other woman was already on the move pulling James to his feet.

"Let's go. You're up."

The familiar stone that dropped in James's stomach prior to battle surfaced.

"I'll need some weapons."

"We've got plenty," Fatima said, walking toward the pill room.

James followed her, trailed by Liam and Rhia. They arrived at one of the rock faces, and Fatima opened it with a swipe of her HOLO. Inside rifles, body armor, and ion batons sat at the ready.

"Help yourselves. I'll pull some shields out for us."

"I'll help," Liam said. "Could you grab me some gear, Rhia?"

"Rifle or baton?" the techie asked, throwing a large piece of body armor on the ground next to hers.

"Both."

"Gamma platform moving," Rex called from the other room.

James pulled the plate vest over his head and checked the rifle. He grabbed extra magazines, clipping them onto his chest and picked up one of the batons. He flicked the power button on and off, watching the blue light lick the edges of the charged stick.

"Ready?" Rhia asked.

James nodded. "Always."

Five minutes later the ion shields were up and running, covering Rex and Claudia in a transparent gray haze.

"Thirty seconds to omega platform entering the chamber," Rex called out.

James gritted his teeth and watched the ceiling. Whatever came through would be a step ahead of them. They couldn't fire from the ground until they confirmed who was on that platform. But the second they did, they needed to move fast. If there was one Sentinel, the entire battalion would come through and tear the Resistance to pieces. James checked his baton charge again.

"Ten seconds."

"Wait until you confirm the platform before taking any shots," Claudia shouted from her place behind the HOLOs with Rex.

Her voice repulsed James, and he separated her persona from his emotions.

"Five, four, three two, entering the chamber," Rex said, counting the circular disc into view.

James's finger hung at the tip of his trigger. He watched as the edge of the platform lowered, fixing his eyes on the point above its horizon until he spotted a brunette ponytail poking from the top joined seconds later by Heather's face.

She smiled and gave him a thumbs-up. Relief flooded his system.

"Gamma entering in under two minutes."

"We need to get them off there," James said to Liam who nodded in response, and the two ran to help the new entries.

The omega platform hung its standard foot off the ground. Clint jumped down, helping Divan and Heather off.

James ran up to Heather and threw his arms around her. He was greeted by an equally forceful hug and a kiss on the lips. He let himself melt away for a second as his worry dissipated into the air. She was okay.

"What happened?" Claudia's voice interrupted and the atmosphere shattered as reality returned, pulling James back into the moment.

"No clue. One second, we're fine. The next, Sentinels are fucking everywhere," Clint answered.

"They were searching for something, but it was clear they didn't know what. Started pulling and searching people at random. We had to get out," Divan added. Her black hair was matted flat against her forehead and her eyes flickered with fear. "Talon's not back yet?"

"Will be in a minute," Fatima replied. "Let's get back.

The twin swallowed, catching her breath.

"Did you succeed in the mission?" Claudia asked. Her gray eyes staring intently at Divan who nodded.

"Yes, ma'am."

Claudia nodded. "Good. Go with Fatima."

Divan bobbed her head and hustled after Fatima to the ion shields.

"Weapons?" Heather asked the group.

"Pill room. Ask Fatima to show you," Claudia answered as she walked to her place next to Rex.

Clint and Heather nodded, running to arm themselves.

"Forty seconds," Rex's voice broke through, and James repositioned himself in his defensive spot.

"Goddammit, I wish we were up there," Liam growled. Concern etched into every word, his eyes betrayed his worry.

"They'll be good," James said.

"Ten seconds."

Clint and Heather crouched behind rock outcrops, their rifles pointed at the ceiling as Rex counted down the platform's descent.

"Five, four, three, two, one, entering the chamber."

The bottom of the platform appeared. The wait was crushing as the lip of the platform revealed nothing until Teresa's form came into view. Her stocky body cast a giant shadow blocking the light.

"Atta girl," Liam mumbled.

The platform continued to descend, and Talon walked to the edge as Teresa moved back.

Something was wrong. An uneasy ripple moved through James's stomach. A vague fear clawed at the back of his throat and he focused on the approaching team.

Talon's face grew more distinct as he neared the chamber floor. Worry and dread clouded his eyes. Finally, the platform settled in its spot.

James approached, followed by a muted crowd.

Teresa knelt on the other side of the platform. She stood and hopped off.

Liam enveloped her in a hug. "You okay?" he asked.

Teresa nodded into his chest. "I… We broke up… He's breathing but… Bob."

James's mouth ran dry. His hands lost circulation, and he looked closer at the platform where a still form lay. Without waiting, James hopped onto the platform and dropped to his knees.

Deck's eyes were closed and his mouth parted at the side. James bent an ear to his friend's chest. A *thump* murmured in a low but rhythmic patter. Momentary relief calmed his mental state and reality sunk in. *Bob*. The name circulated in his brain while he watched Deck take shallow breaths.

"What happened?" Clint asked. The bulky engineer knelt on the other side of Deck. James could hear and feel Heather's calming breath over his shoulder.

"We had to break up. Deck and Bob took off and distracted a bunch of them… I stuck with Talon… We waited in the shop." Teresa's eyes searched the faces of everyone in the room seeking penance for a perceived wrong. "Deck sprinted in and made it in time. Bob never came. Last thing we heard was a crash outside the doors."

Pain, fear, and guilt tore at James as he listened to Teresa's words. He looked up at Centria, breathing in the cavern's dusty air, hoping Bob was still alive.

# PART II

# Chapter Nine

The med bay of the *Kaleidoscope* radiated a feeling of home to James.

*Guess that's what weeks at sea will do to someone,* James thought, breathing in the salt-tinged air of the cavern mixing with the ship's filtering system. Gunmetal-gray plates lined the room along with a single porthole in the ceiling propped open to ventilate the space.

"How's it look?" James asked.

"I have a bunch of pain meds running through his IV. Concussed for sure. He took a nasty hit to the noggin. Luckily there's a nice big bump. Besides that, all other signs point to a healthy if not severely scarred young man." the ship's doctor pulled off her latex gloves and threw them into the waste basket. "That's one hell of a burn scar under his elbow."

James grinned, thinking back to Deck's most recent fireworks display. "Too much fun at Christmas. It's his risky time of year."

"I'd like to go to one of those parties," the doctor replied with a smile. "Either way, you can expect him up in a couple of hours."

"Thanks, Doc. Consider yourself invited," James said, looking at his unconscious friend.

"All done?" Wally asked, brushing past the doctor as he stepped into the room. Heather and the rest of the Federation crew followed with concerned faces.

"You bet, thanks."

"Thanks Doc," Wally said, guiding the doctor from the room.

The rest of the team took up spots along the edge of Deck's bed watching his chest rise and fall.

"He'd love this," Clint said, "It'd be his favorite thing in the world—all of us watching him. Waiting for him to wake up. Jackass." The bulky engineer mumbled the last word as he stepped back from the bed to lean against the wall.

"Any news out there?" James asked. It had been three hours since the platforms' return. With Clint's help, James had taken Deck to the med bay of the *Kaleidoscope*. Without a proper medic in the Resistance HQ, he'd needed help from Janus's ship.

"Nothing yet," Heather replied. "We're going to meet in the Resistance HQ in a half hour. Janus is joining us."

*Thank God*, James thought. He was not sure he could contain his anger in Claudia's presence. Every time he thought of the woman, fury consumed him, and he had to count heartbeats to bring himself under control.

James nodded. "Good, I want answers."

He walked to the entryway, stopping next to Clint. "You coming?"

The mechanic shook his head. "I'll stay here. We'll never hear the end of it if he wakes up alone."

"Thanks," James said, clapping his friend on the shoulder as he walked through the door.

Half an hour later, James was seated at the HQ's meeting table. The room was packed with the Resistance teams, his group, Janus, and necessary members of his crew. Most of the underground population stood around the space, leaning against dashboards or standing with their arms crossed.

James glanced at all those assembled before focusing his eyes across the table on Claudia.

"What's the play, Claudia? This is on you," James said, hoping to convey a bitter tone.

Claudia ignored the barb and pulled up three HOLO screens. Blue haze reflected off her gray eyes. "We need to locate Bob and bring him back within twenty-four hours. If he's already incarcerated, that job will be infinitely harder,"

"Why twenty-four hours?" Liam asked.

"He'll either be dead or…" Claudia trailed off.

"Dead or…what?" Liam pressed.

"Under Raspin's control. After that it's too dangerous."

"So they won't touch him for twenty-four hours?" Heather asked.

"I didn't say that," Claudia responded. "But within that window, we've got a shot at getting to him first."

"Let's get moving. What do we need to do?" James asked. An urgent pleading in his voice underscored the uselessness he felt.

Claudia glanced at him. "We wait." The focus in her eyes was reminiscent of James's last conversation with Stacie. She turned and walked from the room.

Pangs of anger and worthlessness raged within James with each step of her rubber-soled shoes clicking against the rocky path as she disappeared.

Entering the room, Teresa, red-faced with emotion and chugging a bottle of water, said, "That was fast. What's the plan?"

"We wait. Need to get to Bob within twenty-four hours or he's gone," James answered sharply.

"Fucking ridiculous," Teresa mumbled.

"There is some good news."

Rhia's voice from the front of the table momentarily distracted James. Rex stood behind the dashboard controls, and Rhia nodded towards the engineer as he worked the keyboards. Live images James had never seen of Centria's harbor showed on the screens.

"What the fuck?" he breathed.

Manipulating the screens, the slender woman said, "Mission was a success. This is a live feed of the harbor and a fully triangulated area surrounding the mothership."

"The *Odyssey*," Rex corrected her absently.

"Whatever. We've got it, James. We're inside Centria."

"This is live?" Fatima asked.

"You bet. You're seeing everything in real time with less than a one-second delay."

"Holy shit," Teresa said, leaning into the back of Heather's chair.

The rest of the group stared at the video feed capturing a close-up view of the BZ's city.

At first glance, it looked like any typical Federation city. It was a largely quiet scene. People walked casually as birds floated in the air, and water lapped against the bulwarks. However, upon closer inspection and as the camera continued to scan the area, another world came into focus. The *Odyssey's* holding dock towered in the background. Although the entire ship was too big to be seen, a wall of gray revealed to James what floated in the water.

The cameras captured different angles of the harbor as they cycled through their feeds. The details became clearer with each pass. James focused on the people. Initially they seemed to be normal humans ambling through a harbor on a pretty afternoon. But not these people. There was an intensity to their movements. Everyone walked with a purpose.

"Not very casual, are they?" Liam said, confirming James's observations.

"Forced evolution doesn't allow for lazy afternoons," Fatima replied. Her eyes were glued to the screens. James realized this was probably the first time she'd seen the BZ since she defected over two decades ago. His stomach twisted imagining how painful it must be.

"Anything in particular we should be looking for?" Teresa asked the Resistance group.

"That building. Notice anything special?" Divan pointed to a gray rectangular structure sitting in the center of the harbor.

"Not really," Heather replied, glancing at the squat building.

"Look closer," Talon added. James fixed his eyes on the image.

Rhia zoomed in, and suddenly James saw them. There were hundreds of Sentinels lurking on the roof, swooping down to rotate with those hovering across the front of the entire building.

"What is it?" Heather whispered.

"The Sentinel HQ. If Bob's in the Order's control, he's there."

James's heart sank as he watched the Sentinel at the door animate and scan a group of people as they entered before disappearing back inside its disc and floating off to join the others.

Anxiety gripped James as he realized there was no way to get inside that building alive. No bargaining chip in the world could get them access. Bob was trapped.

Hanging his head, he stood from the table and walked aimlessly out of the room. Eventually someone guided him to a bench. Heather's smooth hands enveloped his as he looked at the long kitchen table.

"We'll get him back." Heather's words echoed in the back of his mind, but James could barely hear them, unable to focus on anything other than Bob.

*What did I do?* He blamed himself for not demanding to go on the trip. He should be there, not Bob. Guilt tore at him as he fought to keep his thoughts from spinning out of control when a loud *THUMP* jolted him.

He startled and looked up to see Deck grinning back at him.

"Miss me?"

James grinned. "Sleeping Beauty. How're you feeling?"

"Been better. Bit of a headache." Deck sat on the bench across from James. Heather's protective hand stayed on James's arm as he sat up.

"Shouldn't you be in bed?" James asked, confused and alarmed that a recently unconscious patient was up and walking around.

"Doc said I'm fine. Look, I'm a modern marvel. Can't stop this," Deck replied, balancing back on the bench.

"Nope. That is definitely not what she said," Clint added, joining them in the kitchen, "She told him he should stay in there for another couple of days. Deck said no, took out his IV, and left."

"Sounds about right," James said, grinning at his friend.

"Well, looks like I may be needed. When are we going for Bob?" Deck asked, picking up an apple from the basket on the table.

"I dunno. We don't even know where he's being held or what. I just I don't—"

"Ahem." Claudia stood at the doorway and cleared her throat.

James looked dully at the woman, his initial anger subdued after the revelation of the Sentinel HQ and Bob's possible imprisonment inside it.

"I confirmed he's being held by Centria."

Dread pooled in James's gut as a wave of hopelessness swelled in his thoughts. *What now?*

Quiet enveloped the room as the Federation people stared at the ground. Throughout their careers in war, each had been in situations similar to this. For the moment, futility owned the room.

"Do we have options?" Rhia's voice cut through room.

"Not many," Claudia said, shaking her head. "We have twenty hours and a single shot at pulling him out. There's only one way to temporarily disarm those Sentinels long enough to make it in the room, but it will destroy our plans for taking out the *Odyssey*."

James lifted his eyes and looked at the woman's emotionless face as her eyes glinted in the recycled light.

"Rex can overload the Sentinel system. It's a back door he built in years ago. Our plan was to use it to sink the ship, but if you want to use it now, we'll run it to save your friend. This is your call."

Claudia's odd change of heart surprised James. *Why was she ok with him calling the shots?*

"We'd be able to get into the building?" James asked.

"Can't promise that, but the Sentinels can be turned off for half an hour. Then they're back on and we lose a part of our winning hand. Like I said, later we'll need to find a different way to disrupt the Sentinels to destroy the *Odyssey*. It could be putting that entire mission in jeopardy. Your team, your call."

James broke eye contact with Claudia and glanced at the others in the room. They would be sacrificing the grueling months of travel across the most dangerous ocean to run a mission and change the entire course of the war. All to free Bob. All to save his friend. He searched the faces of his team one by one, finishing with Deck, who nodded from across the table, his eyes steel.

Heather squeezed his hand as he looked up at Claudia. "Let's get Bob."

# Chapter Ten

The zipper on his suit caught as he yanked it up his rib cage. He freed the cloth and finished zipping. Pulling a T-shirt over his head, he checked the sidearm and baton strapped onto the sides of his waist.

*Secure*, he thought tugging at the ionic rod.

"When you get up top, get yourselves to the harbor. Does everyone know the way?" Claudia asked.

"I got it," Deck said. "Steel trap." He tapped the side of his head.

"Once there, emit the signal with your alarm. Rex will trigger the overload. We'll tell you when the Sentinels go dark. You won't know from looking at them."

"That's me," Heather said, holding the alarm device aloft.

"What if they act up?" Liam asked, slapping an ionic band on his wrist.

"Run," Claudia replied. "Make your way inside. Find Bob, get out of the harbor, and go to the second platform."

"Why two platforms? Why not use the same one?" Teresa asked.

Fatima answered for Claudia. "Too risky to use the same entryway. They might have learned about our tunnels after Bob. Safer to change them up."

"Right, stay together. If you have to split up, run evasive maneuvers and keep an eye on your HOLOs. We'll try to communicate with you, but if it's too long after you leave the harbor we may not be able to."

"Why's that?" James asked.

"The first thing they'll do when the Sentinels come back online is shut down everything in the city."

"Can we use some of your connections up there?"

"We're prepared to make that decision." Claudia's answer was noncommittal, but James nodded.

*I'll take it*, he thought. Any promise beyond that would be pulling teeth.

"Other questions?" Claudia asked as she looked at the group. Her words echoed off the hollow stone walls of the cavern. "Good luck."

Claudia joined Rex, Divan, and Talon who were working frantically behind their HOLO dashboards.

Fatima gave James a thumbs-up following her leader.

Janus lingered by the platform glancing at each of the soldiers one by one.

"Any advice, Captain?" James asked, adjusting the fabric of Rex's custom-made suit.

"Keep your heads down and move as fast as you can without attracting attention." Janus concentrated as he spoke. "Move smoothly and conceal your weapons. Once inside the harbor building, do whatever you need to get your friend, and get out. Do not hesitate."

"Yessir."

"See you in a few." Janus nodded and joined the others.

"Taking off in three, two, one." Rex calmly counted down their exit. James lost his balance for a second as the platform began to rise from its hovering position. A *whir* accompanied their ascent, and James glanced over the edge. The HOLOs seemed farther away than he expected from this high up. His perspective watching the platform leave earlier was much different when he was the one flying upwards.

"Freaky how high we go on this thing," Liam mentioned as he leaned over the edge.

"Wait for the lights to turn out," Clint said.

James glanced above to the tunnel, a dark abyss and portal to another world. He gritted his teeth and took a deep breath as everything went dark.

A blue haze lit up the edges of the platform. In the shadowy glow, his friends' faces appeared, their eyes illuminated like beacons of neon white light.

"Freaky, right?" Deck said, grinning with white, shiny teeth.

"Not my favorite," James replied.

"I hope it's not radioactive," Deck mumbled casually inspecting his hands.

After a few minutes, James sensed the platform slowing. Their transport came to a stop and James looked at his team. Immediately, his mind jumped to the worst-case scenarios. *Bob was broken by the BZ, and they know where we are. Or the team below was overrun and we're about to slam back to the ground.* Visions of himself splattering into a paste 1,700 meters beneath the earth formed in his mind until he saw movement. In the pitch black of the tunnel, a thin slice of light was slowly widening above.

"What is going on….?" Teresa said. Her voice trailed off as the lighted line grew wider and wider until the top of the tunnel opened and the platform rose through it.

James glanced around their location and breathed a sigh of relief. *First step*, he thought.

Claudia had told them they would arrive in a basement beneath an apartment building. It was active with tenants, but the sub-basement had been sealed off for decades and was one of the safer entrances to Centria.

"I'd say welcome to the BlankZone, but that sounds lame," Deck said. When the platform leveled with the basement floor it stopped moving and they stepped off. After the team disembarked, the platform disappeared beneath the floor, and the tunnel's mouth closed.

*Clock started,* James thought as his mind jumped to the next part of the plan.

"Everyone remember your pairs?" James asked. Affirmative nods responded. James looked at Deck. "You and me, buddy."

"Love it," Deck said. The scout patted him on the back and walked to the door in the corner of the room.

"Wait two minutes and send the next grouping. See you all at the harbor." James looked at each team member in turn.

"Good luck." Heather pecked him on the lips, and he smiled joining Deck.

Without hesitation, Deck turned the knob, opening the door to cement stairs on the other side.

"After you," James said.

"Such a gentleman." Deck curtseyed taking the first step.

James shut the door, and Deck bounded to the top of the steps to another door. Holding his breath, James waited in the middle of the staircase as Deck cautiously pushed it open.

Deck motioned for James to join him. Before them appeared a rust-stained white-tiled bathroom with cement floors that smelled of rotten water and dust.

"No wonder no one inhabits the sub-basement," Deck said, stepping carefully over a mound of mold growing along a groove in the floor. "Who puts a shower room in the basement?"

"If that's what it was for…"

"I'd rather not think of alternatives," Deck said as they passed three disintegrating rusty metal tubs.

"I'm with you."

Deck pushed on a heavy metal door opening to another staircase. James waited partway up the staircase as Deck opened the door then followed the scout into a gray hallway.

The building directory, written half in English and half in unfamiliar letters, sat in a glass display case next to a single wooden chair with a faded blue cushion and a house plant in a white vase.

James touched the leaves of the plant. *Rubber*, he realized as the fabric squeaked between his fingers.

"Hood on. Follow my lead," Deck said absently.

James donned his head cover and looked at his friend, "Your show bud."

Deck pushed on the glass doors to the street, and James took his first steps into the world of the BlankZone.

An unhurried scene waited on the other side. They watched a car drive idly by, and two older men strode purposefully past them to the end of the block taking a sharp right turn and disappearing behind an apartment building. The area was absent of other activity, and James strained to hear anything unusual. Silence reigned supreme in the space. Concerned by the absence of sounds, James immediately became suspicious. Four hours earlier, the Order had captured a Federation operative on their soil, so where was the defense force? What was going on?

"Wouldn't even think we'd been here," Deck said, repeating James's thoughts.

"Too quiet," James agreed.

"Keep your guard up. This way."

Deck took off in the opposite direction of the men who had passed, and James followed.

As they made their way through the city, James took note of everything around him. The city itself was mostly the same as those he had visited prior to the war with large glass-fronted buildings, corner stores, and old brick structures that had been beautified by time. It was like any other, simultaneously a footprint of the past and a glimpse into the future. Although it held all classic makings of a city, it lacked the sense of humanity that should exist in such a large population.

Traditionally James thought of murderers, killers, rapists, and people with no regard for their fellow humans as lacking humanity. But the behaviors of Centria's population showed James a different aspect of inhumanity. Devoid of any meaningful interaction, these people were even less human than the monsters James generally linked with the soulless. No sounds. No smells. Nothing unique. So scrubbed of imperfections the city itself was imperfect. The opposite of what a city should be.

He scanned the buildings, looking for a shred of normalcy, and, seeing something out of place, did a double take back to the corner of a building's edge. Inspecting more closely, he saw exactly what he'd sensed—a Sentinel. The dull metal shone in the cloudy afternoon light. Upon first glance, they were unimpressive, metal frisbees hanging in the air. But James knew all too well the horrors contained inside their bodies. They were ruthless weapons designed and deployed to tear apart flesh and demand submission.

James turned his head to avoid detection in the thinning crowd. He grabbed Deck's elbow and lightly guided the scout across the street.

"All good?" Deck asked, his body tense at James's touch.

"Sentinel behind us," James replied.

Deck chuckled. "I see six covering these two blocks. If they know we're here, they're not doing anything about it. Follow my lead."

*Six?!* James slowly looked around and saw the other Sentinels materialize. They meandered in the shadows, perfectly camouflaged by the darkness in the empty spaces. *Good thing Deck's here*, James thought, shaking his head.

They continued their walk towards the harbor, keeping pace with Centria's population. As they approached the harbor, the buildings became shorter and the number of Sentinels increased. All around, bands of the floating weapons hung in rotational patterns leading to the waterfront.

This was the only indication anything might be afoot. Otherwise, it appeared as if nothing in the world had changed.

Salt hung in the air as they neared the water. There was an underlying feeling of a cleansed humanity. The odors of a harbor, gasoline, iron, sweat, blood, wood, smoke, oil, and rotting fish had been neutralized. The aura of a working dockyard had been stripped of anything that resembled defects.

Without warning, a shadow broke over James. Fighting to calm his reaction, he looked up at the sky but found nothing blocking his view. Confused, he looked around and saw Deck pointing ahead.

"It's her," he said quietly, and James looked ahead to see a monstrosity looming in the distance.

Cold metal glinted off the top of the manmade behemoth sprouting over the edge of the water like a mountain range. James had only seen the machines from a distance. Their size had been awe-inspiring miles off the coast. Up close though, he was shocked into silence.

"I know," Deck said. "Come on. T, Liam, and Rhia are in position. Let's get ourselves situated."

"Where's the building?"

"This way," Deck said, and he walked out from the mothership's shadow. James followed, fighting the impulse to glance back at what he intended to destroy.

They slowed their pace as they neared the squat gray building James recalled from Claudia's presentation.

A cloud of Sentinels provided an impenetrable security blanket to the structure, and James dared to think about what would happen if Rex's plan failed. *What if they installed a fail-safe? What if they expect the attack?* Visions of Sentinels emerging from their carriers and tearing him limb from limb distracted him for a second until he caught sight of Clint and Heather.

Heather gave him a slight smile turning away and walking towards the building.

"Here we go," Deck said, and they followed the pair. "God, I hope this works."

*Me too*, James thought, moving with Deck.

His heartbeat sped up with each step. Paying close attention to the Sentinels and taking deep breaths helped him focus his energy and control his bodily functions.

*What will be different about them when they lose power*? James gazed at the gray metal discs, trying to discern a change in their actions, shape, or floating mechanism. Would they drop from the air? Pause midflight? There was no way to know.

*Have to trust them,* he thought as he watched, thinking positively with each step that Rex was as smart as James thought.

"Look," Deck whispered. "They're circling weird." The scout pointed in the direction of a group of Sentinels patrolling the corner of the building. Two of the Sentinels would circle one another, turn the corner, and double back. James scanned the building. Sentinels covering the face of the structure mimicked their counterparts, repeatedly making odd, unscheduled changes to their rotations.

"They did it," James said, hearing the surprise in his voice.

"Half an hour," Deck said.

James nodded, and the two quickened their step.

Heather and Clint entered through the plate glass doors, which shut silently behind them. James was greeted by his reflection as they made their final approach to the building.

A swarm of Sentinels hovered overhead. He was unnerved by how close he was to the lethal cloud of devices that had brought death and destruction to his life.

"Inside, buddy," Deck whispered, holding the door as James entered.

On the left side of the lobby, Heather and Clint sat casually in a back row of seats with people watching a HOLO announcing numbers on its screen. Quiet shuffling defined the ambience of the room. Drafts of recycled air from the HVAC carried the muted scents of everyone inside.

Deck guided them to a bench on the right side of the room. They took stock of the people sitting with them as Teresa entered.

The room was a semi-circle with three diagonal hallways extending back to the center room. The main lobby had one floor, but hallways only had a second floor. Each staircase had two guards on patrol at the top. Four guards watched from positions on either side of the front entrance while three guards milled about the room inspecting the people.

**46A-323**

The red block symbol flashed from the front of the room and James watched as a young woman approached one of the counters. She spoke briefly with the blank-faced man before walking away. Her eyes remained on the floor as she exited the building. The door closed softly and James wondered what kind of news she'd received.

"Hey." Deck broke James from his distraction.

*Keep it together man*, James thought, chastising himself. "Sorry. Showtime?" he asked, running his hand under his shirt and grasping the hilt of the baton hidden along his rib cage.

Deck signed to Rhia who popped a HOLO emitter from her pocket. James watched from the corner of his eye as the slim techie operated the device without looking. Thirty seconds later, she replaced it. She splayed her hand out, and James tightened his grip on the baton. He counted in his head. *Five. Four. Three. Two...*

"Showtime," Deck growled.

*CRACK!*

The overhead lights exploded in shards of sparks and James jolted from his seat. His baton slammed into the head of the guard standing closest to him. The guard's body crumbled in a heap instead of dissipating into thin air as was usual when his weapon made contact with his victim.

Hazy yellow lights flipped on as James turned and saw Deck standing over the other guard. He wiped his baton on his pant leg, and a black smear appeared in the distorted light.

"Gusher," Deck said. James glanced at the growing pool coming from the man's head.

"Chains?" James asked, and Deck produced three of Divan's bands. He gave one to James.

"You take the far door."

Without replying, James walked swiftly to the far side of the room. He threaded the band through the door's protruding handles and tied it together, yanking on it to check its hold before running back to Deck at the center door.

"Almoooost…done." Deck stepped back eyeing his handiwork and inspecting the ceiling. "That'll hold. Creepy lights, huh? Very zombie horror."

"Let's hope not. Come on," James said.

He walked to the center staircase, and Deck split to the right. James joined Liam, who was engaged with a guard. One already lay in a pile at the edge of the staircase.

"Here," James announced to Liam.

The bearded man ducked as James took a full swing at the head of the second guard. A *crunch* met his weapon followed by another fall.

Two more guards descended from their position on the second floor. James ripped into them without mercy, pummeling the soldiers. A strike glanced off his shoulder, and he retaliated with a vicious snap of his wrist. A grunt came from the guard as he landed on the banister and rolled to the floor.

"You good?" Liam asked, taking stock of the situation in the room.

"Great. The floor guards out?"

"T got 'em."

James nodded. He looked at the other two chambers. All was going according to plan. Heather and Clint were halfway up the stairs, and Deck was pulling a limp body from the bottom of the other staircase that had blocked their access.

"Lead the way," James said. Liam leapt up the stairs two at a time.

Covering their backs, James followed backwards up the staircase while scanning the room. The patrons sat huddled in their chairs. No one had made a sound since they'd entered. Guards were sprawled across the floor, some with pools of dark liquid expanding in halos around their heads. The yellow light combined with the shadows sent dark orange hues into the recesses of the room.

His foot slipped when he arrived at the top of the stairs, and he grabbed the rail to keep from falling.

"Doors are closed."

James cursed under his breath. They had hoped the rooms would stay open to avoid any unpleasant surprises.

"Clear 'em out," James said as he brandished his baton.

Liam lined up on one side of the door, and James nodded before he bashed his shoulder through.

Lime green walls shined in the yellow lights. A single desk with a chair on both sides sat in the middle of the room along with an unoccupied HOLO emitter.

"Next up," James said. They repeated the process up the length of the hallway. They took turns ramming the doors inward, but every space was empty. After moving back and forth across the hall through ten rooms, they finally stumbled upon their first person.

A woman sat in a desk and tilted her head in curiosity as James and Liam entered.

"We're looking for someone," James said. "We believe you're keeping our friend prisoner."

"We don't do that here," the woman said with a pleasant smile. "Everyone wants to be here. Just wait. I'll have someone help you."

His baton moved before he could think, smashing the emitter to pieces. Heat rose in the back of his throat as he spoke again and demanded, "Where is our friend?"

Confused, the woman shook her head. "We don't have your friend. We are the Order. We are one."

"This is useless," Liam muttered over his shoulder. James turned from the woman and went to the next door. He slammed his shoulder against the structure. It held.

"It's locked," James said.

"Let me try." Liam backed away and did the same, trying to force his way inside. The door held still.

"Thank God for Rex's little gadgets," Liam said. He pulled a paper bundle from his pocket and took out a putty-like material. He pasted it around the edge of the door handle, lit a match, and touched the edge of the substance. Within seconds the putty disappeared and a hole appeared.

James pushed and the door opened. There was a table next to the entryway and a chair sat in the middle of the room.

A man sat in the chair, his legs and feet bound while two men in business clothes stood on the far side of the room. Curiously they looked at the people who had entered.

A groan came from the bound man and he lifted his head, sending a ripple of shock and joy through James's stomach.

*Bob.*

# CHAPTER ELEVEN

Fear, pain, relief, and confusion flashed across Bob's face.

"Bob, you okay?" James asked as he stepped into the room.

The men behind Bob moved forward. Their expressions mirrored that of the woman behind the desk in the other room—blank uncertainty.

"Who are you?" the man on the right asked, placing his hand on Bob's shoulder. James's anger broke. He took another step towards Bob, pulled back his hand, and whipped the man's temporal lobe with the baton. Liam followed his lead, lashing out with equal vehemence at the other sentry.

James heard the man's body crumble to the floor. He knelt and undid the clasps around Bob's ankles.

"What…? What is…? Wha…?" Bob's voice cracked as he tried to speak.

"It's Liam and James, buddy. We came to get you," Liam said.

James glanced at Bob's face. Recognition fought to escape to his mind.

"Wha…? How…? Wha…?" Bob stammered, jumping between syllables, unable to sync them together. Dark liquid trailed from his ears down his neck with a HOLO collar attached.

"Fuck," James cursed under his breath and glanced around the room.

"What?" Liam asked.

"One of the BZ's fun little tricks." James noticed an emitter sitting on a metal table tucked into a corner.

James grabbed the device and swiped across the screen to open it. The tablet's dashboard shook for a second as the arrow recentered. *Locked.*

Ideas on how to break into the machine raced through James's head.

"We've got to go," Liam said.

"I know. Give me a second."

"We don't have time, James. Breaking all those doors ate up our grace period."

*Dammit.* Liam was right, but how the hell was he going to get Bob outside and back to the Resistance HQ like this?

He glanced at the medic whose mouth babbled mutely as he stared at the two unfamiliar men. Every few seconds he emitted strange muttering sounds. Whatever the BZ was doing, they had already made progress.

"Can you carry him?" James asked. He inspected the collar behind Bob's neck but found exactly what he expected—seamless.

"Yeah, what are we going to do about this thing though?" Liam asked, pointing at the collar.

"We'll figure that out," James said as he stuffed the HOLO emitter in his pants. "Let's go."

Liam nodded and pulled Bob's arm around his shoulders, grunting as he stood. "Christ, Bob's heavier than he looks."

"Likes to eat."

"I'll say."

Bob emitted a low *wha wha wha* sound as his legs swayed next to Liam's.

Before they left, James searched the room a final time. He bent to get a closer look at the men on the floor, rifling through their pockets and pulling a band off one of their wrists. He stuffed the apparatus into his pocket and gazed at the lifeless eyes of the man whom he had cracked on the head and the two growing pools of inky liquid. He felt nothing.

Liam was halfway down the hall, and James jogged to catch up to the bearded man. Rhia and Deck waited at the top of the stairs. Deck took Bob's other arm over his shoulder to aid with the descent.

"You guys get held up by those fucking doors too?" Deck asked.

"Pain in the ass," Liam replied.

"Not out of it yet. Hey, Rhia," James pulled the HOLO emitter from his pants and the screen sprang up. "Can you break into this?"

The techie inspected the screen. She tried the familiar swipe and analyzed the monitor and its emitter. Seconds ticked by as he watched her. "I can, but I need a clean HOLO. What's on it?"

"It'll take this off," James said pointing at the collar secured around Bob's neck. "We need to release it ASAP."

"What's it…do?" Rhia asked leaning in for a closer look.

"I don't know about this one, but I never had very pleasant experiences with them," James said. The loss of air and repeating blackouts haunted his mind. He hoped the BZ would not do anything before they had a chance to detach the torture device.

"Get me a HOLO on a secure network. I'll have it off in seconds."

James nodded, buoyed by her confidence.

"Ready for exfil?" James heard Heather from behind and turned to see her marching towards him with a baton in both hands. Clint trailed her closely. His moist skin glinted and his shirt was soaked in red liquid reflecting black in the amber light.

"Christ, were you in a butcher shop?" Deck asked, rearing back at their appearance.

"Apparently we picked the guards' quarters," Clint said, wiping a streak of blood from his eyebrow. "None of its mine."

"Take a bath when we get home," Deck said, stepping away from Clint.

"We're going to have to move fast out there. How long do we have?" James asked.

"Ten minutes," Teresa said checking her HOLO.

"That's not enough time to leave in different groups. We're all going at once. Deck, take lead with T and Rhia. Clint and Heather, you stay in back and shout if there are followers. I'll carry Bob with Liam in the middle."

James switched places with Deck and pulled Bob's limp arm over his shoulders.

"Good, Bob?" James asked.

Bob rolled his head from side to side and looked back at James, expressionless.

Fear twisted his stomach into a knot. It had been only a few minutes since taking their friend, but he was getting worse. They needed to get that collar off. Who knew what the BZ could do with them now?

"Get us home, Deck."

The scout nodded and pulled the bands off the center door. He took a cautious step outside, beckoning for the rest of the team to follow.

Bright blue skies and a fading afternoon sun greeted them on the other side of the plate glass.

The Sentinels maintained their imperfect movements, hovering in the air. One of the discs paused and stuttered. James's hand went to the sidearm at his waist. Adrenaline pumped in his veins, and he counted how many shots he could get off before the weapon became useless.

As if remembering something, the Sentinel continued along its original course, bending around the edge of the building doubling back on itself and repeating the pattern.

"Those things won't hold long," he muttered to Liam.

"I'm guessing Rex's timing wasn't perfect science."

"Safe assumption."

Deck walked briskly ahead of them as Rhia and Teresa trailed at a short distance widening the team's pathway. Faces paused as they looked at the odd formation of people making their way through the city streets, but there was no physical reaction.

*How has no one said anything?* James glanced at his blood-stained shirt and looked at the crowd with suspicion.

Bob's head lolled side to side as they walked, murmuring under his breath, trying to form questions, but something blocked him. The collar was either still active or had already done some damage.

"Time?" James called over to the techie who glanced at her HOLO.

"Seven minutes."

James gritted his teeth. They were never going to make it, and their route left them too exposed.

"Deck!" he called, but the scout held up his hand.

"I'm on it," Deck replied, and he dipped into the closest side street. He pulled a HOLO from his pocket and swiped across the face. James glimpsed at the pop-up map on the ground. He hoped their data was up to date.

"This way," Deck announced as he led them down an alleyway.

Bob's arm slipped and James grabbed it, righting Bob's limp body.

"Good over there?" Liam asked.

"He's getting weaker." James said, noticing for the first time that Bob had stopped walking all together.

"Gotta get his new jewelry off," Liam said, yanking Bob's arm to a more comfortable position on his shoulders.

James nodded. Liam had no idea.

A steady wind blew through the alleyway, and Deck changed direction, pulling them into a shadow-strewn street. They passed short gray concrete buildings, different from the glass ones that dominated the scene closer to the harbor.

A huddle of people passed expressionless, momentarily drawing a semblance of confusion before emotionlessly continuing on their way, intent on their task.

"Rhia—"

James was interrupted by the peal of a siren. Its shriek cut through the stillness of the city.

Liam glanced at him over Bob's head. His eyes said everything James already knew. The Sentinels had returned.

"Deck, get us somewhere," Teresa said, turning in a full circle to scan the area.

"We're five minutes to the tunnel. We have to cross a street..." Deck's voice trailed off, and he stared at the screen quizzically. "Over here."

The scout turned and ran up an alleyway. James followed, watching each door warily.

"Goddammit." Clint's voice caused James to turn around. They had ended up in a crossway of alleys. Two sides ended with streets and one in a dead end. Their side of the alley stretched behind the block of gray buildings until it banked into another set of alleys down the road. Clint's alarm had been warranted as James saw a line of Sentinels waiting at the ends of both alleys. From their position, the team was hidden in a blind spot, but there was no doubt the defensive weapons would start their way at any moment.

James took Bob's arm off his shoulder. "Can you take him?"

Liam hoisted the medic's body over his shoulder into a fireman's carry. "I've got it."

Teresa ran past in Clint's direction with Rhia close behind. James stopped the techie and gave her the HOLO from the harbor office that he'd stowed in his shirt.

"Follow Deck. We need you to take care of Bob's collar the second you can."

Rhia accepted the emitter and took off after Deck while Liam lumbered behind her with Bob bouncing on his back.

Without hesitation, James turned back to the rest of his team waiting with their weapons drawn.

The Sentinels had converged on the center alley, and James huddled behind a dumpster with Teresa while Clint and Heather stood with their backs against an indented doorway on the other side.

Heather signed: *How many?*

Teresa responded in kind: *Twelve total. Four in front and eight in back.*

Clint added: *Do they know we're here?*

Teresa replied: *I don't know.*

James chest thudded as the silent killers continued through the alley. He touched his hand to the ionic switch on his baton and breathed in and out.

He signed to the group: *When they pass, wait three seconds. Use sidearms to take out the discs before dealing with their HOLOs.*

Clint and Heather nodded.

A shadow was cast across the center of the alley.

*Here they come.* James tightened his grip on his pistol.

The dark circle moved away from them as their attackers approached until a gunmetal-gray disc broke the edge of James's hiding space.

It hovered in the air, unaware that James sat only paces away from its cold metal body. James counted the seconds in his head as it passed. They would have to move instantaneously to catch these things and avoid initiating any sort of tracking. Either way, the gunshots were sure to bring every Sentinel in the city crashing on their position. He aimed at the lead and flipped off his safety.

*Three.*

*Two.*

*SWOOSH!*

James was blinded by a beam of blue light.

A *clunk* of metal crashing to the ground sounded in James's ears as he fought to regain his sight. A hand grabbed his forearm and a familiar voice yelled in his ear, "Come on. We need to get inside. They'll help us in there."

James knew Deck's voice anywhere, and he grabbed his friend's shoulder as his vision struggled to return. Other figures and voices sounded as he moved. His foot hit something, stubbing his toe.

*Dammit*, James thought, gritting his teeth through the immediate pain. His eyesight was not getting any better, so he closed his eyes to avoid the swirling colors.

After walking in silence Deck spoke, "Watch your step."

James squinted, and through a swirl of purple dots made out a short metal staircase leading into a building. He entered a door, and Deck ushered him to another staircase leading to an inky black bottom.

"Hold the wall and keep going. I'm going to get us out of here. We're safe."

James nodded and held onto the stone wall, moving as quickly as he would allow himself.

"Anyone else there?" Clint yelled.

"Me," James replied.

"Same here," Teresa echoed.

"Heather?" James's heart hammered in his chest as he waited to hear his girlfriend's voice.

"Don't worry, I'm here." Relief flooded James as her hand grasped his shoulder. He covered it with his.

"Can anyone see?" Teresa asked.

"Blind as a bat. Purples and blues are all I got," Clint replied.

"Same," James and Heather said.

Teresa sighed. "Let's keep going. Would've been nice to have *someone* with sight guide us through here. Damn husbands."

James chuckled as he stepped down the hall using the grooves between the rectangular stone blocks of the wall's tunnel to guide him.

A damp, but not unpleasant odor of fresh soil emanated. *Dirt.*

"Where the hell are we?" Heather asked. Her hand brushing against his shoulder every so often to make sure he was still there. James liked the reminder.

"Underground," Clint said sarcastically.

"Genius," Heather said, her tone revealing the roll of her eyes. "Really though. Where are we?"

"I'm hoping it's the Resistance," Teresa replied. "Otherwise…"

James had not considered this yet. What if they were in a Centria-controlled tunnel? What if this was all a trap? It was not out of the question for Raspin to kill and imitate his friend. An unpleasant scene of future violence flooded James's brain.

"It's not," Heather said, increasing James's anxiety.

"What's that?" James asked, squinting ahead at a growing beam of yellow light in the distance.
Purple and blue dots blurred the edges of the light, but its center was unobstructed.

The yellowish glow was unmistakable. Voices grew louder and James concentrated, trying to discern the sounds.

"Move him here."

"Yep, up… No! Watch his head."

"Okay, lay his feet. Wait, let me pull out…"

A bevy of chaos bounced off the stone walls. James pushed open a metal door and flooded the tunnel with incandescent light.

The blues and purples blocking his vision dissipated, and he found himself in a windowless room of cement stone walls and a smooth concrete floor.

"Pull his head back and strap it riiiight there." A young black-haired woman, her locks pulled in a tight bun on top of her head, was instructing two younger men arranging Bob on a metal table.

A drain was placed under the table, and James followed a streak of stained liquid to the edge of the scene where Liam and Rhia watched. Their bodies were rigid with apprehension, and James tapped Rhia's shoulder.

"What's going on?"

Rhia shook her head. "Needed more than a HOLO." She did not look at him as she spoke, and her lip bled from chewing it.

The rest of the team filed in behind James.

Teresa wrapped an arm around Liam. "Who are they?"

"Resistance. Deck got us into the building, and we were rushed here. They put him on the table and have been getting things set up to operate."

James nodded and stared as one of the men strapped an unknown device around Bob's head covering his ears in steel muffs.

"Is he in?" the woman asked as she flicked open a HOLO.

"He's in. I've got the jaws." The man on the far side of the table held up a large pair of clamps with spiked teeth at the ends that he placed on a table set up alongside Bob's head. "Ready when you are."

"Hopefully you don't have to be. Here we go."

The woman's hand brushed upwards on her screen, and a low hum entered the room. Bob's body went stiff.

"I'm in," the girl said, and the two men on either side of Bob gripped his forearms tighter.

Confusion and anxiety rippled through James while he watched helplessly as his friend was operated on in a windowless room by complete strangers. The odor of stale water hung in the air mingling with the scent of dried blood on his shirt.

"Annnnd we're there…" The woman's voice trailed off as Bob's body convulsed. The unconscious medic's jaw clenched, and blood bubbled around the seams of the metal ear covers. Muscles and tendons strained against the restraints, and Bob's mouth opened, emitting a guttural roar of pain.

The noise ricocheted off the walls and embedded in James's brain, echoing. With each second the screams grew higher and pain rippled through the air tearing more than Bob's vocal chords.

One convulsion was so strong it threw an attendant off Bob's arm, and James jumped in to replace him. He clamped his hands on Bob's arm while Liam and Clint assisted with the other limbs. Heather stood next to James helping the other man hold down a leg as they watched in terror while their friend's back arched in agony.

"*ARRGHHHHH!*" Bob's eyes bulged in terror. Veins pulsed and reflected red against the opaque white of his eyeballs.

"Almost there!" the woman shouted over the turmoil. Each scream leapt from the cement, tearing at James's psyche. His friend was being torn apart.

Suddenly, Bob's body flopped onto the table, and the blood bubbling from his ears slowed to a trickle. Drips of liquid sounded off the pool that had formed on the floor.

James glanced at the woman behind Bob's head who heaved for breath. Silence hung in the air. She placed her fingers on his neck and murmured to herself pulling her hand away.

"He's alive."

# Chapter Twelve

"Hand me those grips." The woman pointed at the forceps on the table next to James.

He picked up the tool and passed it across the table, surprised by its lightness.

"What was that?"

The woman moved Bob's head to the side and placed the opening of the teeth around the HOLO collar. A *snip* removed the device from Bob's neck, and the metal implement clattered to the floor.

James glanced at the device with a deep-seated loathing. Rage washed over him as he looked at the gunmetal-gray object that had created so much pain. A simple item causing the most visceral damage. A circle of metal that had nearly broken him resurfaced in a new world.

"You good?" Heather asked, putting a hand on his shoulder and startling him back to the present. Her face a mask of worry, albeit concealed from the rest of the group.

"I'm good," James replied, forcing himself into the moment.

"He'll be good," Liam said, patting his shoulder gazing at Bob. James was glad the real reason for his concern remained unknown.

"Let's hope." The woman retied the ponytail holding her hair back. "It's been a few hours, but they went for it. He was deep by the time I got in there."

"What does that mean?" James asked. His friend's placid face and thin parted lips pulled shallow breaths into his lungs.

"The scoop. They take everything out that they can and replace it with themselves. Usually, the process takes a full twenty-four hours to complete." She watched Bob as she spoke, "With the speed they took with this one, I'm surprised we were able to help at all."

"What's recovery like?" Clint asked.

"No telling. This was…unique."

The people in the room observed Bob breathe. James half-expected his friend to sit up and ask for food. He imagined the smile they would get when he awoke. But the longer Bob lay still, the less likely it seemed that would happen.

"Kema, they coming with us?" asked one of the young assistants standing expectantly next to the table.

During the aftermath of Bob's surgery, James had not noticed the cleanup happening behind the scenes. The pool of blood under Bob's head had been swept into the drain, replaced by a ring of rusty brown residue. The people in the room were all the evidence that remained.

"Wait for Theo to come back. He and Wilma will need to help guide us through the crypts."

"I can do that."

"Barry, I love you like a brother, but your sense of direction is nonexistent," Kema said.

Barry scowled at the young woman as the doors squeaked open. Deck's head popped through the doorway followed by an older man and woman.

"How's the patient?" Deck asked, approaching the table.

"He's alive," James replied, repeating Kema's words.

"Low bar." Deck touched Bob's shoulder lightly.

"They have to know it's us. She said they've never seen anything like this," James said, racking his brain for answers. Raspin—or an extension of him—recognized something with Bob. Too much of a coincidence to move that quickly with a random person.

"If that's the case, we need to leave." The older woman moved swiftly across the room. She ran her hand over a random spot on the concrete wall.

Seams appeared and the concrete structure opened, revealing a hidden passageway. A tunnel appeared lit with dim bulbs hanging from the ceiling.

"Come on, people. Who's carrying him?"

"We've got it," Barry and the other young man spoke simultaneously. They each picked up an end of the table and collapsed the legs underneath, turning the surface into a gurney. The opening to the corridor widened, and Barry stepped over the descending wall into the tunnel.

"Come on, we'll explain things when we get there. Stay quiet," the woman instructed. James peered at her skeptically, but a glance from Deck told him they were okay. Not waiting for a response, she brushed past the gurney to lead the group.

Faint yellow lights illuminated the path as he stepped into the tunnel. The walls of the corridor were constructed of old cut stone that reflected the bulbs overhead into a semblance of candlelight. James touched one, noting the similarity to the bricks he had followed blindly in the dark. *Nice to see it this time*, he thought.

The scent of sweet decay radiated, giving more credence to the ancient feeling of the stone passageway. They snaked through the tunnel, passing offshoot paths as they walked. James watched Barry and his friend maneuver the gurney around tight corners with ease.

He noticed that the lights in the ceiling were ensconced in balloons of glass hanging along a string of electrical cord.

*Retro*, he mused.

The incandescent bulbs offered a charming appearance to an otherwise terrifying ordeal and left James with a sense of history as he walked beneath the city of their enemy. The passage's turns became more severe and James paid close attention to his guides as forks added a new level of complexity to their navigation.

An unexpected archway of molded steel appeared and wrapped itself around columns of stone. James inspected the crafted doorway as he walked through it.

Boughs of steel snaked around the rock as if grown naturally, like some sort of massive vine. The combination of the two created a unique blend of misplaced elegance. The image of a metal tree hung in the back of his mind when they entered another old chamber. Instead of cement or old bath tile, the walls of this tunnel consisted of huge stone blocks stacked upon one another, creating a narrow room that deepened as they walked down the platform steps into the structure buried beneath the earth.

Enthralled, James turned in a circle. It was as if a cathedral stood under the earth. He stared at the domed roof, held up by fitted stones wedged into one another.

"Where are we?" Teresa asked, taking the words out of James's mouth.

"There have been many wars for power in our world, and someone has always existed underground," the older woman said with her eyes on the ceiling. She dropped her head and nodded in the direction of Bob and his couriers. "Come with me. Let's talk."

The woman led them through a door of the chamber into a stone room outfitted with modernized machinery. Dashboards of HOLOs sprung up in the tiled space bathing the room in a blue haze. She swiped across one of the HOLOs and typed furiously on the transparent keyboard.

James moved forward to stand protectively by the gurney behind the woman. The screens bounced from one image to the next as she mumbled unintelligibly to herself.

"What've we got, Wilma?" the old man's voice carried from the doorway, and he joined the woman at the HOLOs. "Jesus," he murmured, putting his hands on his hips. Anxiety twisted up James's spine.

"Have you ever seen that?" Wilma asked.

"Not in my time," the old man replied, shaking his head. "If they could've done this back then, Rex, Toma, Jengi—the whole lot of 'em would've never made it through."

"He's holding…somehow."

"He's asleep."

Wilma pursed her lips and nodded. She turned to James and the team. "Kema did a great job stopping the Order's progress, but they moved fast. Looks like they've developed a few new methods since the last time we had to run one of these exercises."

"How often is that?" Clint asked.

"More than we like." Wilma sighed. "Still, we stopped it. We'll let him rest a bit. Try to wake him later. You all hungry?"

"I could eat," Deck mentioned idly. "Eggs and spinach, I assume?"

"Beans too. Or bean curd," the old man replied. "Come on, I'll get you something to eat." He waved for them to follow and walked in the direction of the main chamber.

Everyone but Wilma left with the man. Bob's face glowed from the reflection of the HOLO's emitters, and James wondered where his mind was.

"Come on, buddy," James whispered.

"I'm glad you got there when you did," Wilma said from the opposite side of the table. "Ten or fifteen more minutes and he'd be completely gone."

"What does that mean? Gone? Dead?" James understood dead. Ten years' worth of bodies piled up came to mind.

The woman shook her head. "Not that simple. You've seen the way people up there behave? Moonfaced and confused all the time. Years ago, the Order realized they needed a way to control their population. Their existence depends on using us as the means to the end, but a perfect society needs to be molded by perfect people. And humanity is anything but. They began scooping individuals soon after, pulling out the pieces they didn't need and embedding themselves inside.

Wilma paused and turned Bob's face towards James. She pointed at a bruise that had formed under his earlobe. "They used to cut right back here. Feed a HOLO hookup directly to the brain stem and reconfigure the chemical makeup. Now they do everything through those collars."

Unconsciously James put a hand to his neck. He was aware of the collar's ability to penetrate the body without needing to break the skin.

"The collar is breaking his mind?" he asked.

"Controlling, breaking, and replacing it. That's the standard, but with him"—Wilma shook her head—"they were going for a different angle. They knew who he was. They were trying to break something out of him. Guess he wouldn't let go."

"Guess not," James said. He tried to ignore the blooming guilt pressing against his every thought. He should be on that table, not Bob. Their mission, so positive and full of promise hours ago, had diminished to nothing.

"Come on, let's let him hang. He's comatose right now. Kema gave him some extra sedatives in case the Order messed with something we missed." Wilma came around to James's side of the table. She pulled his shoulder lightly and turned him to the door where Heather waited.

Wordlessly, Heather slipped her arm into his and guided him out the door.

His experience of being strangled with the collar in endless torture sessions was far different from Bob's. He wondered if this had been Raspin's intent the first time they met. If that's what would have happened had the Federation not intervened. He could not wrap his mind around the alternate universe in which those thoughts sat and followed Heather into a room echoing with voices.

Tables were set up randomly, and Deck leaned against the far wall, holding court. He talked between bites of a tan substance. "So you were the one who sent me those directions? Sonofabitch! How'd you pull that off?"

"Limited local network. Hard to get going, but possible if the HOLOs are on the right frequency."

"Theo, you are one smart cookie," Deck said, winking at the old man who returned a thumbs-up.

"He knows a thing or two," Wilma said, entering behind James and Heather. She guided James to a chair, and Heather sat next to him. His host walked to one of the fridges in the corner of the room.

"So you had a random map pop up on the HOLO and followed it?" Liam asked, shaking his head in semi-disbelief.

"Crary, ri'?" Deck spoke through a mouthful of food chased with a glass of water. "Pure instinct took over. We were blocks away from our platform and never would've made it. You saw how those Sentinels positioned themselves in the alley."

"It was the right move," Barry spoke up from his seat next to Theo. "The whole fucking city is on alert."

"Glad it wasn't suicidal," Teresa added with an eye roll.

"Same!" Deck said, genuinely happy, "I mean, that could have been…bad. Eesh."

James grinned at his friend's ability to roll with the punches and accepted the spork that appeared in front of him along with a bowl of the tannish brown substance.

"Bean curd," Kema said. "Enjoy."

He took a cautious bite and was pleasantly surprised by the taste. *Anything's better than the food on the boat,* he thought, scooping another helping into his mouth.

"Enough about us. What is this place? And how did you know we were out there? Who the hell are you?" Deck asked, as he realized all the unknowns regarding this group.

"That is a long story," Wilma said. She looked to the ground, her eyes lost in time.

"We figured that," Clint said, leaning back in his chair and pushing his empty bowl to the center of the table.

"We're a part of the Resistance. Surface operators. After the Order broke Rex, they came for everyone, and I mean *everyone*. Hunted us like animals throughout every city. Hordes of Sentinels and soldiers ripped us from our beds, slapped collars on us, and threw us into the interrogation rooms at the harbor. Centria, Maldona, Kovo, Welshire, everywhere.

"I was lucky to be working on a siloed project under the surface with Claudia, Fatima, and Theo. This place was brand new, and we were rewiring Rex's brain in the room Bob's lying in now. Without warning, all our systems went wild and SOS calls came from everyone." Wilma stopped and looked at the wall. Theo reached out a hand and patted her shoulder.

"Like Wilma said, we were protected here, but there was little we could do to help any of our friends. We used the tunnels under the city to find their children. You've met a few already." Theo gestured at the younger population in the room. James nodded, beginning to understand the gap in ages.

"We, of course, were now stuck under the ground forever, but they were so young the Order had not catalogued them for service yet—military, Sentinel-mind, or otherwise. Our group of youngsters became expert spies traversing the city and acting as the eyes of the Resistance."

"Naturals," Wilma said, interrupting and patting Barry on the leg eliciting a blushing smile from the young man. "We've been here for decades. We venture into the city whenever we need to access the platforms, but never for long."

"How many others are there?" Heather asked.

"Some…" Wilma replied with a cagey smile. "Our job is rebellion against an enemy that rips minds from people's bodies and molds them to fit their needs. We don't reveal facts."

"They don't know about these tunnels? They're ancient," Deck said. He ran a hand across one of the stone blocks, inspecting its eroded surface.

"Yes, they are," Wilma said. "Our world has been engaging in rebellion and war for generations. They would probably be museums in different times. No doubt, the Order knows they exist, but imperfect scans left a lot of the structures undiscovered. Secrets of a lost city buried under the surface. They were in rough shape when we found them, but with the help of some tech and a great deal of construction we were able to spruce up their infrastructure."

"They're an unknown honeycomb of passages beneath the city, broken on occasion by exposed or demolished pieces when the Order got involved," Barry added.

"Why not put a platform in here? I mean it would make sense to have transportation running to and from your base and Claudia's, right? Especially if the tunnels don't connect," Teresa asked.

"Too dangerous," Theo answered.

"If somehow they discover us and a platform system, the next thing you know, they'd uncover the rest of the Resistance," Kema added.

"Safest to keep things separated as much as we can," Wilma finished. She glanced around the room waiting for further questions.

James turned the new information over in his head. He imagined decades of spying, planning, watching, and waiting in separate but connected operations all towards the goal of destabilizing and destroying the Order.

*Dedicated.*

"What's the long game plan for you?" Deck asked and, receiving blank stares from the Resistance members, continued. "I mean, you've been running intelligence operations for more than twenty years *literally* underground. What's the next physical move?"

"I think that would be you," Theo said with a smile.

"Theo's right," Wilma added. "But this war won't get won overnight with some big explosion. The Order's too stable for that."

Silence filled the room as they contemplated her words. James nodded. She was right. Centria's operation controlled the entire population. A single mission led by a foreign enemy already under attack by the Order's military wouldn't be enough to upend their world.

"Enough story time," Wilma said, leaning back in her chair. "Bob's going to need to rest here for a few more hours. We have plenty of food and can shorten your exposure above ground. When we're done, Kema will take you to the nearest platform in a more remote part of town. I'll send a message to Claudia letting her know you're with us. Get some rest, and we'll reconvene in a few hours." Wilma spoke with maternal authority.

"That sounds great," Deck said. He stretched his arms over his head. "Where's a good place to lie down?"

"Barry? Terrence? Could you help our guests?" Theo said.

"I've got it," Barry replied, standing with the other young man who had helped carry Bob. He walked towards the door, talking over his shoulder to the group, "We have some extra cots for visitors this way."

"Oh, I love me a nice cot, don't I, Clint?" Deck said, draping an arm over Clint's sagging shoulders.

"How are you this awake right now?"

"I'm not. Just deliriously tired," Deck replied, disappearing around the corner followed by the rest of the team.

Rhia scrolled though a HOLO, entranced by the screen.

"You good, Rhi?" Heather asked.

"What? Oh yeah," she replied distractedly, "This local network thing… It could work."

"For what?" Heather asked, glancing over the techie's shoulder at the screen.

"I don't… Too early to tell. I need to do some more digging."

"Okay." Heather shrugged at James, and the two linked arms following the rest of the group.

When they reached the door James stopped and turned to Wilma, still seated and gazing thoughtfully at the ceiling.

"Why'd you help us? You've taken such precautions to hide yourselves. Why us?"

Wilma looked James in the eye. "Every empire needs its executioner." She smiled and pulled a HOLO screen up on her lap as James let Heather guide him to rest.

# Chapter Thirteen

"He's awake."

A hand nudged James's shoulder. He flipped over, making eye contact with Wilma, who nodded at the door.

"Come on," she whispered, "You should be there."

James nodded sleepily and pulled the thin blanket from his body, careful not to disturb Heather.

Wilma was gone by the time James's feet hit the ground, and he flexed his toes on the stone floor, forcing himself awake. He had no idea how long he had slept, but still exhausted, guessed it couldn't have been long.

*Power through*, James thought, and he slapped his face lightly.

The bed creaked when he stood, and Heather patted his thigh when he bent to kiss her.

"Good luck," she whispered and rolled back to sleep.

He picked up his shoes and tiptoed from the room. The rest of the team did not need to join him. This was not their job but something he needed to do. And unlike Heather who understood this intuitively, they might not.

The light blinded James when he entered and he blinked at the sudden exposure. When his eyes adjusted, he took in the scene, categorizing the space and its contents.

Theo and Wilma stood on either side of Bob's bed. They fiddled with HOLOs and checked the screens hanging around the medic's body. Kema sat behind a series of HOLO screens in a makeshift dashboard. Her hair rested in a tight ball on top of her head and her eyes flicked to James as he examined the space.

Everything had been removed from the room. All that remained were the HOLOs and a chair for each person. The machinery heated the enclosed space, and James's mouth filled with warm, dry air.

"Seat at the end of the bed is yours," Kema said, her gaze focused on her HOLOs.

"Thanks," James replied.

Bob's eyes remained closed and his chest rose evenly.

*Doesn't look awake,* he thought.

"We're forcing him into a state of semiconsciousness right now. We wanted you here before we did anything," Wilma said as if reading his mind.

"What can we expect? Is he…still Bob?" James asked, unsure about the situation.

"From what we can tell, the scoop was deep enough for the standard removal and manipulation they use for soldiers—autonomous, human machines, their sole purpose to follow orders. Other than sacrificial battlefield movements, they present with blank stares and respond to simple commands. They're cannon fodder at the end of the day."

Images of soldiers from the battlefield at Midway mingled with those of the confused people working in the harbor facility. People walking into blatant gunfire and the looks of lost travelers stuck in his vision.

"Okay, what else?"

"Bob's original self is there. We located that piece of him, but they took a chunk of it. We can bring it to the surface and may be able to make that the overriding persona. We'll need to wake him though to get started."

"Overriding persona?"

"The primary personality. The scoop removes the function in the brain that lets humans realize the self. It's how they manage control," Theo explained, sitting in his chair.

"What's worst case?" James asked, directing his question at Theo.

"There's next to nothing left. He'd be a shell, owned by the Order and manipulated at their whim."

"And best case?"

"We can pull Bob's persona to the front and cut out everything the Order did."

"Sounds good. Anything else?"

Theo and Kema glanced at Wilma whose eyes remained on her HOLO.

"There is something we haven't seen and can't explain at this point. If it's anything, we'll work it out together," she finished. Her answer was vague, but James nodded anyway. He wanted to get started.

"Let's get moving." James said, bracing himself mentally and physically gripping the steel bed frame.

"Kema, you're up," Wilma said.

*Whoosh!* The woman's fingers darted across her screens and keyboards with intense but practiced speed.

He turned his attention to the patient propped in a sitting position. Anxious seconds ticked by as the *whir* of generators filled the stone tiled space.

Suddenly, Bob's eyes flipped open. The brilliant browns and greens of his hazel eyes converged to create an amber hue and the light caused his pupils to widen, resembling drops of ink in a bowl of honey.

James held his breath as sleep fell from Bob's face, and he cocked his head to the side with a questioning look. Thus, James's first question about who he was about to encounter was answered.

"What's your name?" Wilma asked.

Bob faced the woman. His expression portrayed distance and confusion, but uncaring at the same time. As if he did not care about answering and could not understand how.

"I don't know." The reply came out cold and robotic, sounding similar to the people James killed hours earlier when breaking his friend from their imprisonment.

"Where are you from?" Theo asked.

Bob's head twisted to stare at the new voice.

"I don't know."

"Do you know where you are?" Wilma asked.

"In Centria."

"How do you know that?" Theo asked.

"I have no reason to believe otherwise."

"Do you know where in Centria?" Wilma asked, continuing the round of alternating questions.

Not bothering to examine his surroundings, he answered curtly, "No."

"Do you want to guess?" Theo asked.

"No."

Wilma lifted a hand in the air, and Kema moved her fingers across the keypad again until Bob's eyes closed. His head lay on the pillow, and James glanced around the room. "So? What did that tell you?"

"Standard so far," Wilma replied, typing on her HOLO.

"He's responsive, unquestioning, and open to suggestion. Textbook Order."

"Is he too deep?" James asked, with a glimmer of hope.

"Not that I can tell. Kema, get him to his natural self. Let's see what Bob knows," Wilma instructed.

Kema nodded, her fingers moved again.

"I have to warn you, James, Bob may not be the person you knew. He'll be frightened, confused, irrational, emotional, and possibly violent. Stay calm and listen to us. Know we have his best interest in mind," Theo said. His eyes conveyed deep sympathy, and James bobbed his head in response.

"Okay, wake him," Theo instructed.

*Whoosh!*

Bob's eye's blinked and his expression changed. The pale white orbs vibrated drastically searching the room in terror. The pupils, serene a moment ago, represented pinholes, barely distinguishable from their hazel ring.

Bob sat up and flipped his head side to side. His eyes landed on James at the end of the bed. Horror, confusion, and pain registered on his face. Guilt drove into James's gut.

"What the hell is happening? James? Where are we? Who? Who…?" His eyes darted with a touch of insanity to the sides of his bed and to the stack of HOLOs over which Kema's hair appeared in a haze of blue light.

"Do you know your name?" Wilma asked.

Bob swung his head towards the woman. She looked at him calmly and waited for the response.

"What is…? What…? I was running, and I got hit in the side. How am I? We were in…" Bob stammered. His eyes shifted as he tried to wrap his mind around what was happening.

"Do you know who you are?" Wilma repeated her question. Her voice remained level and Bob stared at her with feral eyes.

"Who the fu—? James?!" Bob looked pleadingly at his friend.

James gritted his teeth. "It's okay. Answer her."

His words seemed to work, and Bob's eyes stopped their mad circle of the room. He took a deep breath and sat back on his pillow.

"Yes, I do."

"What is it?" Theo asked.

"Bob," the medic replied. He continued to scan the room, examining every corner while James scrutinized his friend. Was anything out of the ordinary? Tics or tells that would indicate something drastic had changed in his friend.

"Do you know where you are?"

"I do not," Bob said, glancing at the ceiling. "Looks old though."

"Do you want to guess?"

"Somewhere in the BlankZone. A building in Centria I'd guess, but who knows? James, what the fuck is going on?" Bob asked again, agitation crept into his voice.

"Wait a second," James said, holding up a calming hand.

"Are you in any pain?" Wilma asked.

"Some."

"Where?" Theo probed.

"My head's killing me, my neck's aching, and my spine's…uncomfortable. Now can you answer some of my fucking questions?" Bob was not having any more of it, and a fist formed in his right hand.

Wilma must have seen the reaction. She lifted her hand, and Bob's eyes went blank as his torso flopped back on the bed.

"What the fuck was that?" James asked. *They turned him off without warning?* James's hands vibrated with anger as he waited for an explanation from Theo and Wilma.

"We'll get him back in time, but we need to figure out what else they did. Everything seems fine so far James, but there's no way of telling until we finish our research. Understand?" Theo said as Wilma typed on her HOLO.

He settled his racing heartbeat with a long slow breath out, *keep it together*.

"Okay. Kema, go slow. No clue what this one is about."

"On it," Kema said. The engineer's brow furrowed until the standard *whoosh* broke the silence.

Quiet owned the room as the four of them waited in anticipation. Bob remained still, his body flat against the pillows. His eyelids motionless. The rise and fall of his chest indicated he lived.

Seconds ticked by. James focused on his own breathing, counting each lungful in sets of four, maintaining a steady heartbeat.

"Maybe we sho—" Theo was cut off as Bob's head pitched forward, eyes closed and back straight.

James eyed his friend watching the medic's chin dip to his chest and bobble, detached from the rest of his body.

Without warning, Bob's head whipped up, and he cocked it to the side. He looked straight ahead and opened his mouth in a loud scream.

The shriek pierced the air, bouncing off the stone walls. The sound of its inhumanity lodged in James's brain. He covered his ears to block the sound. A line of blood appeared at Bob's ears, and James stood, moving towards Kema to shut things off when the noise stopped.

Bob's face leveled again, and he turned his head in James's direction.

His bloodshot eyes opened and James stared into misty orbs of red and black.

"Hello, pleasure to meet you." An unnatural smile perched on Bob's lips and disappeared, replaced by a slack face.

James did not respond but squared his shoulders and looked intently back at his friend. Emotionless, he balled his hands into fists. Bob's damaged eyes followed him as he walked back to his position at the bottom of the bed, wrapped his hands around the frame and nodded at Wilma.

The woman started her questioning. "Do you know who you are?" Her voice had lost its confidence. This was new for them.

"I'm Bob. Well, not *me* but…this is." Bob motioned at his body, and James's mind transported back to the woods in the Federation and his encounter with an Exil.

Bob opened his jaw in an unnatural motion, and James made eye contact with Wilma. Her face concealed her emotions, but her eyes gave away her true thoughts. Something was deeply troubling.

"What do you mean by 'not me'?" Theo asked, continuing the line of questioning. His voice remained steady, impressing James with his poise.

"I don't know how to explain it other than that. Or I don't want to," Bob said, indifferently shifting his body. The medic inspected his hands and wrists, rotating the joints and flexing his tendons murmuring to himself. "Fascinating. They weren't kidding."

James, overcome by terror, felt adrenaline flood his nervous system. Muscles tightened and his eyes grew wide watching his friend's body. Scenes from the frozen tundra after the ambush by a group of Exils filled his mind. In particular, the body of the woman Raspin had occupied. The out of sync uncontrolled body movements, arms jutting out at weird positions, and the lack of comfort within his own skin were all too familiar. The blood coming from Bob's ears increased as the person inhabiting his body touched a finger to the liquid running down his neck.

"That's unexpected," Bob's body said absently rubbing the wetness between his fingers before smearing a streak of crimson on the aged bedsheets.

Shock reverberated through the room. Bob's possessed body inspected the room with its blackened eyes.

"Who are you?"

"I said I don't feel like talking about that," Bob responded.

"Did Raspin send you?"

Halting the examination the eyes settled on James. Recognition dawned on Bob's face and the smile returned. "Ahhhh. Someone I may know."

Keeping his composure, James returned eye contact gripping the edge of the bed as he waited for a response.

"You must be James."

Silence engulfed the room as James waited for the response to his question.

"No answer. I must be right. Edgar said you were like that. I was hoping it had been you that we grabbed. This whole thing would have been easier. No more dealing with underground societies bent on taking the world back. We're here to step forward. I mean, look at your friend. At the very least, you must admit this is impressive."

Bob glanced at his torso, and a well of nausea rose in James's throat.

"I don't think your friends know what's happening though." Bob's head nodded between Wilma and Theo. "Have you told them? About your chat with Edgar? I suppose not. Withheld? Hmmm, doesn't seem so given what I know of you, James, but could be. You're known to keep things close to the chest. Hell, three months of torture, and we never broke you. That's impressive really."

The person manipulating Bob pulled his legs beneath him in a cross. His back stayed straight and blood continued to flow in a trickle from his ears. Drips of liquid hung from his lobes like wax earrings dripping to his shoulders and staining the edge of the pillowcase.

"I will say, you seem out of place here, James," Bob said suddenly, his head cocked to the side. "Never expected to see you in Centria."

"How do you know we're in Centria?" James replied.

"Assumption. Judging by the room, I'd say in one of the lost tunnels under the city. Resistance has been there for years. Not worth sniffing them out though. They'll mess it all up eventually. You know as well as I do, there are bigger things at stake in lands far from here."

"How so?" James asked. Bob looked away again, and James took the opportunity to glance at Kema. He

mouthed for her to follow his lead and motioned for her to
duck beneath the HOLOs. The younger woman complied
dipping lower in her seat.

"The Federation is as weak as we can get it. Factions
of Exils running the western borders and NOLA teams
backing up what's left of the military. It's time for us to act.
It's what we do."

"Take over people's bodies."

"To be fair, we thought we had more time."

"Why did you do it in the first place?"

"Because we can. And we figured the fastest way to
you is by burrowing into the mind of a friend."

"Get to me?"

Bob smirked. "Edgar did say you don't get it yet.
How much they need you. Yes, James. To get to you. The
last true leader of the Federation."

"There are others," James said, suddenly defensive.

"No. There are not. Philip knows that. Better than
anyone I'd guess."

"Philip?"

"You know him as the general. But we go farther
back than titles." Bob smiled again. "You've stepped into a
long history."

Tired of the circular conversation, James held up a
hand. "Enough. I'm done with you. It's time to get my friend
back."

"Fine by me," Bob said, shrugging. "I got what I
need."

An unsettling smile perched on his lips as James
nodded at Kema. Her hand flipped across the screen and
James watched his friend's body collapse on the cot.

Nerves gripped James's stomach. He walked to the
side of the bed and checked Bob's pulse, wiping blood away
from his ears with the edge of the worn yellow pillowcase.

"Bring up Bob."

"Wait, before we do—" Wilma started, but James cut
her off.

"No. We need to get Bob. Kema, now please."

"On it," the woman replied.

"You've seen this?" Theo asked. His eyes were a mask of horror and bewilderment as he stared at Bob's motionless face.

"Once. Ended quickly."

"What happened?"

"A bullet."

*WHOOSH!*

Bob's eyes flew open in terror. He panted, and James held his friend's hands firmly on the medic's heaving chest. The red lines around his eyeballs had dissipated, and pupils retracted to their regular state.

"What the fuck was that? Who the hell is inside of me? James? Who were you talking to?!" Bob cried in panic as his head twisted searching for an answer.

"It's okay. We subdued whoever it was. They implanted someone inside you, Bob. We don't know who or why, but—"

Bob interrupted, "I got that! I could hear everything. I could hear other voices too. People analyzing the room. People talking in the background they were…listening along."

James's brow furrowed. "What do you mean?"

"They were here, James. They were talking. About you. About me. About this…place."

"What did they say?" Wilma asked. Her expression hardened. "Can you remember? Anything at all?"

"I can't. I…can't," Bob replied. Exhaustion plagued his voice, and his face dropped to stare at his blood stained sheets.

His friend's despair elicited a surge of anger and sympathy in James. He swallowed, struggling to control his voice. "Anything at all, Bob. We need some answers."

"Just try," Theo said softly.

Bob nodded, and the group held their breath while the medic concentrated.

"They were talking about the people in the room. They knew who James was."

"Anyone else?" James asked.

"Her," Bob said, pointing at Wilma. "They didn't say a name, but they thought they recognized you too." Bob pointed at Theo. "The only one they talked about at length though was James."

"Did they say the name of the person who was talking through you?"

Bob shook his head.

"What about Kema?"

"They didn't see her. Or the person—I think a woman—inside me didn't see her," Bob said.

"Why?"

Bob could barely lift his face from the bed, "I could feel their mind. It was…different."

"A woman?" Wilma asked. She glanced at Theo. His eyes hardened, worried.

"Anything in terms of indicators or names, Bob? Could you tell what they wanted?"

"No. It was a…blur. I was in the room, but not present." Stress crept into his voice, and James walked to the head of the bed. He put a hand on his friend's shoulder. "A few more questions, man."

"I know, I know. I want to sleep so badly. I feel like I haven't slept in weeks."

"That's the scoop," Kema added from her post. She leaned to the side of the screens and observed Bob with a worried look. "A full scoop can take weeks of recovery for people to regain physical stamina."

"He was only in for a few hours," James said, surprised.

"It must be the extra piece that's causing it," Kema surmised, shaking her head. "More stress on the mind eating up any energy it can. He's going to fade fast."

"Alright, we're done," James said. He guided his friend's shoulder back to the thin cot.

"Not yet," Wilma said.

"Yes, yet," James replied. Anger and frustration bubbled to the surface. "He's given you everything he can at this point."

"What did you see in the room, Bob?" Theo asked, ignoring the confrontation.

"I said that's enough," James growled. "Kema, knock him back out."

"Bob, what did the room look like?" Wilma persisted, ignoring James.

Furious James turned to the woman and snatched the HOLO emitter from her hands and hurled it at the stone wall. The metal object exploded on contact as James's chest heaved with rage. "Shut up," he said menacingly and turned to Kema. "Turn him off, or I'll rip those fucking HOLOs from the wall."

"Bob, we need to know the room," Theo said, his voice still calm.

"I said enough!" James shouted.

A door opened and Deck entered the room. "What the hell is happening. Bob? James?"

"Bob. The room," Theo repeated.

"Goddammit." James lunged for the HOLOs, but Deck blocked him.

"Easy, man. I've got your back, but you need tell me what's happening," Deck said. He looked around the room with caution as James attempted to control his anger.

A cool hand touched his arm and pulled him away.

"Settle down," Heather said. James's heartbeat slowed at the sound of her voice.

"They did the same thing to Bob as they did to that Exil in the woods."

Deck and Heather glanced at one another, fear filling the space between them.

"Are you sure?" Deck asked.

"They're in there," Bob said.

His normally cheery face dripped with sadness.

"That doesn't explain why you're acting like this, James," Heather said calmly. "Like Deck said, we're on your side. But what's happening?

"He needs rest. They keep running questions at him."

"We need to know," Theo replied with composure.

"Know what?! You haven't explained shit!" James yelled.

"If it's her. If it's them," Wilma said.

"Who's 'them'?" Deck asked moving coyly next to Kema who looked ready to pounce.

"The Order's leadership. Raspin's boss, if you will," Theo said. The old man's eyes sank to the floor. "If it's her…."

"What?"

"If it's her, we're in deep trouble," Wilma said. "So Bob, I want to help, but please tell me—what did the room look like?"

Bob scrunched his face, and the rest of the room held its collective breath.

"There were mirrors—no, not mirrors. They were screens, HOLOs. I couldn't tell what they showed, but they were everywhere. And there was a round table with individual boxes that looked like old emitters before each seat. Everyone was huddled around me—or her, or whoever it was—and they were watching…" His face paled and James glanced around the room, anxiety building with each second.

"I knew I wasn't actually there though," Bob said, taking a tired breath.

"Why's that?" Theo asked quietly.

"Because I was looking at me through my own eyes. And I could feel her thoughts."

"Anything specific? An emotion?"

Bob closed his eyes. The room waited a moment in breathless silence before he opened them and looked Theo in the eye. "Triumph."

A loud *BEEEP BEEEEP BEEEP* split the room in half.

Kema flew from her chair out the door.

Wilma made eye contact with James. "They're coming."

# Chapter Fourteen

"Destroy the emitters. Theo, you have the HOLO tracks?" Wilma stepped decisively across the room, opening a cabinet on the far wall.

"I'm on it," Theo replied. His face reflected the light from a HOLO as his fingers flew across the keyboard.

"We have three minutes," Wilma shouted over the alarm.

"Who exactly is coming?" Deck asked. He held his hands over his ears while sirens ripped through the stone room.

"The Order. They must have tracked us here inside Bob's mind," Wilma replied. She pulled an armful of batons from the cabinet. Heather ran over and relieved her of the load.

"How are we going to move Bob?" James asked, looking at his helpless friend lying on the bed. The blood from his ears had dried in rust-colored streaks along the frame.

"Stretcher." Theo motioned to the corner, jutting his chin so he could keep typing.

"Thanks," James said, eyeing the collapsed gurney they used to bring him through the tunnels.

"What the fuck is happening?" Clint's voice broke into the room. He took in the devastated state of the present company. Liam, Teresa, and Rhia peered over his shoulder.

"We've gotta move," Heather said, jogging across the room and dumping the ion batons into Liam's outstretched arms.

"I figured as much," Liam replied, juggling the weaponry shoved against his chest.

"Seriously, what happened?" Clint repeated his question, stepping farther into the room and glancing at Bob's head haloed in blood.

"The Order broke into Bob's mind, and they tracked us here. We've gotta evac now," James said, moving to the corner of the room. Picking up the folded stretcher, he spread the plank to its full length. The two polls connected with a thin strip of tightly bound cloth, and clips hung off both sides. He laid the stretcher on the bed next to Bob, balancing it with his hip to keep it on the twin mattress.

"Clint, can you help?"

Clint joined him by the bed. Teresa stood at Bob's feet as James took the shoulder opposite Clint.

"One, two, three!" With a *humph* they lifted and lowered their friend onto the stretcher.

"HOLO portals wiped, emitters burning as we speak. Everything that could be sent below is there," Kema said, breathless, running back through the door, a gray pack slung over her shoulder and an ion blade stuck in her waistband.

"You guys have any Sentinel rounds? Or grenades we can use? Anything to keep them further back?" Heather asked the room at large.

"You think I'd have handed you a bunch of fucking batons if we did?" Wilma asked. "This is the best we've got. Besides, we won't be able to fight them for long."

"Why's that?" Deck asked as he tested his ion baton's balance and charge.

"They'll send hundreds down here."

"No pulse pillar?" James asked.

"What's that?" Kema asked, her face twisted in sincere confusion.

"Never mind," he replied, turning his attention to the rest of the room. "We're going to need to move around Bob. I'll carry him in the middle of the pack with Clint. Heather and Deck should be up front with Wilma or whoever else is leading. Sound good?"

"You're no good to us carrying Bob. I'll take half the stretcher," Rhia said. She handed her baton to James. "Clint and I've got this."

"Yes, we do," the mechanic said, nodding.

"Alright. Liam and T, we'll take rear guard."

"Yessir," T replied. She flipped on her baton, smiling as the static crackled up the side of the weapon. "Been a while."

"Wilma and team, you'll need to guide up front but stay behind Heather and Deck. They'll handle things if we run into a problem."

"We can *handle* things ourselves," Kema said with a false confidence James admired.

"No. We cannot. This is their work," Theo said, patting Kema's arm, "Listen to them and watch what they do. Where are the boys?"

"Here!" Barry said, sprinting into the room.

"Pres—" Terrence's voice cut off as he fell face-first into the room. A pool of crimson liquid leaked from the back of his head, and glistening white bone shone through his skull.

Liam reacted instantly, grabbing Barry before further rounds ricocheted around the room. Teresa followed her husband's lead and grabbed Terrence's body pulling him from the entrance while Deck dove at the door slamming it shut.

"Looks like we're not leaving through there," James said. He glanced at Wilma who stared in pain and horror at the young man's body.

"Wilma! Where to?" James understood her agony, but they were running on borrowed time.

The woman shook her head and took in a deep breath. She pulled up a HOLO, and after a few swift movements the wall behind them opened. Rounds continued to hit the heavy wooden door of the room.

"Through here," she spoke with a cracked voice.

"Quite a bag of tricks you've got there," Deck said, impressed.

"Deck and Heather, you're up."

"Right on. Let's go. Theo, Wilma, who's leading?" Deck asked.

"This way," Wilma said. She pulled Barry's arm as he stood staring at Terry's body.

"See you there," Heather said. She kissed James's cheek and entered the stone-walled tunnel.

Rounds thudded against the door, sending puffs of dust from the ceiling.

Clint and Rhia heaved the gurney to their shoulders and ran into the tunnel.

"Time for you, Theo," James said as a projectile from the other side of the wall sent splinters flying across the room. James moved behind the stack of HOLO emitters where Kema sat minutes earlier.

"No can do. I've gotta seal our exit."

"All together," James said. "T, Liam. Hit the road."

*BOOM!* Rumbling shockwaves reverberated shaking the space and the door flew off its hinges.

James dove to the side, avoiding further explosions and landed next to Theo.

A transparent arm pulled itself into the room but was cut short when Teresa jumped from the corner and slammed her baton into its throat. But rather than instantly dissipating, the Sentinel fell back into the other humanoid figures clambering to enter the room.

Horror mounted in James's gut as he tried to wrap his head around the impervious Sentinels.

"Get into the tunnel!" Theo shouted, he pushed to his feet and stood next to the entrance of their escape route. The old man held an ion blade in his hand and crouched, ready for the Sentinels.

The Federation couple sprinted with unconscious synchronicity to the opening. James followed and reached the edge of the door as the other Sentinels became acclimated to the room.

James looked back at the mass of transparent bodies forcing their way into the demolished space, their weightless feet stepping lithely over Terrence's motionless blood-soaked body lying on the floor.

When he ducked his head under the entrance to join his friends, a hand gripped his shoulder and slammed him into the wall. His head thudded into the stone, cracking his skull against the concrete seam. Despite blurry vision and shock, he batted at the ironlike grip with his baton.

Without warning, the arm vanished and a different hand grabbed him, pulling him farther onto the underground pathway.

"Still know how to do a few things," Theo said with a wink as he flicked off the power on his ion blade.

"Thanks for that," James said, taking a breath.

"No time for that. Your friends are ahead. Come on."

James nodded and followed the spry older man down the pathway through the tunnel, listening behind them at all times.

"Around here," Deck's voice echoed, and James breathed a sigh of relief when the static of a baton rebounded throughout the chamber.

"Close it!" Heather cried.

Three Sentinels rushed at the front of the party when James turned the corner. Deck nimbly moved and hit the first in its throat before lodging an ion blade under its chin.

The second surged forward, but Heather cracked it on the back of the head with her baton, and Kema plunged her knife through its ghostlike chest.

The third avoided Wilma's swinging baton, and she flew into the wall, pushed aside by the electric-bound monster. Hazy outlines of arms hung in the air as the figure reached for Bob. Instinctually, James grabbed the ion knife from Theo and whipped it at the creature's head. As he watched the blade embed in the humanoid's back, James realized he hadn't flipped on the ionic mechanism. Without skipping a beat, Rhia dove towards the Sentinel, powering on the blade's handle, and the Sentinel vanished in a crack of static.

"Everyone okay?" Heather asked, lifting Wilma from the ground.

"Gotta remember to turn those things on first," Deck said across the crowd.

"Good looking out there, Rhia," James replied, giving Deck the finger.

"Anytime," the techie replied, nodding at him.

"No time to waste. We've got to get out of these tunnels. They aren't the secret we thought they were," Theo said, walking over to check on his friend.

"He's right. Wilma, you ready?" James asked.

"Through here." The woman swiped up on her HOLO, and the wall opened to their right. "When we get to the end of the tunnel there's an opening to the outside. The brick building on the right has a platform installed under it. We need to get there."

"You heard her. Let's move."

Deck and Heather led without waiting.

*BOOM!* Another explosion traveled the length of the tunnel, vibrating the walls.

"Can you walk?" James asked Wilma who gingerly tested her ankle.

"I think…" she replied, wincing in pain when she put weight on her foot.

"Liam," James said.

"Come on up," the bearded man said. He lifted Wilma onto his shoulders and jogged through the tunnel, following Rhia's thin figure bobbing in the darkness.

"Stick with him, T. We'll seal things up here," James said.

"See you on the platform," Teresa said, running to catch up to her husband.

"Any other obstacles we can put up, Theo?" James asked, surveying the area.

"I can blow the lights, but that won't do anything except make our lives worse," he replied, scanning his HOLO for options.

"All good. Let's get the hell out of here."

He pushed Theo ahead of him, checking over his shoulder to avoid another ambush and watched as the old man closed the entrance behind them.

Theo led the way, bracing his body on the stone wall. James held out an arm for the older man.

"Here," he said. "Might be faster."

Theo shook his head, accepting the arm. "Used to be a time I could run these tunnels with my eyes closed." He sighed. "Now look at me."

"Hopefully you can run outside again one day," James said.

"If wishes were horses, then beggars would ride."

They reached the end of the tunnel where an opening sent a whiff of fresh air into the musty depths of the underground.

Dim light dusted the edges of the exit, and James approached, careful to stay in the shadows. He peeked around the edge and watched Liam enter a door to a brick building on the left side of the street held open by Teresa. James popped his head into the light and waited for the stocky woman to notice him. When she did he signed: *Go ahead.*

She nodded, and the door swung shut behind her.

"We're up. Ready?" James asked, glancing at the old man taking deep breaths.

"As I'll ever be," Theo replied, holding out his hand. James grasped it and pulled him through the tunnel exit. Inky black sky cloaked the light from the streetlamps adorning the road.

They ran as fast as Theo's aging body would allow. Relief swelled in James's chest when they made it to the entrance of the brick building.

"Give me a second to close that up," Theo said, pulling out his HOLO.

James's heart pounded. Seconds and heartbeats ticked by as James waited for the man to finish.

"Everything okay?" he asked after the count in his head had reached thirty, and Theo's placid face had furrowed into a frown.

"The connection's off. Let me just..." Theo swiped across his screen again, and James glanced up and down the quiet street. Adrenaline amplified in his system, accentuated by the quiet state of the world and the darkness hiding what he could not see.

*Thump.*

His eyes spun to the tunnel's exit while the invisible door closed.

"Done! Now we can—"

"Hey!"

A shout from the end of the street cut off Theo's voice. James's stomach dropped and his muscles contracted. Every hair on his body stood.

"Hey! Who's there? There's a mandatory curfew. Come over here."

Scenarios ran through James's mind when a hand shoved his chest, pushing him into the shadows.

Theo walked into the open space.

"Apologies, I am an old man. I mean no harm."

"You need to come with us. Did you receive the message?" questioned a different voice.

*There're at least two of them*, James thought, crouching against the pillar.

"I don't think I did." Theo held his hands near his chest, and James watched his thumb loop through a ring under his jacket.

*What's he doing?*

"Are you alone? We thought someone was with you?"

"Just me." The old man hunched his back to emphasize his age and conceal his hands. James peeked around the edge of his pillar. Six gray suited soldiers with rifles drawn walked towards the entrance to the building. The two closest were trained on Theo while the other four swept the area.

A bead of sweat dripped into James's eye, blurring his vision, but he dared not move.

"We thought we saw someone else."

"Nope, only an old man who missed a message."

James smelled the alien scent of the BZ soldiers— grease, sweat, and washed polyester.

"You should come with us. Let me help you."

"I'll go back inside."

"Not possible. We're under orders to bring anyone outside back in."

"That's a shame," Theo said. Sadness tinged his voice, and James's heart slammed into his chest.

"What? Stand up straight. You need to get over here."

"He's on the other side of the pillar. Good luck," Theo said.

"Wha—"

*BOOM!* The explosion rocked the area, sending a wave of explosive energy into the glass doors, shattering the barred windows.

James jumped to the other side of the brick pillar where an unmasked soldier leaned in a daze. He tilted his head in confusion towards James who did not hesitate and grabbed the soldiers jaw, slamming his enemy's skull into the edge of the pillar with a satisfying *crunch*.

He picked up the soldier's discarded rifle, gazing at the spot where Theo had sacrificed himself. Alarms shrieked in the background accompanied by the sounds of soldiers converging on him from around the city. With a final glance at Theo's final stand, James ran through the door.

He entered another open doorway at the end of the hall and locked it behind him sprinting to the bottom of the stairs.

Deck's head popped out at the bottom of the staircase.

"What the hell happened? Where's Theo?"

"Gone."

"What?"

"Group of soldiers came on us. He was wired and took them out."

"Fuckin' hell," Deck said, shaking his head.

"Hell is right. Everyone else on?"

"We're there," Deck said, leading him into a small concrete hallway. Another doorway at the end of the hall led to the final staircase of the sub-basement.

Wilma's eyes were the first James caught when he entered the room. She already knew.

James stepped on the platform, and Kema shuffled to make room between herself and Heather.

Heather gripped his arm and the floor beneath them opened.

"We're with you all the way," Wilma said, choking back emotions.

"I know," James replied, clenching his fists, resolve coursed through his brain, sharpening his focus. The platform moved, descending into darkness and illuminating the walls of the tunnel in its eerie light. "We're not done here.

# PART III

# Chapter Fifteen

Drops of water echoed off the bathroom walls with a *plink*.

Tendrils of dark red liquid faded to light pink swirling down the drain. With mild curiosity, James inspected his head. He located the source of the bleeding and pulled back the hair. Dried blood ensconced a gash on his head

*When did that happen?* He then remembered the Sentinel slamming him into the wall. *Goddamn Sentinels.*

He examined the cut, wondering how he hadn't noticed it. It wasn't deep but could cause a problem. Inspecting closer, he realized he may have reinjured a simple scratch during his shower, creating an open wound.

"Dummy," he muttered, observing the fresh flowing blood.

He patted the cut dry with his towel and walked into his room to look for something to help stop the bleeding.

Searching through his chronically disorganized bag, he found his med kit buried under a stack of extra ammo magazines. When he unzipped the canvas bag a bottle of quick-stitch adhesive along with a bio-bandage sat at the top.

"Bingo."

He returned to the mirror and began the process of applying the glue-like substance to his scalp.

"Need help?" Bob's voice bounced into the room. The medic stood next to Heather in the hall leaning against the doorway.

"I think I'm good," James said. He dropped a piece of the sticky liquid into his hair, grimacing as it dried into a bead of hardened resin. "Okay, yes, maybe."

Bob grinned and pointed to the toilet in the corner. "Sit backwards on the crapper. Pants on please."

Heather took a spot next to the mirror above the sink maintaining a line of sight towards the door. James noted her heightened awareness.

"Thanks, Doc," James said, handing Bob the medical supplies.

He settled on the covered seat of the toilet and waited while Bob washed his hands.

"What're we dealing with?" Bob asked.

"Opened a scratch when I took a shower. Started bleeding everywhere and thought I'd try to seal it up myself. That quick-stitch dropper isn't very accurate though," James said. He touched the side of his head wondering how he would deal with the ball of rubber cement stuck in his hair. *Guess I need scissors.*

"Let's take a look." The medic pulled back James's hair. "Yeah, it wasn't big. You really shampoo too hard, man."

"I've told him that," Heather chimed in.

"It's been a long day. Needed the cleaning."

"No shit."

Syrupy liquid pooled on his scalp, and the tear of a wrapper followed quickly by pressure on his wound completed the job. "Aaaand done. Make sure you're careful, James. It's not bad now, but if you keep shampooing like you do who knows what could happen?" Bob clapped him on the shoulder and turned the faucet back on.

"I'll keep that in mind." James inspected the bandage in the mirror. *I could never do that*, he thought, realizing Bob had cut the bandage to size and applied it so it only covered the wound.

"Any other ailments?" Bob asked, drying his hands.

"Nope. How're you…doing?" James asked, unsure how approach the question. *What do I say for a status update on an outside force that tore his mind apart with no potential repair?*

"Not bad. Got this one attached at the hip," Bob said, nodding at Heather. Her cheeks blushed.

"It's not like that, Bob…" Heather started to say.

"I know. The others are nervous," Bob said, waving away her explanation. "I feel fine though. For now." Uncertainty colored the end of the statement. Helplessness rose in James's chest while Bob repeatedly washed his hands, scraping at a dab of quick-stitch on his thumb.

"It's hard to miss the amateur-hour spy game going on." He gave up cleaning and dried his hands with the towel hanging from the rock protrusion next to the sink. "I mean, the obviousness of it."

"I told you that's why *I'm* here," Heather said.

"What are you two talking about?" James asked. Some from Claudia's group had expressed concern about Bob walking about the complex alone, even after Rex had cleared him. As the old techie described, Bob's mind had not been plunged enough to control from the outside. Down here, at least, it would be next to impossible. They all had agreed to let Bob walk free.

"Claudia's got the younger team playing babysitter on our buddy," Heather said. She nodded at the doorway. James looked in time to see a shadow move out of view and around the corner.

Anger rose in James's head, "That fu—"

Bob's hand caught his chest. "Stop. It's not worth it. They're worried. Claudia just watched an underground base get turned over in the span of two hours along with losing two of her operatives—one a close friend. I get it." He sat on the edge of a benchlike rock formation. "Besides, Deck and Heather have stuck with me the whole time in case they try anything weird."

"Weird?" James asked.

"I dunno," Bob replied, shrugging. "But Deck got that look in his eye like there was an easy target for him out there. He had Kema and Talon running circles around the base for a half hour dropping hints and clues I had escaped to the *Kaleidoscope* a couple of hours ago. It's entertaining at least."

James grinned, imagining Deck spinning his web around the younger operatives. "All that aside, anything new?"

Bob paused. His face fell to the ground. James glanced at Heather out of the corner of his eye, and the two waited for Bob to collect himself.

"It's hard to describe," Bob said, shifting his weight uncomfortably.

"Try," Heather said in a firm tone.

"It's… Have you ever seen an ant hill? Of course you have, but have you watched one? Long lines leading to a hole and the tunnel system underneath. It's incredible. The ants collect food and bring it back to feed their ant kingdom. The queen signals the kingdom to do everything. Each ant collects food to make sure everyone is cared for, and the entire purpose of the colony is to make sure the colony survives. It's fascinating. The way the BZ, Centria, the Order—all of it—works reminds me of that, like an ant colony. But to achieve their goals, they need to remove a piece of you. They need long lines of unquestioning greater good service." Bob paused and took a breath. "As much as I try to ignore it, there's something at the back of my mind, a nagging piece drawing my thoughts elsewhere. But it's not like I'm having thoughts. I'm…being thought for. I still have control right now, but for how long? That's what I don't know." Bob shook his head, his eyes still trained on the ground. Silence hung over the trio of friends, Bob's words heavy in the air.

Sorrow burrowed into James as his friend actively grasped to control a mind not entirely his own. The sorrow bled into fear and a flutter of distrust which ultimately plunged his conscience into guilt.

*It's Bob.*

"Bob, I—"

"Nope. Nothing. Nothing you can do," Bob said, cutting him off. "I've gotta figure this one out."

James bobbed his head in dull recognition. Conflicting emotions clashed in his brain, but he held them at bay. *If anyone could figure this kind of thing out, it was probably Bob.*

"Maybe I should be watched," Bob said, shrugging.

"I've always thought that." Deck's voice broke the tension and the lean scout entered, flopping onto the bench next to Bob. "A guy drawn to examining bodies the way you do is terrifying."

"Solid point," James said, appreciating Deck's ability to disrupt painful conversations.

"You got into it for a while there," Bob retorted.

"As a field medic, Bob. What you do is very different." Deck stood and took up a spot on the other side of the mirror, watching the doorway with Heather. "Either way, I'll keep tracking you for a while longer." Deck winked at Bob who gave him a middle finger.

"Well, one thing they didn't take away was my hunger. Anything to eat?" Bob asked, rubbing his stomach.

"Eggs and the newly added bean curd," Heather replied, pushing from her spot on the wall.

"Bean curd?" Bob wrinkled his nose.

"It's not bad when all you've eaten is spinach and eggs for weeks. Better than the *Kaleidoscope*," Heather mentioned as the two disappeared around the corner.

"I know, don't remind me. The frickin' worst."

James grinned as their voices faded down the hall.

He collected his used medical gear from the sink. "I hear you're having fun with our friends." He shoved the quick-stitch into his med kit, crumpling the remnants of his bandage casing and tossing it in the incinerator bin under the sink.

"The young ones are always funny with this stuff."

"They're like five years younger than us, Deck," James said, rolling his eyes at the exaggeration.

"Young in *experience*, my old friend. I've taught nine-year olds from Rio Negro better surveillance than these kids."

"Your child army."

"You know, I think that's a genius idea, but let's not go there. What'd you think about Bob?" Deck asked. He settled on the far side of the room, ignoring the door for the first time since he'd entered.

"Bob said some weird stuff at the end there."

"Yep, not your normal Bob this time around. The ant thing…"

"I didn't get that," James replied. Bob had cut himself off and jumped to the end before finishing, leaving James puzzled.

"He's feeling that pull—whatever it is that keeps the BZ people doing what they do. This whole place, man."

Deck shook his head. "I'm ready to get back home. Could use a little Cristina in my life."

It was the first time James had heard his friend mention his wife since they'd left the Federation, and he nodded solemnly. Before leaving, Cristina made James promise he would watch out for Deck. He already lapsed one time. He did not need another.

"I'm sure she misses you."

"Of course she does. I'm delightful." The scout stood quickly to escape the unwanted conversation. "Wilma's in the console room. She wants to talk with you. I think they're planning a base-wide meeting too. Janus and the crew are joining. I'm guessing it's about the mission. Didn't want you to miss Claudia's invitation." The smoldering contempt James held for Claudia flared as Deck held up his hands. "Reign it in, buddy. I'll see you later."

James nodded as Deck stepped towards the door. "Deck."

"What's up, tootsie pop?" Deck stopped, looking back at James earnestly.

"We'll get back there," James said, forcing conviction into his voice.

"Yessir." Deck tipped an imaginary hat towards James disappearing around the corner.

James tossed the med kit into his pack. *I'll organize that later*, he thought, lying to himself as he left the bathroom to find Wilma.

The dashboard room was empty and quiet save for a corner where three HOLOs illuminated the space. Wilma sat alone, her eyes reflected the HOLO's blue haze. Her pupils shifted from screen to screen, moving in steady progression.

As he approached, James trod louder to avoid startling the isolated woman.

"You made it," Wilma said. She turned from the screens and motioned to a chair next to her.

"Deck said you were in here. Wanted to talk," James said, accepting the invitation. He glanced at the HOLOs.

Lines of code James did not understand ran across the screens. In her lap Wilma held a notebook filled with inscriptions on each page with arrows and bullet points connecting her ideas. The older woman's eyes flickered between the screens and her notepad as she scribbled what she saw, seemingly without purpose.

"Need someone for code analysis? If so, you've got the wrong guy," James said, leaning back in his chair, attempting to break the uncomfortable stillness.

"Nope, almost done here," Wilma replied. The scrolling on the left screen stopped, followed seconds later by the other two in rapid succession. With a flourish of her pen Wilma jotted some final notes and tossed the notepad on the table under the HOLOs.

"Thanks for waiting," she said, rubbing her eyes. "I hadn't gotten a chance to look through Kema's downloaded code sequence from Bob's reading earlier today."

"And?" James asked, interested.

"Complicated," she replied with a tired smile.

"Care to elaborate?" he asked. He knew she was exhausted, but they needed answers now.

Wilma grabbed the notepad off the table and tossed it on James's lap. He opened it, stonewalled by the indecipherable symbols filling its lines.

"We've spent years reconfiguring the way the Order disrupted the wiring of their soldiers. Rex and Theo translated it into a readable code," Wilma said, nodding at the screen.

*Readable to who?* James thought, staring blankly at the endless lines of symbols.

"Fatima, Rex, and I think we have a chance of flushing out what the Order did. They were aggressive in their approach but hadn't made enough progress to make their edits irreversible."

"So there's hope?" James said. Tepid positivity filled his thoughts.

"Some," Wilma replied cautiously. "Claudia's not convinced."

Clouds returned to James's vision. Why was he not surprised?

"Not a fan of Claudia?" Wilma asked with a grin as she accepted the notebook from James's outstretched hand.

"We've had our differences," James replied, careful to avoid insulting the woman's friend.

Wilam snorted. "Claudia has differences with everyone. It's her leadership style. Her way or no way." The older woman shook her head lightly. "She's been bitten more than once but seems okay living with the pain of her mistakes. It's what I wanted to see you about. Partially at least. Make sure you understand a few things."

"She's done this?"

"All the time. If someone has an idea, you bet your ass Claudia's brewing up one of her own at the same time. Drove Theo nuts." Wilma looked away.

"Has anyone ever tried to take over? Doesn't seem like she's working out," James asked.

"No, never. She's the only one that wants it. She cares more about this fight than anyone else in the world. And she cares about the whole fight. Finishing the Order. I…" Wilma's voice trailed off.

"What?"

"We've been fighting this war for decades now. Twenty years underground and another twenty buried within the Order's forces. As wars go, this has been one of the longest in modern history. You and your team have fought, for sure, actively battling an intruding force, but we've lived this our entire lives. We've been a part of conflict longer than we haven't. It's hard to imagine a world that exists without being constantly pushed forward by an enemy. I'm not sure Claudia knows how to get that out of her mind. Maybe I don't either. But there is one thing I do know. Destroying that ship will not end the Order. It will take much more than that."

James stayed silent as Wilma pulled up an image on the HOLOs. His mouth dropped in disbelief as the screens panned over the heads of millions of gray-suited soldiers walking shoulder to shoulder onto the ships.

"This was when they first attacked. Entire populations turned into ruthless killing machines, filed onto the boats, transported across the world, and dropped in your lap. Destroying a ship or two won't win this battle, James, and it will not win the war. To do that you need to root out the core thought at the base of the Order. What they believe in. You need to stamp out the idea that brought about their existence because they have thought through it all. They've known you were coming for decades and are ready for it." Wilma stopped and looked at James with quiet resolution etched into the lines on her face.

"So we have to destroy them all? We already knew that," James said, confused. He knew that in order to win, more would need to happen. That was the point of going after the ships in the first place. *What is she getting at?*

Wilma shook her head. "The Order or at least something like it will always exist. Even destroying their military and winning back the Federation won't stop that. You can't win that battle."

Stubbornness rooted itself in James's gut. "So you don't think we can win?"

"I think a balance must be struck to save humanity that goes beyond the war with the Order. The entire ethos of the Order is to recreate humanity in an image that suits them. A vision *they* believe is most beneficial to human evolution. Humanity has been influenced by its environment to adapt and evolve for thousands and thousands of years. The Order wants to shift that and design the world so that humans develop in ways that are beneficial to both. Sadly, that's not how things work.

"Claudia is right, there is no winning the total war. There will always be those who believe in the Order or something like it. You can't eradicate disagreement from people. It's what makes us real. The ability to keep secrets, lie, cheat, steal, fight, anger, love, cry, hope, and hate. All those pieces are central to humanity and traits the Order wants to disabuse us of and cut from our general psyche. That is a war that will be fought forever and caused by the same qualities that define us as human. But she is wrong."

"About what?" James asked, hoping for a glimmer of hope from the woman.

"The Order will fall." Wilma gripped James's wrist. "Like I said the first time I met you, every empire needs its killer."

"If we can't win it all, what's the point?" James asked.

"The point? The point is to fight for the side that believes in the simplicity of human existence. We are not the owners of time and space, but inhabitants of its design. We evolve as our environment predicates us to change. But to push from the other direction knocks off the natural balance of the world. *That* is why the Order is wrong. *That* is why you will win. The hard thing is, you're actively fighting to save the very thoughts that you are fighting against. Little paradox for you." Wilma winked at James with a grin.

"Beyond the theoretical, do you think we can win?"

"The Order has never fought when something unexpected has happened. Their plans are based on the predicted and predictable. They play probabilities to their advantage, and winning is a certainty in their minds. They do not foresee the end, and because of that, the Order is stronger than it has ever been. By destroying one of their greatest strengths, you change the tides of war. But they will overplay in the future, and *then* you have a chance to destroy them," Wilma replied.

"Overplay?" James asked.

"They will bring unimaginable destruction to the Federation if you succeed on your mission. I'm certain the rest of your military is aware of that, but you're the only one who understands how deeply the Order holds its people and how ready it is to fight. If you succeed, be ready to fight."

James nodded his understanding. "They'll bring everything they've got."

"Nothing will be left behind," Wilma said wistfully. "Your victory here will change everything, James. I wanted to make sure you knew it."

# Chapter Sixteen

HOLO lights flooded the space. Three groupings formed at the table. James sat with the Federation team across from the Resistance folks who watched his group cautiously. Janus's crew—including Kady, Wally, and a few sailors James did not know—joined at the end of the table.

Bob observed it all with a detached demeanor, and James made a point to keep an eye on the reactions to his friend's presence.

While he waited, James combed through the pages of notes Claudia sprang on them minutes before the meeting was set to start.

"God, I hate reading through all this crap," Clint muttered, brushing his finger up his HOLO's screen.

"Nature of the beast, my man," Deck said, propping a knee against the table and wedging himself closer. "Gotta read to get the lead."

"What the hell does that even mean?" Clint asked.

"I don't know if it applies, but I wanted to make a point using rhyme, and that sounded the best."

The table chuckled as Claudia walked into the room. The mood shifted from tepid congeniality to isolated skepticism. The HOLO's lights changed to slate gray, and James's attention was pulled to the front of the room.

The Resistance leader stood at the head of the table, supporting herself with her hands and hanging her head towards her chest. She looked at the assembled groupings, settling on James. "The platforms are shot."

The younger members of the Resistance whipped their heads in two directions. First towards Claudia in disbelief and then to the Federation team across the table.

"What do you mean?" Wilma asked. Her leveled tone countered the injection of drama Claudia dropped into the room.

"They're done. We can't use them anymore."

"They're not working?" Fatima asked, confused and glancing at Rex, who looked similarly perplexed.

"Not for us. They're too much of a risk. Having found our base, I don't know what the Order knows. At this point, we have no way to get up there undetected."

James sensed an angry current in Claudia's words and stole himself.

"There's no way back up top?" Kema asked, looking dejectedly at the table.

"For now, at least. We cannot use them. Consider them shut off."

"Claudia…" Wilma looked at her friend over the long table. "It's ho—"

"No!" Claudia's voice rose as her hand landed with a jolt on the table. "We've lost one goddamn base after twenty years. We've spent nearly half a century fighting this thing. They come in, and it all goes to crap in a few days, Wil. Days! How? I'll tell you. *They* don't know what we fight for and have no goddamn clue how to beat the Order. They don't even call them the Order! The platforms are out of the question. I won't risk that for their mission anymore. Do not push me on this." Claudia's chest heaved. She stared with feral intensity at the people watching her. Silence reigned and tension ratcheted up with each second.

"She's right." James spoke with authority. He eyed the groups around the table, ignoring Claudia's surprise hidden under a mask of self-righteousness.

"How else do we get up there?" Kema asked. The young woman's expression wavered between frustration and sorrow at being told she could not go home. James understood both emotions and needed to use them to his advantage.

"There's an entire sea of water surrounding our target. I'm not so bold as to risk the *Kaleidoscope* or her crew with a head-on collision, but we can utilize the strengths we have available."

"We're using my ship now?" Janus asked, amused.

"Hear me out." James walked to the front of the table. "May I?" he asked Claudia, reaching out a hand to take the HOLO controller.

The woman handed him the device without a fight and assumed the empty seat next to Wilma. James inspected the device and glanced at Heather out of the corner of his eye. She nodded at him with a slight grin. Deck leaned across with a thumbs-up under her chin. James smiled and found the images he was looking for. He swiped up and displayed the overhead maps of the harbor.

"The ship, as you all know, is too large to sit in the harbor. Even when it appears next to shore, it's actually in open water. There are over a hundred yards of runway from the harbor all the way out to the offshore dock where ships sit to restock and refuel." He pulled up an aerial shot of the docked mothership. "Its tarmacs are as wide as those needed for a C-5's wingspan with nowhere to hide. Pure concrete all the way except for a few small warehouses in between that they use for restocking. On top of that, there's constant surveillance and Sentinels on ultra-high alert swarming every inch of the city."

"James, we know all this," Teresa said, eyeing the rest of the room as patience wore thin on Claudia's face.

"I know. This all confirms that we can absolutely not go above the waterline or try any sort of onshore attack"—James turned to Claudia—"proving you right. But why does the ship sit so far offshore?" James turned to look around the room. Each group member glanced at the others in their team, but quiet reigned. James realized his fear of becoming a middle school teacher was coming to life.

"It's too big." Kady's voice sprang from the end of the table.

"Exactly! But why? Why is it too big?"

"The engines," Kady said cautiously.

"What about them?"

"They're too deep."

"Yes! Exactly. The ships can't get closer because the shelf is too shallow for its engine cooling mechanism. Nuclear reactors, even small ones, need a way to cool, and by keeping them deep under water, they're using their ship's environment to its advantage." An image of the ship's reactors popped up on the screen with architectural diagrams of the ship's bottom next to it. "Rex, I hope you don't mind that I borrowed these from you. Now, the ship's reactors are broken into eight separate compartments running power to their own grid on the ship. The reactors are built independent of one another in case of problems with different reactors. They can shut one down or cut it off entirely without risk of destroying the whole ship. But if four of the reactors were to explode simultaneously…"

"At different parts of the ship," Rex said finishing James's sentence and standing up to walk closer to the screens.

"Then we can take it all at once," James said, finishing with a final shot of the reactors. Four of the reactors were highlighted in red. He was proud of his little design addition at the end of his presentation. He had seen Caitlin do it during meetings and enjoyed a second of self-congratulation.

"Okay, but how do we get there? They'll spot the *Kaleidoscope* in a heartbeat," Janus challenged. His face remained unreadable as he examined the screens.

"It doesn't need to go all the way. If the *Kaleidoscope* can drift us close enough to the surface to shorten the distance from the seafloor we can swim up to the reactors, board the ship, plant our explosives, and leave. We get back in the ship and are out of the harbor before the Order even knows what happened."

"Timed explosions?" Deck said. The scout joined Rex at the front of the room, looking at the screens.

"Timed would be too risky. We need a remote detonation."

Claudia snorted. "This plan won't work. There's no way we can get a signal in there, let alone a simultaneous one that can set off explosions in four different reactors."

"Why not? You piggybacked their network earlier," James said, annoyed at her derision.

"She's right, James. Remember, we can't use the same trick twice." Fatima looked at him apologetically, and hope drained from James's chest.

"You're wrong." Rhia's voice bubbled through the crowd, and all eyes turned to the slim techie. She sat engrossed in her HOLO. Without looking up, she continued.

"Theo did some pretty cool stuff in your base. After I looked at his tech setup, I was impressed."

James was taken aback by Rhia's rare compliment. She did not hand them out lightly.

"Can you explain?" Rex asked. His eccentric body movements played perfectly against Rhia's smooth, robotic demeanor.

"Theo linked multiple networks and hid the base's activity beneath Centria's own set of signals. It was genius, but I didn't understand how he did it all until now. We can use that concept to create connections with each of the detonators and send the signal that way. The Order will never see it coming."

Rhia had hacked James's control of the monitors to display network diagrams overlaying James's plan, animating what he talked about in real time.

*Showoff.*

"Okay, so four teams take off from he—" Wally started, but James cut him off.

"No. One team. Me and my people. There's too much risk involved. This is something we have all done."

"You've destroyed one of these things?" Wilma asked, raising her eyebrows in genuine surprise.

"We've run these kinds of ops. It should be us doing this whole job." James looked around the room receiving nods from all corners.

"And contingency?" Claudia asked, cutting James's celebration short. "What happens if you fail? Or get caught? Or lose connection to the detonator? How are you going to handle something like that?"

"Local detonation if needed. That's what I'm here for," James said. He knew this was the part that people would argue against. He was prepared.

"James…" Heather's voice trailed off, and she looked at him, annoyed. "That's not the way this goes."

"It's my plan. I need to stick by it. Okay?" James glared around the table, daring someone else to challenge him, but all eyes were concentrated elsewhere except Bob, who met his stare and nodded.

James returned the gesture. "Alright, anything else?"

"Is he going?" Claudia asked. The room shifted in discomfort and skin pricked on the back of James's neck. He knew who she referred to but wanted to make her say it.

"Who's *he*?" James glared at the woman across the table.

The Resistance leader held his gaze and replied, "The one whose brain the Order installed themselves in. The one who blew up a base we've held for twenty years. That one." Her eyes remained on James, but her hand rose to point at Bob.

Bob cast his face to the table doing his best to hide from the room.

Spasms of anger coiled in James's brain and hot rage flowed through his veins. "Listen to me when I tell you this, Claudia. I know what you think of me. I know what you think of Bob and what we're doing here."

"Oh?" Claudia replied, amused. She folded her arms across her chest and tilted her head.

"Yes. We're outsiders to you. People who came over here and are ruining the world you set up for yourselves. But here's the deal. We're the only ones who have done more than watched from the sidelines. We've *been* the ones fighting the Order in our country. I've watched friends be ripped to pieces by their Sentinels same as you, and I've seen our cities razed to the ground by their soldiers same as you. I've lost family and have seen my entire world destroyed. I understand you have lived this for forty years, but our experience falls in line with yours. Just in a different timeline.

"Bob's been with me on this since the very start of this war. This is the beginning of the end, Claudia, and I want you to be on our side. So please, give it a break and get on board with us." His emotions hung on a tightrope, and he ground his teeth as he awaited the older woman's response.

"James, I—" Claudia started to speak, but Bob interjected.

"Let's have a chat if you wouldn't mind, Claudia." Bob stood from the table and locked eyes with the woman.

"Bob…" James tried to intercede, still hopeful Claudia would  listen to reason.

"You said your piece. Let me talk with her." Bob did not shift his sight from the woman across the table, and Claudia gestured towards the door. The two walked from the table while the rest of the audience sat in awkward silence glancing at each other with furtive looks.

"Bold move by Bobbo," Deck said, nodding his head, impressed.

Anxiety, annoyance, and anger rippled through James's psyche, each taking hold of the waves of nausea cutting through his stomach.

"Way to hold back there," Liam said, clapping James's shoulder.

"I would've knocked the bitch out," Teresa said, loud enough for the other Resistance members to hear. The other teams sat looking at anything other than the Federation folks across the table, and James grinned at the stout woman's brashness.

"Good work," Heather said. She squeezed his elbow as Claudia and Bob walked back into the room. Bob led the way and gave James a thumbs-up as he took his seat again on the other side of Heather.

"So, Bob will be going on the trip, and the Federation team will run things. Are we set?"

James did his best to keep his jaw from dropping to the floor. Bob's eyes focused on the HOLOs at the front of the room.

"What do you need from us, James?" Janus asked.

Still reeling from the immediate turnaround, James stumbled over his words trying to answer, "Um ,well. I, uh, I think we'll…"

"We're going to need you to get us to a depth that's safe enough for a quick ascent without risking pressure illness. And if you have any light scuba gear, we can use that'd be perfect," Heather said, taking over for her stammering boyfriend.

"We can work with that. Wally?" Janus turned to the lanky sailor who winked at the Federation team.

"I've got that all worked out for you. Air recyclers should do the trick. Short life, but you'll be moving fast." Wally shrugged. "Or at least you'll have to be."

"Do you have handheld propellers?" Clint asked. "That's going to be a long swim without something to help us pull through the water."

"We have…" Kady started, but her words disappeared as conversations broke out around the table.

The sudden flurry of questions, movement, and whispered voices twisted James's mind in a hundred directions. He looked around the table and down to the flat surface. He took a breath and Heather's hand covered his, her cool palm relaxing him.

"What about getting inside?" Fatima asked.

"I can help with that," Rex said. An image of the engines sprang to life on the HOLO dashboards, "Which ones are you thinking again, James?"

"Focus on the center. If we get the right shot, we can blow the whole thing."

"And everyone for a few hundred miles," Claudia said, raising an eyebrow. "You plan to destroy the ship?"

"I plan to sink an empire," James replied. He knew the risk of blowing up four reactors right next to one another, even ones as contained as those aboard the motherships. But the BlankZone had left him with no choice.

The room hushed at James's words and everyone turned to watch Claudia. The tension, gone moments earlier, had reappeared as the two leaders sought each other's approval. *Maybe Bob will jump in again,* James thought, hoping a different voice in the room would speak up. When none came he gritted his teeth and rapidly searched his mind for the right words. James caught Wilma's grin hidden behind Claudia's elbow. The older woman nodded.

"This is our shot, Claudia. I've said it and I'll say it again. We will not have the opportunity to destroy their greatest weapon ever again. I know we believe in the same cause. I need you on my side. I will listen to whatever you have to say, but this is the moment we can take down the Order. Maybe not in its entirety, but damage it enough to push it off track. We can win this. I know it. But you and I have to fight the same battle to win any of our wars."

Claudia's eyes danced to other faces in the room as she evaluated his words. Her demeanor was different than before she had left with Bob. Her eyes thoughtful, her attitude less challenging, more open.

*She's listening.*

The Resistance leader took her time and looked back at James. "Let's sink an empire."

# Chapter Seventeen

The odor of drying paint and freshly installed drywall filled James's nostrils. Why those two scents hit, he did not know, but they swept his thoughts to a different time in his life.

His father enjoyed building things in what little free time he had, especially when James and his siblings were young. He constructed a small playhouse in their cramped backyard. The design was simple, but the amount of effort his father took to incorporate all the pieces of a home into it impressed James, even more so now than when he was younger. Custom crown molding and hand-designed woodwork on the door, with moons and stars carved into the shutters so the light cast shadows of their images when it shone on the floor.

He could see the house perfectly, nestled behind a row of pansies in the springtime and zinnias or dahlias in the summer months, potted mums in the fall, and festooned with holly sprigs and long strands of pine each winter. The house never lost its allure, acting as a plaything he and his siblings used for hours as children and through their teen years when James used the house's closets to hide beer and cigarettes from his parents' watchful eyes.

Soldered metal seams and bolted steel beams stared at him from his bunk on the ship. He did not know why he had suddenly been transported back to memories of a house built by his dead father, but anything was possible when sleep kept itself at bay.

Glowing light emanated from under the door. The ship never slept, and normally that meant the crew too. Always something to do on a ship. Someone needed to keep watch, maintain engines, or simply clean up. Tonight seemed different. Silence engulfed the ship's populace. Even the lights under his door shined undisturbed, a sign of inactivity. Normally someone yelled on deck, or banging erupted from a machine, interrupting sleep. He wished the same distractions would surface now as he lay in bed, searching for the cure for his insomnia.

Thoughts drifted everywhere. The mission preoccupied most of them, already less than twenty-four hours in the future. Claudia and the Resistance team let him and the *Kaleidoscope* crew plan out the details, only calling in specific HQ residents as needed. James wanted tight control over their plans, and with Claudia in the room, pushing anything to a state of completion would have been difficult. Rex and Fatima stuck around, as did Wilma whose knowledge of the Order's defensive structure aided in their planning more than James had expected. Kema hung around in the background, watching with interest. James's first inclination had been to ask her to leave, but after glancing at her notes, he realized she wasn't spying on them for Claudia but instead wanted to learn more about their methods. She may have only been half a decade younger than James, but her entire life had been subjugated to underground activities, none of which would prepare her for the real world of battle. It was good she learned from them.

Now, after four days of constant diagramming, tech consults, and scenario-building, they were ready. Tomorrow night was a go, but James's mind would not let him rest.

He turned to his bedmate, but Heather's breathing remained steady. She was either very good at faking sleep or actually sleeping. Given the next day's events, James decided not to check. He slipped from under the covers and grabbed a shirt from the back of the chair in the corner of the room.

The door opened soundlessly on its greased hinges, and James pulled it shut behind him, careful to avoid making noise.

*One of us needs to sleep*, he thought as he walked barefoot to the mess.

No one moved in the halls, and James padded quietly across the ground. He did not want to get blamed for waking up the entire ship. Teresa, in particular, was unpleasant when her sleep was interrupted.

The mess hall stairs squeaked as he climbed and, looking up, was surprised to see halogen lights emanating from his destination.

*Maybe someone forgot to turn them off*, he thought, puzzled. The scent of frying eggs hit him seconds later, activating a well of saliva that pooled in his mouth. *Maybe that's why I couldn't sleep*, he thought, running a hand across his stomach.

He knocked the side of the doorframe with his hand as he entered the room and looked at the stovetop. "Hello?"

"James?" Bob's voice carried through the room. His friend sat at the table gripping a fork with one hand as a steaming plate of eggs and bean curd waited in front of him. Guilt hung on his face.

James grinned. "Haven't lost that appetite."

Bob returned the smile. "I'm always hungry. I'd offer you some, but…I don't want to."

"I'll make my own," James said, giving his friend the finger and walking over to the fridge. He collected eggs, placed them on the counter, and flipped on the power to the induction burners. He placed a pan on the stovetop, dropped in a spoon of oil, and cracked the eggs in one by one.

"Can't sleep either?" Bob asked.

"Not on nights like these—right before a mission, and I have no idea what goddamn time zone I'm in anymore. Above ground, below ground, at sea, underwater—I'm all over the place."

"I know what you mean. I never know if I'm supposed to eat breakfast, lunch, or dinner. Doesn't matter though. It's all the same—bean curds and eggs. Or the fucking rations on this ship." Anger crept into Bob's tone at the last part. "Why have these beautiful cooking appliances if all you freaking eat is crap? Makes no goddamn sense." Bob shook his head and took a big bite of his egg, chewing in indignant rumination.

"Pisses you off, huh?" James said, suppressing a chuckle.

"It's nonsense."

It was rare that James saw Bob annoyed or emote anything other than calm, but he loved that food was still one of the things that got him going. Over the last ten years, Bob's reactions to Kevin's cooking after long trips apart were some of James's favorites to watch. Dogs didn't get as excited to see their masters as Bob did to eat his friend's cooking. The sudden memory of his friend reminded James of his other team members working across the sea trying to destroy another mothership. James stopped himself. It was the wrong time to lose focus.

"I'm glad we're on the boat," Bob said. "I feel more at home here."

"Agreed. I'm not meant for underground.

"Yeah, I'm also not loved by the Resistance crew. Or at least one of them."

"Fuck her," James said, waving his hand over his head in dismissal as he raced to grab a plate and flip his eggs out of the hot pan. He forgot how quickly the stoves heated up and hated hard yolks.

"No, she's doing what's right. I don't like it, but it's her job. You'd do the same."

"Bullshit! I'd at least let you walk around, not treat you like a werewolf during a full moon," James said. He took a seat across from Bob. "I'd like to think I'm pretty reasonable when it comes to this kind of stuff."

"Right, right, and the group of Nomads we ran into outside Detroit?" Bob asked with a grin, "How long did you make them walk in front of us?"

James blushed. "That was a different situation. They were coming directly from an Exil encampment and knew that entire minefield. I had to do that, or they would have let us blow up the city. Or what was left of it." James cut into his first egg and a creamy yellow oozed from its center. "Besides," he continued, pausing to take a bite, "we let them go in the end."

"Yes, but you did what you did because that was in our best interest. You had them lead us through the city and dig up the mines along the way. Not out of cruelty, but you believed they would do us more harm than good if they were allowed to walk away. And you wanted to make sure we could safely guide ourselves back during a return trip without surprises. Hell of a thing to subject someone to. But it's a leadership thing, James. You've got it. Claudia's got it. Hell, Croyton's got it. But man, you've got it bad," Bob finished, breaking into a smile, and James shook his head at his friend's impressive logic.

"Thanks for my grouping," James said sarcastically.

"If the personality fits," Bob replied, shrugging.

"That what you were telling Claudia? I'm a stubborn leader?" James asked, partially in jest. Bob had not divulged any of the conversation.

"Something like that," Bob replied mysteriously as he focused too much on his food.

"I knew I smelled eggs! I told you." Deck entered the room swiftly, then turned and pointed an accusatory finger in Clint's face as the muscular engineer followed him into the room.

"Man, everything is not a competition, Deck. But yes, you did smell eggs. Congratulations." Clint rolled his eyes and walked over to the fridge. "You want any?"

"Two please. Over easy, my man," Deck replied, and he flopped into the chair next to Bob. He reached over to spoon a piece of bean curd from the medic's plate but was batted away by a fork.

"Easy, man. I just want a little taste."

"More in the fridge. I'm starving. Mind making me a couple more, Clint?" Bob asked, eyeing Deck's hand inching closer to his plate. "Deck, I swear I'll stab you through that pretty little hand of yours if you move another inch towards my food."

"Just a bite? Those people up there have made you overly protective," Deck said, pointing at Bob's head.

"I'm eating for three now," Bob replied, taking a large bite of egg.

The room laughed, and Deck relented, hopping to the front of the fridge and ducking his head inside.

"How many you want, Bobbo?"

"Three more."

"I'll have three too," Clint added, turning the induction burners back on.

"And with both of your inspiration, I'll change my order to three and will add one for good luck. James, you sure you're good? Two more and we're at an even dozen."

"I'll pass. I'm stuffed as it is."

"Suit yourself."

"No one could sleep?" James asked the group between bites of his bean curd.

"I could, but Fidgety over here wouldn't stop moving in his bunk." Clint tilted his head toward Deck.

"Sorry, I was busy reviewing plans to keep us *alive* tomorrow," Deck replied, scooting across the floor to Clint while holding ten eggs in his shirt like a kangaroo pouch. "Need to have a muscle memory with this stuff. Those timelines…" The scout shook his head, and he handed the eggs one at a time to Clint, who cracked the shells, emptied their contents into the pan, and threw the remains in the compactor.

"Too tight?" James asked. He knew they would be scraping by with only seconds to spare between various stages of the plan as it was, but to hear Deck voice his concern was not normal. For James, it was troubling.

"Probably. That's why I need to know everything," Deck answered. Clint finished filling up the second pan, and Deck returned to his seat at the table. "Who knows though?"

"I'd hope you would," Bob replied.

"Good point. I do know, and time will be tight. And *that* is an understatement."

The group nodded collectively. *Now I'll never sleep,* James thought, reviewing each part of the plan for the thousandth time.

Four engines—each needed to be detonated simultaneously. Afterwards a fight to their exit since there was no way to run interference with the Order's servers long enough to get out of the engine rooms and back to the *Kaleidoscope* without one. The longer it took, the harder that fight would be, assuming everything went perfectly from the start. One idea had been to blow one of the engines early and force the Order to focus on protecting the others while tending to their damaged vessel, but they were only able to manage a single connection to the detonators. That strategy required one detonation to occur manually and three more to happen remotely as planned. It'd cause the most damage, but James squashed the idea once Rhia told them about the network limitations.

"Plates up, Deck?"

"On it, chef," Deck replied, hopping up and giving James the distraction he needed from his internalized torture.

Clint plated the remaining eggs and joined the table.

"Grea' wor'," Deck said through a mouthful of eggs while Bob nodded furiously and gave a thumbs-up.

"Anytime," Clint said as he dug into his plate.

James took the moment of silence to look around the table at his friends. Three people who had been with him since the beginning. Connected by twelve years of war, battling an enemy traveling thousands of miles across the country, and over an ocean to even things up on their own terms. If they could pull this off, everything would change.

He remembered it all. Those days in the dorms, waking up in a haze, trying to figure out which way was up. Learning how to lead a group of people he didn't even know he was leading. The icy mornings of pain and fatigue in the camp with Croyton. And the humid nights hanging out under their palm umbrellas in the jungles of Rio Negro. It had brought them to this point, and he wondered where he'd be the next time his memories greeted him.

"Oof, that helped." Deck sat back in his chair, holding his stomach. Bob spread his arms behind the seats next to him, and Clint let out a burp.

"Lovely." Deck grimaced at Clint. "That's a way to show your roommates love. We're practically living together you know."

"Through necessity," Clint said.

"We're a fun little bunch of guys living it up," Deck said. "We'll go on to do a lot more in the future, but we'll always have our caves."

"I can't wait to get back to NOLA," Clint grumbled as he cleared Bob and Deck's plates. "I'm headed back to bed." He deposited the plates in the sink and walked to the door.

"I'll join. Bob, James?" Deck said, pushing off his chair.

"I'm with you," Bob said, sliding out from behind the table.

"I'm going to hang here for a bit," James replied, waving them off. "Sleep tight."

"Don't stay up all night!" Deck said as he disappeared around the corner.

"Night, James," Bob said. He patted the doorframe with his hand and followed the scout's loud footsteps down the hall.

James pushed out his chair and approached the faucet. He cleaned the dishes, going over the plan again and again, step by step, until he had it memorized perfectly. Coincidentally, the dishes and his thought exercise finished at the same time.

He leaned against the sink and looked at the empty room, replaying the meal with his friends, wondering if it would be his last.

"Find out tomorrow," he said and walked out the door, shutting off the lights behind him.

# Chapter Eighteen

*WHOOSH!*

"Watch it!" Wally shouted and dove across the tight space. His hand clamped onto the back of James's air recycler. "Gonna want that, bud. Here, you'll need a refill." The lanky sailor unclipped the armored container.

Embarrassed, James tried to brush it off. "It'll be fine. It was only a few seconds of air."

"That translates to a minute of breathing depending on the volume you released," Wally said as he screwed the device into the pressurized air pumps. "Only takes a couple of minutes."

"Thanks," James mumbled, trying to hide his reddening face.

"No worries. Gotta lock these things is all," Wally replied over his shoulder.

"You messed up big," Deck whispered, and James pushed the scout to the side.

The crew of the *Kaleidoscope* and the Federation team prepped with Rex and Rhia, ensuring they were well-versed on the pieces of the plan requiring any technical expertise. James had already walked through everything he needed to with Rhia while the Resistance engineer worked with Heather and Clint who would lead the other part of the charge. The small room shrank with the extra bodies, but that would change soon. James had already given the ten-minute warning when only operation personnel were allowed to remain. He needed absolute focus.

"Alright, how's everyone feeling?" Claudia asked, entering the prep room and scanning all the faces.

"Solid," Heather replied. She inspected the bands of her suit hanging on the wall and checked her gear hookups for the fiftieth time. "Ready to get moving."

"Yep, good to go," Bob echoed.

Claudia nodded at the medic, who returned the gesture. James's body relaxed as the interaction passed.

"Should we do a final walkthrough while we wait for James's air?" Claudia asked. James sensed a ripple of sarcasm in the older woman's voice but squashed it when he saw her face grilling the team.

*She's not one for gentle ribbing.*

"Blow up engines, return to ship," Teresa replied, reviewing a HOLO diagram of the controls to the torpedo-like devices that would propel them to the mothership.

"Some more detail maybe?" Wilma prodded, stepping in behind her friend.

Her usually calm face carried a more serious expression as the women waited for their answers.

"Allow me," Deck interjected, stepping to the center of the room. He whipped out his HOLO emitter, and seconds later a 3D image of their current location appeared in the center of the room.

"Dubbed Operation Night Riot, trademark pending, we're going to lay charges in these four engines of the Order's mothership, the *Odyssey*. Everyone with me?" Deck scanned the room and skipped past Heather and Teresa's heavy glares as the monitor illustrated their explosives' targets. "I'll take silence as a yes. First step is to get onto the *Odyssey*. Using old ship blueprints, Rex worked out some neat little tricks for us to bypass their security and get onboard. We timed their surveillance routines to the second to board without them noticing. Liam and Clint cooked up a couple of things to keep the Order busy later on. We'll drop what we need into the water, get on the ship, and lay our bombs. The first two engines are on the same side. Using Rex's maps and outlays we're going to hit the halls, break into the side paneling, and travel through the wall space, ceiling gaps, and anywhere not out in the open to the second engine room."

"What kind of distractions?" Kema asked confidently, becoming embarrassed the moment she spoke. Her cheeks darkened as she looked at the floor, reminding James of every other young soldier's reaction the first time they asked questions.

"We'll have timed charges next to the engines we're not hitting," Liam explained, saving Kema from dying of embarrassment.

"What if they go off early?" she asked. James appreciated her questioning. *She'll need to know this stuff one day.*

"It doesn't matter," James added. "If they go off and we're still working engine three, no big deal. We still get the benefit of a distraction."

"Won't that ruin your timing?"

"We'll have to move fast." His tone ended the questions, and James nodded at Deck who picked up from his last spot.

"Hit the nail on the head, Kema. This is where things are going to be tough because the timeline only allows for three engines. However, all four have to be blown up simultaneously or the connection Rhia's creating won't work properly. Soooo James and Bob will take care of numbers three and four while the rest of us use the paths behind the walls to create hell for the rest of their crew. Buuuut there's no way to get out of there without a gunfight. When the final bombs are planted, we'll have timed charges go off in whatever gathering places we can find—a mess hall, HOLO room, hell, maybe we'll randomly stumble upon their entire leadership team and end the war without even trying. Anything's possible. Either way, first timed charge is to get them running in one direction."

"Then you exit?" Wilma asked, staring at the board. Concern, confusion, and outright doubt colored her expression.

"That's right. We get off the *Odyssey* and kick our asses off back to the *Kaleidoscope*."

"What about the scooters?" Claudia asked, dissecting the plan with shrewd eyes.

"They won't stay put under water. We'll drop them at the escape netting," Heather replied.

"Exactly, so it's just us," Deck said. A picture of seven people swimming underwater and giving a thumbs-up while something exploded behind them appeared on screen. The scout looked at the crowd expectantly, hoping someone would appreciate the bit of flare he had added. After a few moments of silence, he shut off his emitter and asked, sulking, "Any questions?" Then under his breath: "Artless idiots."

"There's no way you can get off that ship without a firefight?" Wilma asked as Janus pulled out his emitter. They watched it cycle through the plan across multiple screens.

"We need to hit all four engines, or their defense mechanism will still be intact."

Claudia's eyes narrowed. "What? Why does the defense system need to be down? Killing the reactors should be enough to blow the thing up or cause enough damage that it will take years to rework."

"Exactly. They could get it running again," James said, stepping forward. "Janus and his crew are going to fire torpedoes as we're enroute back. They'll aim for the engines we hit. Their cores will be unprotected. A direct shot and that thing will never sail again. Their problem turns from years into decades. A timeline *they* can't afford."

The Resistance leaders glanced at one another. Claudia turned to James and nodded. "Good luck." She stuck out her hand, and James accepted it. The arguments queued in the back of his mind fell to the side.

"Thank you."

"Cast off in twenty minutes, folks. Smoke 'em while you got 'em," Wally announced, refocusing the gathering.

"I've gotta piss. I know I'll be in the water but feels nice to use a toilet before these things," Deck said, walking out of the room.

"I do too. Wait, do you pee in the water?"

"Of course. It's my ritual."

"God bless your wife."

"You understand how to use this?" Rhia's voice caught his attention, and James turned to find the slender woman with Rex. Ignoring the man's peculiar facial movements, James accepted the network extender for the detonators.

"You and I walked through it a hundred times. I've got it, Rhi." He knew she meant no disrespect, but he had that piece down.

*Maybe she does mean a little disrespect*, he thought remembering other inane questions she had asked him regarding the tech as if he had the intellect of a squirrel.

"You need to link each deployment. Got it?" She ran through a mini demo without verbal explanation, walking through each piece with her hands. "See?"

"I got it. Really," James said, gritting his teeth to stop himself from snapping. Heather waved at him from over the crowd and he started in her direction.

"Okay, good luck. Don't forget the process," Rhia tittered behind him, and James glanced back at the slender woman's gloating and smiling face illuminated by her HOLO's glow.

*Goddamn techies.*

"Walk?" Heather asked. James nodded. He needed to get out of the room for a minute. They'd be under the most intense pressure in the known world for the next few hours. Walking down a hallway with Heather would help him relax one last time. He caught Bob's eye over the heads of the crew and pointed at the hallway. Bob gave him a thumbs-up.

"Let's go," he said, and Heather ducked around the corner leading the way.

"Rhia giving you instructions?" she asked with a grin.

"She thinks I'm a moron."

Heather barked out a laugh. "She probably does. Don't take it personally."

"I spent the last twelve years with Jon as a close companion. I can handle any negativity thrown my way."

"Good point. Rhia does have a special way of demeaning you though."

"The constant doubt whether I can even turn on a lightbulb is where mine starts," James said, turning the corner and brushing by a cart of weapons heading back to the prep room.

"Once she showed T how to start a HOLO emitter for a presentation." Heather chuckled. "Teresa broke the emitter in half and threw it out the window. Rhia took out another emitter and tried to show her the right way to break it without using as much exertion. Liam had to drag T out of the room before she broke every piece of tech in there."

It wasn't hard to imagine Rhia's stone-cold expression delivering an endless list of advice to Teresa. He knew how she must have felt and found himself wishing Liam had not intervened.

"Rhia aside, you ready?" he asked, turning the final corner in their short loop.

"Sure am. Not enough prep time, but we knew that'd be the case."

"Resistance team seems on board."

"Even Claudia," Heather agreed. Another cart filled with ammo rolled past them. They reached their final corner. James knew they'd need to head back soon, but he wanted a few more minutes alone with Heather. He looped his fingers through hers, and she drifted closer to his shoulder. The grassy scent of soap washed over him, and James picked up an undercurrent of lemon emanating from her body. Evidence of the special bar of face soap she'd brought along, her one travel indulgence.

"Must be doing something right," James said. The doorway to their go-room reappeared, and empty carts filtered from the tight space, making room for final preparations.

"How's Bob?" Heather asked. James had thought about his friend most of the day but wasn't sure how to answer. The even-keeled medic seemed to be his normal self, but every once in a while, a far-off stare or misplaced pause when he spoke made James pay closer attention.

"As good as he can be." James shrugged.

Heather nodded. "Keep an eye on him in there."

James bobbed his head. "I will."

The line of carts entering and exiting the room stopped its endless procession, and the hallway grew quiet. James glanced at Heather who stared at the ground. He lifted her chin, so her face was inches away from his. "I love you." He kissed her, soaking in her scent while her lips pushed against his.

"I love you too," she whispered. Hand in hand, the couple walked back to the room.

During their short walk the atmosphere in the room had changed dramatically. Clint, Liam, and Teresa sat in a corner wordlessly going through a 3D diagram of where they'd set charges.

Meanwhile, Deck sat with his HOLO, walking through the ship's blueprints, perfecting his path. Bob sifted through his medical bag, checking over his instruments and debating if any changes to his supplies were needed. Everyone had their way of dealing with the moment.

James cleared his throat, and the eyes of the team greeted his. He pointed at the row of equipment waiting against the far wall. "Gear up."

Silently the team donned their mission suits. The suppressor was the last thing James screwed onto his sidearm holstering it on his combat suit. He flipped a rifle onto his back and looked over the team.

Six cold determined faces stared back at him. He focused on each one in turn, ending with Bob. James turned, ignoring the mini spasm in the medic's face as he addressed the team.

"I won't repeat myself with the dos and don'ts of this mission. You all know the stakes. Let's stick to the plan: get in, get out, go home. Any questions?"

As usual, silence answered him.

"Let's go. Clint, would you call the essential personnel back in?"

Clint gave a thumbs-up.

The team finished last-second preparations, rechecking each other's gear and securing loose items to their person.

Deck turned around wordlessly in front of Heather and James and pointed to his back. Heather looked him over, tapped him on the shoulder and turned around for the same treatment.

James toyed with the ammo magazines strapped across his chest and the baton on his hip. The *Kaleidoscope* crew had provided them with a few anti-Sentinel devices, and with Rex's help, they'd been strengthened to ensure they could stand up against the monsters the Order kept closest to home.

"Ready?" Janus's calm voice ended James's self-inspection. Kady, Wally, and Rex walked into the room. Clint followed and guided Rhia through the door, tapping her knee so she would lift it and not trip over the entryway.

*She's focused, that's for sure*, James thought, watching the slender techie take an unassuming place by the wall.

"Ready as we're going to be," Deck replied. He stood behind James and adjusted a strap for his friend.

"Thanks, bud."

Deck clapped his shoulder in response. His talkative nature disappeared in moments like these. He was locked in.

"Submersion chambers ready to go," Wally said, opening the hatch leading to the pressurized room they would use to enter the water. "The scooters are hooked up under the boat outside. When we get your signal, we'll start our rise. Once we hit three hundred meters from the surface, we'll stop and open the floodgates. Then it's up to you. Last minute questions?"

Wally's lean face searched the crowd, but he received only shakes or murmured nos.

"Alright, good luck," Wally said. James realized this was probably his first time in this kind of situation. *Not many people have been involved in such a high-stakes operation*, James reminded himself. That was hard for him to remember after running dozens of these a year, totaling in the hundreds at this point. Nothing quite like this, but the early days in the Southwest involved the same element of danger. *Hotter and dryer though.*

"Anything from you, Kady?" Janus asked, glancing at his engineer.

"Watch the throttle on the scooters. They'll create too much churn if you go over one thousand rpms. You won't go fast, but you'll be harder to detect at a slower pace."

"Thanks, Kady. Let's get you all in the chamber," Janus said. He motioned for the team to enter. James stepped through the hatch, followed by Deck and Heather. The rest of the team moved into the tightly cramped space around

James, shuffling to keep at least a foot apart from one another. James was surprised. *Bigger than you'd think.*

Janus calmly gazed at the team, and a slender face poked around the edge of the tall captain's shoulder. Rhia pushed a strand of the captain's hair to the side and watched them with forlorn wanting. James knew she wanted to come with them, but he needed her on the ship. She was the one who had invented the new network system, and Rex could only handle so much.

"Come back," Rhia said. She looked Bob in the eye. "You too." The techie hid her face from the team and returned to her spot on the wall, getting a reassuring pat on the arm from Wally.

Bob looked at the floor, and James glanced questioningly at Deck who shrugged.

"We'll be ready when you call," the captain said.

"Thanks, Janus. We'll see you soon."

Janus swung the hatch shut, and the maglocks thudded against their steel counterparts sealing them inside.

Red light flooded the room until a low *buzzzz* reverberated around the metal space. The light turned green, bathing the team in an eerie glow, and pumps dumped water into the space. Pressure filled James's eyes and nose in random spurts, neutralizing as his body acclimated to the underwater environment they were about to enter.

The first of a trio of white lights blinked on the door, signaling them to start the process. Wally had taken James through their deep-sea submersion training the first time they boarded the ship, and the rules had been drilled into his brain over the last twenty-four hours. As Wally put it, without them, he'd bubble up like a balloon and die.

He attached his recycler mask, tightening the plastic rubber straps around the back of his head until the seal stuck to his face. A tap from Heather asking him to check her work gave him the chance to ask for the same. Her thumbs-up told him what he needed to know. He was good.

The air hose coiled at his hip and attached neatly to the top of his tank. He clipped the other side into his mask. His fingers turned the dial until the O2 monitor blinked a solid green. *Another check.*

Light number two blinked over the door. Water lapped against his thighs, and James took the extra oxygen tank from his belt and clipped it to his face mask. He breathed in and out twenty times and stopped. He threw the bottle to the side joining the discarded cannisters from the rest of the team floating in the water.

By now the salty liquid was above his waist. The third light flashed, and he ran the final check of his equipment going through the progression in the exact steps drilled into them by Wally, Janus, and Kady. Air tank first, then weapons, then tech gear, then mask, then air tank again and repeating the steps two more times.

The routine complete, he clicked on the comms earbud, opening the channel between James and the team. They would not be able to use them when they got inside the *Odyssey*, but until that point, the team needed to take the risk and coordinate over their network.

"How's everyone doing?" James asked. He glanced at the masked faces of the room. Nods and thumbs-ups returned. His heart beat calmly in his chest, and adrenaline coursed through his veins. He breathed in and out, combatting the natural fight-or-flight response. It was too late for one of those options.

"See you all out there," James said. Teresa bobbed in the water, and James's face dripped with salt water stinging his pores.

Water rose, filling his ears and cooly rushing through his hair, submerging his body.

To help remain calm, he breathed in and out, accepting the enormity of the moment as he waited for the signal.

Red lights flooded the space.

The door to the ocean opened, and their room merged with the sea.

James waited until the door finished its ascent. With a final shudder the flap stopped moving and the lights turned off replaced with a single bar of white light, and the room flipped back to green before shutting off entirely.

James had requested they flip them off immediately to avoid any Order sentries stumbling upon their ship. He floated out under the boat and looked up at the looming belly of the *Odyssey.*

# Chapter Nineteen

Darkness permeated the liquid world in which James floated three hundred meters beneath the surface. But even in the light-deprived depths of the water, the presence of the mothership dominated the space.

Clint and Liam performed checks of the scooters while the others hung in the weightless environment. Seconds ticked by in James's head. The ever-present clock signifying failure or success never stopped.

To distract himself he stared at the gargantuan hull of the ship they sought to destroy. He still had trouble wrapping his head around the enormity of the BZ ships. This close, the vessel seemed more a figment of some bizarre imagination rather than a reality. In fact it was probably one of the most significant feats in human history. To have three roaming the world was an entirely different scale of achievement. It dwarfed the efforts of the Babylonian gardens, even those of the Great Pyramids. How do you compare to these structures? Floating fortresses. Cities that cast shadows so wide on the bottom of the ocean that they created eclipses for the creatures below. They were nothing short of astonishing. From his current position, James could not see the edges of the boat. It stretched too far into the distance and with little sunlight to combat the night's blanket it seemed as if the ship was a part of the sea. An inescapable cover blotting out the world above.

"We're ready." Clint's voice crackled over his headset. Seven scooters bubbled in the water, their battery indicators glowed a soft green.

"Time to go," James said. The team members drifted to the devices and tested the controls.

The scooters were essentially caged propellers held in cylindrical tubes with handles on the sides that formed a U-shape under the propeller compartment. The rider held the handles with the device under them to avoid getting blasted with a wave of bubbles. While the propellers sped up their approach, they emitted very little noise, making them ideal for clandestine operations. James had been happy Janus prepared the gear on his ship for any possible situation. Without the scooters, the team would have had a long swim to the boat through a field of potentially deadly surveillance traps. Speed and stealth were key.

James gripped the handles on his scooter, maneuvering so his body floated naturally above his transport. He tested the triggers that controlled the pitch and speed of his propellers. Satisfied, he checked on the rest of the group. "Everyone good?"

A series of black-gloved thumbs illuminated by headlights greeted him in response.

"Great, we're going to lose comms at some point. Remember the plan. Stick to your parts, and if you get into trouble let someone know. Keep an eye out for one another. I'll see you all in the boat. Deck, on your go."

Compact bubbles followed Deck as he took lead and pulled out his HOLO scanner. Kady had worked on modifying the HOLO for use underwater. They were practically invisible, but the Order ran consistent surveillance. The scout's ability to map out holes in the enemy's defense would help them reach the ship's alarm perimeter.

Deck's goggles reflected the light from his HOLO as he examined the screen. With a wave, he pocketed the scanner and started off on his scooter in a flurry of fizz that turned into a torrent of rushing water, invisible to the naked eye.

Without hesitation, James mimicked Deck's path, manipulating the scooter's controls with his fingers. He used his fins to aid the propellers, kicking to increase his speed through the water.

Refracted light cut into the water, and the structure of the mothership became clearer. James had never seen the underside of the ship firsthand, and the mystifying pieces of the *Odyssey* peeled back bit by bit. The light from the harbor illuminated the massive engines. They were the width of skyscrapers with pistons that jettisoned in or out of the water, depending on the ship's movement. During the attack in

Midway, James remembered the ship hovering above the waterline, hanging in midair, defying natural physics. When docked or in safe waters, the engines submerged. The heat from their reactors was too concentrated to stay inside the ship for more than a few days. This was their natural state.

Paneling on the parts of the ship closest to the waterline came into focus—titanium alloy girded by stainless steel to combat the negative effects of the seawater. Admiring the machine on their ascent, James tried to discern the little pieces that made the creation so incredible. Self-sustaining desalination vats that collected, ionized, and emitted fresh water for the crew. Solar paneling embedded across the entire hull, including areas facing the water to ensure no energy was wasted. Even the propellers hung in a web of intricate magnetic fields rather being held by screws and soldered metal. It was an engineering masterpiece.

*Too bad we have to blow it up.*

Deck held up a hand to check their distance. Fifty meters. This is where they would begin their escape route. Liam, Clint, and Teresa handed their scooters to the other team members so they could begin their part of the operation. James accepted Clint's and joined the remaining three to watch them work.

Clint flipped the duffel bag from his back to his front and readjusted the straps so that it floated around his waist. From his bag he pulled a series of thick, three-foot-long cords and hung each one on a hook embedded in the side of the duffel. Two round black objects the size of tennis balls came from the bag next. The balls floated into Clint's hand, and he fastened one at both ends of the strips of cord. Afterward, he hung the cords on a hook under his bag and had them float while he worked on the rest of his gear.

Without warning one of the balls escaped towards the surface. Panic gripped James's heart. Clint grabbed the stray floatie before it could travel far enough to cause a serious problem. Relief swept through James's brain, and a stream of bubbles escaped from Deck's face mask.

*He must have seen it too.*

With the strands of floating explosives ready Clint connected an almost invisible netting to them and hooked reels of high tensile fishing wire to the net. Weights sewn into the cross-stitching held the material from floating until the net dropped. The fibrous material unfurled with its explosive cord wrapped within its face, creating a web of explosive walling directly in the path of the ship. A gap remained from where they would exit. Clint, Liam, and T had set up the first step for their eventual escape.

Once the netting disappeared in the dark water, he motioned for the rest of the team to follow.

Deck led the way while Liam and Teresa returned from their own netting responsibilities, pulling the excess explosives behind them to close the space between their sections and Clint's.

When everyone regrouped, they dropped their scooters. It would be manual swimming from here on out. Not ideal for a getaway, but a net of invisible explosives along their route added the element of surprise if speed was not an option.

The team took off toward the boat with Deck leading, churning his flippers rhythmically. The ship's hull loomed ahead, and James matched their HOLO's schematics with the *Odyssey*'s actual layout.

The first two engines were exactly where they wanted them—underwater and free of any potential Sentinel or human guard. At the beginning of their planning, James hadn't been sure what level of security the Order would have waiting for them, but Rex and Claudia knew Sentinels were not underwater devices. The physics did not work. They had even thought it silly to think a Sentinel could go into water.

*None of it makes sense*, James thought ruefully, approaching the mobile city.

A ringing careened through his earbuds—another expected development Wilma warned them about. The likely culprit was the interference from the ship's communications and the active jamming they ran from Centria's servers.

They moved within ten meters of the ship's defensive perimeter, an infrared alarm system monitoring the ship's safety at dock. Heather joined Deck at the front of the line and, using a scanner, located the boundary. She removed a jammer from her belt and activated it. The jammer fed the infrared signal back into itself to avoid breaking the circle and sending alarms to the ship, unleashing Centria's forces.

Deck swam through first without a hitch. Heather pocketed her device, and the rest of the team followed, pushing along towards the *Odyssey*, now an open target.

Light from the surface poured from above creating a sea of shadows that bounced around the underwater world. *Seems busy,* James thought as a beam of light cut across their path.

Concrete pylons draped in swaths of barnacles towered from the bottom of the ocean to the ship's dock. They searched for the emergency hatches. The schematics showed numerous external entrances to the ship's engineering blocks. *Probably not worried about entrances that sit under the water*, James reasoned while he searched for an entryway.

Lights from the dock highlighted the fused metal plates. Bob patted his shoulder and pointed to a spot at the bottom of engine one. The two swam towards it. Optimism spread through James's thoughts. The wheel. Each took a side of the device. The crank turned, and a panel popped off the ship.

James motioned to Bob: *I'll get the team.*

Bob gave him a thumbs-up and kept working on the panel while James rallied the group.

Upon their return, Bob had the whole panel off and pushed inside the opening. One by one, the crew floated through while James waited at the back of the line. After helping each person enter, Deck swam in. James followed, pulling the hatch back into place and securing it. Without the reflected light from the outside, James found himself in a nearly pitch-dark chamber.

Light shimmered through the water like distant light bulbs. He kicked off the bottom and swam until he broke the surface. The rest of the team removed their sets, and Liam pulled James from the water. Sloshing liquid echoed in the chamber.

They had learned from the blueprints that these rooms served two purposes. One was the mechanic entrance, and the other was as an emergency valve to cool the reactors.

Each valve held a similar vat of seawater used to flood the rooms if something went wrong. He removed and packed up his underwater gear, admiring the space, preparing for the next part of the mission.

Heather and Bob examined a HOLO with intense expressions, watching the symbols on a chart rise and fall. James finished his prep as Heather called to the group, "We're good to talk. Scans are clear."

*Good so far.*

"Nice work, everyone. Any issues with the nets?" James asked his newbie explosives experts.

"Went smooth," Clint answered with affirmative nods from his partners.

"Good. Let's take care of these first two engines then we can start the party. Deck and Heather, you're up top. Keep an eye on the scanner. Clint and Liam, do what you need to do. Bob, T, let's start working on the move to our next target. All ready?"

Bobbing heads, thumbs-ups, and Deck's crisp salute answered the question.

Those members of the team working on the engines went about their readying the initial detonations for explosion and preparing for future parts of the plan.

James picked up his rifle and checked it over.

"The map ready?" he asked Bob and Teresa.

Bob's HOLO cast its screen between the trio. A 3D image of the room came into view. James tapped the icon for their part of the mission. Blue lines indicated their path, and the animated plan played for them a final time. Bob looked at him expectantly.

"This way," James said, and the two followed him down a stretch of corridor leaving the sounds of clanging and twisting of metal as their remaining team members prepared the engines to erupt.

They followed signs along a series of thin corridors winding their way through the engine's inner mechanics. James passed a doorway and moved towards a wall farther along the path. He removed a set of corrosive wires from his bag and attached them to the wall with tape. He hooked a

HOLO emitter into one end of the wire and a series of sparks flew around the outline of the square he had fashioned.

When he disconnected the emitter from the wire Teresa and Bob removed the wall panel, giving way to a crawl space filled with steel girders. James stepped inside. In the tight space he had to stretch in unnatural ways to move. He wedged his way down the wall until he came to another plate. He took out his schematics and walked himself through the steps one by one. The scanner in his pocket showed all clear, and he took a deep breath, resetting his wiring and plugging in the emitter.

Sizzling metal echoed in his ears joined by the scent of burning metal. James's heart pounded. He didn't trust the scanner through this metal, and if it was wrong and people were on the other side of this wall, the mission was fucked.

The coil of wire blackened as it ran out of metal to burn. James disconnected it, stowed it in his pocket. He placed his hands on the newly created entryway, took a deep breath, and pushed the bottom of the panel ever so slightly to pop it from its place.

Quiet filled the air. James held his breath as he peeked out of the square space into the hallway. After taking a second to focus, he confirmed the space was clear. He pulled himself through and landed in the hall of the ship.

James glanced around at the stark space. The design was typical of the Order's lack of humanity. Cut-and-dry lines with nothing but the essentials. No ornate paths or beauty. Austere and functional. Less than simplicity. His lungs strained as recycled air pulsed through the space.

James turned as Bob and Teresa made their way through the hole to join him.

"This place sucks," Teresa muttered, turning in a circle and staring at the ceiling with disgust.

Bob touched a wall and pulled back. "Why's it so cold?"

"Still underwater," James replied. "Doesn't matter. We've gotta keep going. You two start on the wall over there. Judging by Rex's map, that's where the easiest entrance will be. Crawl space is wider."

"Happy to," Teresa said as James hopped back through to the engine rooms.

When he returned to the team, Clint and Liam were watching Deck and Heather finish their final touches on the engine explosives.

"Almost…done." Deck moved his hands slowly away from the black rectangle attached to the electrical input system on the engine block.

"It's not triggered, you know," Heather whispered, looking at him out of the corner of her eye.

"These things can go off at any minute," Deck answered, backing away and treating the bomb with a healthy level of respect. "Besides, Kevin always did this stuff."

"It'd be nice to have him here," Clint chimed in.

"Him and Jon," James added. "Ready for the first connection?"

"All you." Heather moved away, so James could access the space.

James bent to a knee and pulled the network connector from his pack. It was a simple device that looked more like a band-less slingshot than a high-tech implement that could remote detonate the largest manmade object in history.

"Here we go…" James connected the cable from his HOLO, and a screen popped up. He went through the series of steps to activate the network and get it working independently before he unplugged it and stuck the connector into the top of the detonator. He watched his HOLO anxiously as the gray bar stayed rigid until it flipped to green. His heartbeat steadied, and his shoulders relaxed.

"Next up." He zipped the rest of the connectors in his pack.

"That's it? It's…live?" Deck asked, looking curiously at the Y-shaped stick popping up from the black box.

"That's it."

James moved through the hallway to the wall. He guided the rest of the team into the hole and reattached the paneling to the engine room.

He joined the team in the hallway as they walked uneasily around the space. Something did not sit right with James. Everything stank of an artificial nature, opposing humanity, from the angles of the walls and the slope of the floor to the feel of the metal against his hands.

"This place is gross," Heather said as James approached.

"It's a good thing we're not staying. Into the walls, everyone." James shepherded the team to the next step in the journey, eager to get out of the open.

Once inside, James replaced the panel, trapping them in darkness.

Using a flashlight as their guide Deck led them through the cramped space and, although bigger than the first pathway, did not expand enough to relieve the nagging sense of claustrophobia.

Deck's hand rose. James stopped. He held his breath and watched Deck inspect the scanner.

The scout's hands signed in the light of the scanner: *Mess hall. Two hundred inside. Maybe more.*
Clint signed back: *We'll start here. Meet you at engine two.*

Deck replied with a thumbs-up and padded ahead.

James wedged himself past the bulky mechanic, scraping by Liam's beard. He nodded at the two of them, who returned the head bob. This would be the last James saw them during the operation.

After a series of twists and turns, Deck signaled for another stop. James controlled his breathing and waited for another scanner check. Given the all-clear, James attached another cord to the wall and waited while the charged wiring ate through the material. He popped off the panel as Heather rescanned the area without the wall's interference.

She gave him a thumbs-up. *All clear.*

James hopped into another empty hall and crossed the corridor to the stainless-steel wall. Again, he mounted his wires and created their access panel to the engine room. Once inside the compartment, he turned to Bob and Teresa. "You two hang out here and keep guard. If anyone comes, take them out. If there are too many, hold on until we get back. We'll be two minutes."

Teresa nodded, pulled the rifle off her back, switching off the safety. "On it."

James led the way to the same place as in engine one where Deck installed the first explosives.

"On you, Deck."

Deck knelt and organized his materials. He began installing the pieces one by one.

"Lucky us, running into a mess hall, huh?" Deck said, pulling a black metal box from his pack and setting it on the ground.

"Not lucky for everyone there," James replied, checking the space for lurkers that might have been missed on their scanners.

"Right, I guess not. But strange there were so many people."

"Two hundred isn't that many," James replied.

"Two *thousand*. Not two hundred. Why the hell would I have us stop for two hundred?" Deck asked. He connected the box to the cords and stepped back, "How's it look?"

"Wait…two thousand? They had two thousand people in a mess hall? For what?" James did not trust something. *Why so many people on a ship in port to eat?*

"I dunno." Deck shrugged. "Stocking, cooking, maybe pulling long shifts."

James's mind swirled, and Heather caught his eye as Deck sensed a change in tone.

"What? What's going on?"

"That's a big dinner party." Heather's brow furrowed as the two of them raced to analyze the situation.

"Yeah, that does—"

"ALL PERSONNEL, PREPARE FOR LAUNCH."

Three bells chimed in the background, and steam erupted from the floorboards as the reactors beneath their feet powered up. A door opened above and James looked at Bob, Heather, and Deck in turn.

"Here we go."

# Chapter Twenty

"Why are we moving?" Deck's back straightened, rifle at the ready as the engine noise grew. "What's going on?"

"Bad intel or the Order changed their minds," James replied. He tossed off his backpack and started the network process, forcing himself to focus on the connector in his hands while adrenaline flew through his veins. Meanwhile, his mind raced through the same question. *Why are we moving?*

It was entirely possible they had the ship's sail date wrong… But by two weeks? Something was not right. Maybe the Order got spooked by the recent attacks and Federation presence in Centria. Maybe the other ships were making a move. Maybe something happened with Stacie and her team.

If the last possibility was true, he hoped it was in their favor. *Silver lining.*

The network connector blinked green.

"Done." James zipped his bag. A clang of metal turned the team's attention to the doors of the engine compartment.

James glanced at Deck who put a finger to his lips. The scout pointed toward the voices and moved his finger, pointing along their route as the BZ soldiers walked the hall until the footsteps stopped. A chorus of suppressed rounds echoed followed by the thud of crumpling bodies.

"Clear," Teresa's voice called to the team.

Breath reentered his system. James tossed the bag on his back and followed Heather up the stairs.

Bob and Teresa pulled the bodies to the wall and sat them against the metal surface. Simple shots through the head and chest slicked the floor with blood. James bent to inspect the still figures for devices. He pulled the earbuds from their heads, inserting one to check if anything had changed.

Static echoed and he pocketed them.

"Wall?" Heather asked.

"Yeah, can you all handle that? Bob and I need to get to the next engine."

"We're on it."

"Stick to the plan. Bob, you ready?"

The medic stood to the side staring blankly at the bodies. His eyes swiveled right and left, examining them one by one in a robotic typewriter motion.

"Bob? Hey, man, you okay?" Angst crept into the back of James's mind.

"Bob!" Heather shouted and pushed the medic on the arm knocking him out of his trance.

"What? Sorry. I…I don't know what happened. There's a signal or something or…"

James gritted his teeth. He had picked Bob to go with him against the wishes of Heather and Deck. He hadn't wanted to risk anyone else partnering with their biggest vulnerability. If someone had to make a call with Bob, it would be James.

"We're heading out, buddy. No time to think about it. You're with me. Third engine." James pulled earbuds from a body and tossed them to Deck. "You may want these. We'll see you guys back home."

"Good luck," Heather said.

James nodded.

*CLANG*. The upper-level door swung back open, and Deck dropped to a crouch and disappeared around the corner.

Heather waved James away and signed: *We've got this. Go.*

James wanted to help, but knew they'd be fine. He pulled Bob's shoulder and they moved into the wall's wider paths through the center of the ship.

Electricity hummed throughout the crawl space. James kept a close eye on their route diagrams from Rex's files. It would be easy to lose their way, and James did not want to be trapped on a ship filled with thousands of BZ soldiers sailing towards the final destruction of the Federation.

Two loud bells tolled.

"What's that for?" James whispered.

Bob remained silent, and James glanced over his shoulder at the medic. His friend stood stock-still. His breathing quickened as his eyes opened and closed without control. He chewed on air sporadically while his body stuttered.

"You okay, man?" James asked. His hand drifted to the sidearm tucked in the holster on his belt.

Bob's eyes followed James's hand, and with a great amount of effort, he raised his fist and forced open his fingers.

*Stop.*

"Okay, okay." James put his hands in the air. Fear and curiosity gripped James. An underlying current of guilt prompted him to listen to his friend. In the back of his mind James knew how he would have dealt with anyone other than Bob.

"Bellllsssshhh." Bob growled out the word through spasms, clamping his jaw shut. He gripped the wall with his fist, clawing the metal with his nails.

"What about them?" James needed to know how he could help.

"Sassasiiigna." Bob forced the word, choking on each letter.

The bell tone ended, and Bob crumpled in on himself. Body contortions forced the medic's body into a tight ball. Regret and more guilt poured over James. If he had listened to Claudia, they would have left Bob on the ship for him to work with Rex to find a long-term fix.

Without warning, Bob stopped shaking and composed himself. Shadows from the flashlights showed veins pulsing on his forehead.

"Sorry," Bob said, embarrassed. "Those bells, they're some sort of communication device. One of the pieces inside my brain… It's pushing out. I don't…" His voice trailed off as he rechecked the clips on his pack's harness.

"Come on. Once we down this thing, you'll be good," James said, brushing off his immediate concerns, but Bob's face said otherwise. The medic shone his flashlight forward and followed James with a steady beam cutting through the ship's interior.

They walked in relative silence, twisting and turning until they came upon a stretch of open ventilated ground. James edged himself up to the vents and tested their strength.

"We should be good to walk across. Stick to the cross beams though."

"Look." Bob pointed through the grates, and James knelt  to see through the slats.

Thousands of soldiers marched in full battle gear through the ship's entrance. An endless procession of gray marched in crisp lines onto their transport. James angled himself to get a better look. He was shocked by the number of troops being led onto the ship. There were hundreds and hundreds of lines of soldiers all the way back to the tarmac. He glimpsed another dry dock and witnessed a similar setup with rows of vehicles breaking the lines of bodies at random intervals.

An entire army being loaded into the *Odyssey*, intent on destruction. Programmed to ensure obedience. A rolling parade of death.

"That's a lot," Bob said. His eyes scanned the loading piers stretching into the distance.

"Good," James said. "The more on the ship, the better. Come on." James balanced on one of the beams and tightrope-walked until they hit the other side and slunk back into the walls. After another interminable distance, James checked their diagrams and held up a hand. He began the process of pasting the wires to the wall when a *click* sounded through the metal. He placed the wire on the ground removing a scanner from his pack. Clicking increased as his hands swiped across the dials and waited for an image to come through. When it did, his suspicions were confirmed. A group of soldiers walked the halls searching for something. They trod slowly with weapons raised, examining every corner.

James handed the scanner to Bob who shook his head. "Not good," he whispered.

"Nope. Have to go up and over."

Bob handed the scanner back to James and pulled the bag off his shoulder. "They'll be in the engine rooms too."

"Cross that bridge when we need to blow it up," James replied. He took the spool of wire Bob passed him and let it coil at his feet.

"Works for me. God, I hope they don't blow those charges yet," Bob said as he aimed his grappling hook at the ceiling. Wire unraveled from its coiled heap and trailed the magnetic clamp and connected to the metal with a light *thud*. James glanced at the scanner again, happy their hunters had not heard the noise.

"See you up there." The medic pushed off the ground and traveled swiftly upward on his ascender's power. His friend dangled in the air for a second before he swung forward and shimmied his body into the crawl space. A second later the medic's hand appeared with a thumbs-up.

*Here we go*, James thought as he clipped himself on and shot to the ceiling.

Bob was wedged in a space about twenty-four inches tall. His bag sat next to him and he shuffled to the side, making room for James.

Following Bob's lead, James grabbed hold of the wall and pulled his body in, careful his feet did not clang against the metal barrier.

James glanced again at his scanner when done. *Still good*.

The two stowed their gear and crawled in long smooth movements over the hallway. Their descent caused no issues and after a clear scan, they moved inside their third target.

Unsure of their isolation, James signaled to Bob: *Down the stairs. I'll take lead.*

Bob nodded, and James lifted his rifle, listening for the slightest change in the room's activity. The engines' reactors warmed up for the journey, and their heat jacked the temperature by a solid ten degrees. Sweat trickled along James's brow, leaving a stinging sensation along the inside of his nose. He wiped the moisture, and his hand came back with blood on it.

*Must have cut myself during the ascent,* he thought searching his mind for reasons for the blood on his nose when a *BANG* broke his thoughts.

The pair dove for shadows on opposite sides of the wall. Footsteps echoed off the walls.

*At least twelve*, he thought as a door swing shut. He pointed to the bag of explosives at Bob's side: *You're up. I'll take care of the network.*

Bob shook his head, signing: *I've got it.*

James tried to protest, remembering the medic's reaction to the bell in the engine room. He signed: *It's on me I'll do it.*

Bob broke his cover, moving across the hall to James. The medic dropped the bag at James's feet, "I've got it," he growled. Without another word Bob stole from the shadows towards the stairs.

James padded in the opposite direction until he came upon his target. Emptying his materials from the bag, he took a knee. His entire concentration focused on the work, connecting wires and redirecting others as needed guided by the schematics on his HOLO. He ignored the random burst of gunfire, grunt, or clang of metal. He hoped he'd made the right decision with Bob.

*Trust your gut.*

As he finished attaching the detonation connector to his HOLO, Bob returned. Dark black stains spread in blotches on the fabric of his suit. None of it his. The medic sheathed the knife he had been cleaning.

"Clear." Bob's breath recovered, and his eyes shone steady in the HOLO's reflected light.

The HOLO flipped green. "Done here too."

"Try the hallways? It'll be faster," Bob said, glancing at the ceiling.

James was tempted to say the same, but this had not been what they'd expected in their original plan. Blowing up a ghost ship is one thing. Blowing up a ship with thousands of troops actively boarding was a different story.

"Too risky. It's fine. They haven't even started the—"

The ground shook, sending the metal staircases jingling in the enclosed space.

"You were saying?" Bob grinned.

"They're late," James said, throwing the last charges into his bag. "We'll have a legion of BZ troops running through the halls."

"But away from where we need to go," Bob argued.

"Come on." Unconvinced by his friend's argument, James took off towards the wall exit when another explosion shook the room.

"That was fast." Bob's tone now no longer joking. That was off schedule. They never did things off schedule. There was always a reason.

Scenarios flooded James's mind. *What was going on back there?*

"SECURITY FORCES, SECTOR Q. SECURITY FORCES, SECTOR Q." A calm robotic voice blared at full volume as lights flashed.

"Your call." Bob inspected the room as if expecting BZ to pop out of every corner.

James's mind sped through the maze of options. Speed was the key. Silence no longer mattered after the second bomb. If they went through the halls, they'd have to recalibrate their pathway to avoid major troop points. *We'll figure it out.*

"Hallway." The two moved towards the exit of the engine room. James double-checked his ammo and patted the arsenal strapped to his body. Everything stayed in place. They took up positions on either side of the door.

The scanner gave them an all-clear, and James handed it to Bob.

"We're good for now, but you run this. I'll keep us on track."

"On it."

James counted with his fingers: three, two, one. He opened the door a crack and stuck the muzzle of his rifle through. As predicted, no one waited on the other side. With a swipe of his finger, his HOLO map sprang up in front of him, and he took off down the hall with Bob running behind.

Distant alarms echoed through the ship's hallways as the two friends ran at a steady pace towards their next target. Smoke-tinged air that had escaped the clutches of the ship's filter system lingered.

*Those bombs will keep them busy,* James thought, turning a corner with a quick glance back and a thumbs-up from Bob. He worried about his team. They had not expected a ship full of soldiers. Taking out that many soldiers would change the balance of the war.

Sirens wailed in the empty halls. Perpetual noise prevented the ability to relax.

"How much farther?" Bob asked.

"Two hundred yards, another right, and we're there."

"Good. They're coming."

The scanner's lights flashed in Bob's hand as he held it up for James to see. In the hallway parallel a pack of soldiers marched in formation towards their next target. The sensation of hot metal poured into his stomach

"Fuck," James cursed. He stopped to think over their next move. They'd never be able to hold off that many BZ troops in the engine room, and they needed time to set things up.

He searched his mind for what to do when he remembered his corrosive wiring. He took it from his bag and looped it over his shoulder.

"Sprint for the engine room. You cover me while I get this set up."

"We're going into the walls again?" Bob asked skeptically.

"I'll use it to meld the doors together. Lock ourselves in and buy enough time to set the charges."

"That's why you're the boss," Bob said, racking a round in the rifle's chamber.

James's feet barely touched the ground as he flew towards the corner. Rounding it, he dove through the metal doors of the engine room.

Loud *thuds* sounded over his head as bullets embedded themselves in the steel encased doorframe. Bob knelt in front of James and picked off the front line of the BZ horde bearing down on their position.

Coiled wiring lay on the ground, and James worked feverishly, pressing the adhesive rope to the edges of the door. If he set it along the seam of the doors and pulled it off at the right moment, the metal would fuse together. A bullet tore through the air under his arm. A volley of return fire from Bob dropped the aggressor.

"How's it going?" Bob asked with forced calm. The medic's fingers moved rapidly peppering the BZ soldiers with bullets.

"Almmoooost…done!" James slapped the last piece of filament on the top of the door. He glanced down the hall at the BZ soldiers. Riot shields emerged from the corner and formed into a line facing the door.

Bullets ate into the metal around them, turning the wall into a shower of sparks and steel shavings, burning the skin on James's neck.

"Get in—" Bob yelled, cut short by a prolonged *BEEEP* suspended in the air.

His mouth hung open. Saliva pooled under his tongue and dripped out of his mouth. Helplessly James watched as his friend dropped to the floor, limp.

Bullets continued to fly, and the wall of riot shields drew closer. James grabbed Bob's arm and yanked him through the door.

He dropped his friend behind the metal blockade and slammed the doors shut, activating the corrosive wiring. He watched the wire, listening to the bullets ricocheting off the blocked entryway until the edges of the metal turned orange.

*Done.* He pulled the breaching wire off and slammed his body into the steel plating, pressing his weight against the barrier as lead projectiles thudded into the metal inches from his body.

After pushing for fifteen heartbeats, he backed away, pulling Bob's body behind him. He gripped his rifle. The banging continued against the newly created wall, and he waited for the BZ soldiers to tear through to his side. Finally, it ended.

James breathed out and hung his head, shaking himself. More to do.

Eyes shut and jaw clenched, Bob twitched on the floor. Panic and confusion swarmed James's thoughts. *What can I do?* He bent and held Bob's shoulders as the spasms relented.

A shake rattled the room. James grasped the ground as the floor beneath his feet moved violently.

*Number three.* They needed to be heading to the exits, not dealing with a medical emergency.

He checked Bob's pulse and considered what to do. He turned on the scanner and set an alert in the motion sensor. *If he wakes up or if the sensor picks up anything on the other side of the door, I'll know*, James reasoned.

He flew towards his target location at the bottom of the steps on the second-level platform. With practiced ease, James hooked up their explosive signals and popped on the network adapter.

"ALL HANDS FOLLOW LATEST SIGNAL ALERT. ALL HANDS FOLLOW LATEST SIGNAL ALERT."

The loudspeaker blared the message five times, but James ignored it. He flipped his HOLO screen up and waited as the network connection inched towards complete when a loud *BEEEEP* tore through the air. A crackle came through the speakers and James dropped his HOLO to the ground, jumping multiple stairs to reach the top.

"Hello, James. We meet again. Not exactly like the last time of course. My colleagues and I did not expect to capture one of your people."

James knew Edgar Raspin's voice. *Is he on the ship?* The tantalizing aspect of killing his former tormenter sent a rush of adrenaline through James that excited and terrified him. He had never been excited to kill before.

Gritting his teeth, James tried to ignore Raspin's goading as the BZ leader continued. "You're a long way from home and have made things very difficult for me. I had a feeling you were here for my *Odyssey*. I predicted it really. You've become much more thoughtful in your attacks since our first encounter. You made it too easy."

James hit the first turn and lifted the tip of his rifle in the direction of the door. The silence unnerved him. He expected a legion of BZ soldiers to come crashing through any second.

He turned the last corner and saw Bob sitting cross-legged facing the door.

The metallic feeling in his gut heated and adrenaline spread through his capillaries, pricking the surface of his skin and pushing him into sensory overload. Stale air, iron, smoke vapor, and engine grease caused tears to pour down his face, overwhelming his senses.

"But since our last meeting, I've learned a lot too James. I've come to understand something that is an acute gap in our knowledge. You know what that is? I'll tell you. No hints. I've discovered it's best never to make friends. They end up being your biggest mistake."

The intercom clicked off and James looked at his friend's back.

"Bob? What's on the scanner, Bob?" he asked, stepping closer to his friend.

The medic did not respond, and James inched closer. "Bob, the scanner." His eyes trailed to the knife and handgun gripped in white-knuckled hands. Nausea washed over James.

"Bob?"

Finally, Bob cocked his head to the side. The world stood still as James watched his friend battle against forces in his skull until, with a simple twist, Bob's legs exploded from under him. He lunged towards James with the knife over his head, his eyes disconnected from reality.

# Chapter Twenty-One

Violent slashes forced James to jump side to side as Bob's knife attacked his body. The tight space of the hallway pushed James to spin away from the wall, kicking his attacker back, sending the frenzied medic tumbling into metal piping.

The momentary crash gave James time to get his bearings. He grabbed the sack from the ground, dumped its contents, and used it as a makeshift shield. The rough, waterproof canvas felt like paper in James's outstretched arms. *Come on, Bob, snap out of it.*

Bob, with unseeing eyes and a thin line of blood dripping down the middle of his face, turned to James.

"Bob! You're in there. Figure it out," James shouted, hoping to break through the BZ's mental block. It was useless.

Without hesitation, his friend's body sprinted towards James, swiping at him with his knife. Hopping to the side, he slammed the taut fabric down on Bob's outstretched wrist as the tip of the knife narrowly missed his stomach. He twisted the sack around Bob's wrist to disarm him when a fist connected with the side of James's head. The momentary break allowed Bob's body time to regain control of the knife, and he landed a gash across James's forearm.

"HA!" Raspin cried over the intercom. "Quite the move, don't you think?"

James ignored his tormentor and circled Bob, waiting for the body to make its next move.

Gray-shrouded eyes watched him coldly, and the body moved with no pretense of self-defense. James worked through the situation in his mind. He had to get off the ship, get Bob off the ship, blow up the ship.

*Worst comes to worst, neither of us leaves*, he thought, gritting his teeth, hoping more options would appear.

Bob's body lurched forwards, spinning the knife in his hand, expertly flipping the blade between grips. Acting on instinct, James stepped forward and forcefully shot his knee to the side, catching Bob's hip and eliciting a grunt from the medic, who stumbled sideways. Using his momentum James pursued and, grabbing Bob's knife hand, locked his wrist. The blade fell to the floor. James kicked the steel implement down the hall and flipped his friend's body over, slamming him into the metal grating.

He sprinted to where the knife lay and picked it up, whipping around in time to see Bob's body rise, crack his neck, and turn to James, tilting his head as an animal would inspect its prey.

*Come on, Bob, break through*, James pleaded, but it was hopeless. Nothing would bring Bob back.

"Well fought, James. Bravo!" Raspin's voice bounced off the room's metal walls, reverberating with a sickening tin sensation in the increasingly hot engine room. "I believe it's time to finish this off. We'll have Bob take care of you here, disarm the bombs, of course, and be on our way to the shores of the Federation. Well, not really the Federation anymore, huh? Either way, that's the beauty of this technology. Those memories of Bob's will be…remarkable."

Fear washed over James. *Memories?*

"Ahhh, you didn't guess that piece? Of course not. Why would you? We'll be able to retrace whatever we need here James. All this for nothing."

Panic joined fear in James's mind. Everything they'd worked for to save the Federation crushed by the memories of his friend. Why had he brought Bob with them? How stupid. Risk the entire Federation? His friends, family, NOLA—all of it—because he wanted to prove his friend was good, wanted to save one more person. Lungs heaving, his mind swam as he looked across the humid metal hallway separating him from Bob's body. The rucksack hung limply in his hand.

Bob crouched, knees bent, the knuckles on his fists a pale white.

James watched his friend's body readying itself for a final onslaught. James did the same. He let Bob take the first step, the disconnected brain, refusing to protect its host moved swiftly towards him. James knew what he needed to do. As Bob neared, James lunged with the knife towards Bob's stomach. The body stepped to the side, easily avoiding the move, but James kicked Bob's legs out, sending his torso twisting towards him, off balance and careening them both backwards. Falling on his back, James gripped the rucksack and wrapped it around Bob's throat, enclosing his legs around Bob's thighs.

"I'm sorry, Bob," James whispered, tears streaming down his face and a roar echoing from his throat across the maze of metal-cased piping in the steam-ensconced engine room. James forced the canvas bag into Bob's windpipe. The thrashing continued for an eternity until a final shudder rippled through Bob's muscles and James's friend lay dead on top of him.

Pinned to the ground, with no time to waste, he pushed Bob off as the loudspeakers blared again. "ABANDON SHIP. ABANDON SHIP."

James could not bear to look at his friend, but he found the field kit Bob used since their first days together and stuffed it in his pocket, shoving away the emotions welling in his throat. Alarms cried in full swing and steam from the cooling systems flooded the engine room in clouds of mist. He collected his gear from the pile on the floor.

The network connector fit in his pocket, and he clipped the air recycler to his hip as he moved towards his detonation location. He dropped to his knees, fighting against time and guilt. When the connector turned green, he flew to the stairs, jumping down flights.

There was no time to make his way back to the other side of the ship to retrieve his gear for exfil as planned. He'd have to make the swim solo. The cylindrical shape of the stairwell rebounded noise. Each alarm jarred his psyche and sent him deeper into the abyss of guilt.

*I killed Bob. I killed Bob.*

All James could think of was the last shudder of his friend's body, the *crunch* of his windpipe, and the flailing arms grasping to breathe.

Sweat poured down James's face, and he wiped a forearm across his brow. Iron tinged his lips and his arm stung. He bled profusely and remembered the slash from Bob's knife. While continuing to move, he pulled out Bob's med kit. Blindly he fumbled through its contents until he found the bag of bioclot powder. He tore the packaging open with his teeth, the medicine numbing his tongue on contact. The burn on his wound told him it was working. Guilt racked his brain, thinking how lucky he'd been to have such a prepared medic, but he shook he head.

*Get the fuck off the boat, James.* He gritted his teeth and jumped another flight of stairs.

Steam dissipated at the bottom of the steps where the wheel to the exit hatch sweated in the heat. He yanked open the hatch and, without another thought, bit his air recycler and dropped into the water.

His arm stung on impact, and he could only make out hazy objects in the dark salty liquid. He kicked through the water with long smooth strokes using his arms to pull him downward. Dark corners blinded him. He did not have much time left in the temporary breathing apparatus. Each stroke logged itself in his memory to track his progress and stymy his fear response. It was painful to pull and his breathing became ragged, signs the device's efficacy was slowing. Without warning, an arm gripped him and pulled. He fought, lashing out with a leg that was deftly seized.

Another pair of hands grabbed him while another signed: *It's us. Where's Bob?*

He couldn't tell them yet and shook his head. It already felt like a lie.

The arms guided him, wrapping his forearms around someone's waist. His arm stung when it brushed against the fabric, but he closed his eyes and let them pull him to the *Kaleidoscope.* He had no idea how long they had left, but they needed to blow up that ship.

When they stopped moving, he was led to the decompression chamber. He bumped into random surfaces as his consciousness slipped, his oxygen dangerously low. His body supported itself on all fours as water flowed from the room. Through his eyelids, he made out a red signal, and in a spectrum of diluted light finally saw green. Blinking and breathless he forced out his words. "We need to blow it.

Raspin knows. Blow it now." He heaved for air, exhausted by the effort.

A soft hand touched his face. "What are you saying James? What do you mean?" Heather's voice spoke with a gentle firmness cupping his chin with care.

Finally, he spoke the words he'd been dreading. "Bob's dead. We need to blow the ship up. Now."

"Goddammit," Deck's swore and silence took over the room.

"Alright, tell Janus. Break cover and run. Blow the *Odyssey* now," Heather said, taking command.

"On it." Wally's voice came through the background.

Footsteps echoed. James remained on all fours staring at the ground. His eyes swelled in pain from the saltwater, and his arm ached. Internally, guilt and sorrow forced him into a chasm of self-loathing. He stared at the ground, wishing he was still on the ship.

"Come on, buddy," A pair of arms picked him up, accompanied by Liam's voice as he was guided through the hallway. Heather wrapped her hands around his other side. James could not move his feet.

*What will they think of me when I tell them?*

"Prepare for detonation in one minute." Janus's calm voice emitted from the speaker system, echoing the live version in the room. Energy pulsated on the bridge.

"Strap him here." Heather guided James to one of the jump seats lining the wall. His mind flooded with glimpses of Bob's head lolling to the side. The crunch of his neck. Simple thoughts sent waves of nausea coursing through his gut.

"James, open your eyes, bud." Liam's voice entered James's inner crisis, and he squinted in the dark, blinking through the salt burn. "Tip your head back, buddy. There, like that. Give us a second. We'll get you right. Okay, now hold those eyes open." James pulled apart his eyelids, staring at the ceiling while someone poured a cleansing solution into his eyes. Splashes of the liquid ran down his face, and his senses normalized.

Liam finished the eye flush, and James dropped his head back down, fluttering his eyelids to remove the last of the saltwater.

"Hope that helps."

"It does, thanks," James said, nodding at Liam's blurry, bearded face.

"No problem. Nothing like Bob, but we're about to get them for that." Liam clapped his shoulder, and James's stomach dropped.

"Twenty seconds to detonation. Engines full."

"Engines full," Kady's voice replied. James's back dug into his jump seat.

"Strap in and hold on. We'll be riding the wave to the edge. Hitting the Roll head-on until the other side," Janus spoke with uncanny serenity.

"Ships are in pursuit," a crew member's voice called out randomly.

"Not for long," Deck grumbled, staring at the ground next to James.

"Ten seconds," Rhia announced from the corner of the room.

James glanced at the techie, sitting between six different HOLO screens, strapped into her chair and flipping through the screens with alarming speed. The windows at the front of the bridge showed dark water.

"Five, four…" Rhia counted them down.

Heather's fingers wrapped through his, her hand enveloping his knuckles.

"…three, two, one, engaged."

The result was not immediate. A few seconds of steadiness followed, and the world held in relative calm. The first inclination anything happened was the dull roar echoing in his ears paired with a flash of light far overhead, sending eerie shadows through the *Kaleidoscope's* thick glass. He glanced at Heather and Deck on either side of him, holding their chins high and their eyes shut. Everyone in the room did the same except Janus and Rhia, both focused on their screens.

"Success, shock waves hit—"

The dull roar in the background transformed into a wall of unbreakable screaming that sounded like a thousand nails were being fed through a woodchipper. The percussion from the blast slammed him against the restraints of his seat. He watched as the body of a crew member flew forward, their jump seat harness failed them, and slammed into the window with a crimson splash.

James gritted his teeth. Unrestrained shaking bounced the ship into a world of chaos. They twisted and flew forward at a speed James thought impossible under the water. The tainted sky faded to a dull orange glow. Fire from the reactors' implosions flew into the air, casting a towering inferno, imposing an unmatched power.

Janus's lips moved, but his words went unheard, at the mercy of a force of violence untouchable in the world of man.

His forearm ached as Deck squeezed his fingers into James's flesh. He gritted his teeth and stared forward. Noise grew absent at this stage of the explosion. James was not sure he heard a roar or the sound of his eardrums disintegrating from the force of the blast.

Without warning, the ship dipped down and raced to the bottom. During the dive, James's sense of hearing returned. Alarm bells rang and red lights flickered on and off.

Janus stayed at his spot leading from the center of the bridge, exuding calm as his ship tore through the water.

"We're headed down to use the water as a shield. Kady, can you hear me yet?"

Janus waited. "Kady?"

"Janus, this is Clint. Kady's unconscious. What do you need?"

"Can you operate the engines?"

"Yessir."

"Good. We're going to skim the bottom of the ocean, and then I'm bringing us back up to the surface for the Roll. Understand?

"Yes, Captain. Give the orders. I'll be ready." Clint's confidence put James at ease.

"Good man. Be ready in thirty seconds. Hold on crew."

"I hate this shit," Deck mumbled.

"Almost done, pal," James said. The momentum of the downward travel helped James extract his arm from Deck's vicelike grip.

"This is when I need Bob. At least we got 'em. Up to Clint now."

James simply nodded. A squeeze on his other hand redirected his attention and he saw Heather looking at him.

"You good?" she asked.

James nodded again but knew he wasn't fooling her.

"Clint?"

"Ready!"

"Three, two, one, engines full!"

Another influx of energy sent James backwards into his seat. Janus braced his knees and stood at his controls, towering in the room, daring the sea to challenge his balance further.

"Headed to the surface," Janus said as he pulled the fins upwards.

"Engines at full!"

"Keep them there. Roll in sight."

The Roll loomed ahead of them. A wall of water, sealing them in or out of the BZ's landmass. *How are we going to do this?*

James braced himself, pushing the soles of his feet into the ground. He squinted, readying himself to slam into the next phase of their plan when Janus's voice broke through the noise, shouting, "REVERSE! REVERSE! REVERSE!"

"Reverse?!"

"REVERSE NOW!"

James eyes flew open in confusion. A wall of water rushed out in front of the ship. It was as if one of Saturn's rings liquified and bounded through the sea in a torrent of unbound nuclear energy. The water slammed into the edge of the Roll, creating an explosion of foam and froth. Amazement overtook James as the BZ's protective edging collapsed, leaving a sea of open water.

"Full ahead," Janus said, regaining his calm, replacing the shock that had dominated his face moments earlier.

"Full ahead!" Kady's voice returned to the comms channels, accompanied by a smile from Janus.

"Hold here. Welcome back."

"Holding. And thank you, Captain."

Foam swallowed them, creating a divot of air where an impenetrable wall of water once stood. Mist hung suspended, creating a fog similar to a waterfall, and James drew on the memories of the jungles in Rio Negro.

"What the hell?" Deck's voice muttered. His face had gone slack with wonder, staring at the empty void into which they traveled.

"Waves beyond the edge Captain," a crew member chirped.

"Keep up our speed. Ready the wings. Where's our boundary?" Janus asked.

"Ten kilometers."

"Good. Stay course."

Their ship held on the surface and plowed through the water.

"Ships in pursuit," Rhia's voice popped up from the middle of the room.

"Ready the d—"

"Don't! Stay on top of the water. The loom will pop back on in a minute here Captain. We'll get pinned under," Rhia interrupted.

The hairs on James's arm rose. They waited Janus's response.

"Captain?" A crewmember, held in limbo, glanced back from the bridge.

"Keep position." Janus's voice betrayed nothing if he had felt slighted by Rhia's words. "Pull up an image of our pursuers. How long until the loom reactivates?"

"Two minutes according to their network," Rhia said, looking at her screen.

"I hope you're right," Janus said, with a crisp finish. He was betting his ship on her.

"Always," Rhia replied.

As Rhia predicted, the loom's effects on the water reappeared, and a column of swelling liquid mounted skyward.

Gravity pulled James into his seat as the ship tilted towards the smoke covered skies.

"Pursuing ships within five hundred meters."

"Send torpedoes."

"Launching torpedoes!"

Pandemonium flooded James's system with adrenaline. A mountain of water, percussive explosions, scorecards of hits and misses sounding over the intercom, a climbing ship, and the beginning of the Roll sent waves of energy coursing through James's body. He was alive.

Heather gripped his hand.

"Roll active in thirty seconds."

"Dive!" Janus's voice echoed, and gravity ceased to exist. The boat tipped into the ocean's frothy surface. James's stomach lurched. Speed increased and they fell off the edge of the world.

"I hate this!" Deck shouted, his hair suspended in the free fall.

"Wings now!"

"Wings released!"

A jolt sent James's shoulder ripping into the harness straps, digging into his skin as the ship righted itself before it hit the surface and bounced off the top of a wave crest, skipping directly to another. The boat sailed down the surface of the next wave, and back up the face of the next.

Screens that had shown their pursuers moments earlier now displayed only the wall of water blocking their view of their enemy's territory.

James gripped Deck's forearm, his head still bent between his knees.

Heather's lips found his.

He kissed her back in relief. They had made it.

# Chapter Twenty-Two

Moaning winds spoke to James through the thick glass of the ship's bridge annex. Constant sound reminded him where they were. What they were doing. What he had lost. What he had done.

Palpable sadness etched itself into his gut. Three days had passed since their escape from Centria, and he had not told anyone what had happened in the engine room. Instead, he buried himself in silence, pretending to listen, walking through the motions of life.

The ship tore through the water, the *Kaleidoscope*'s fins cutting across the wave surfaces, moving up and down the liquid walls with ease. Their dive mechanism had been damaged by the explosion's aftershock and subsequent escape from Centria's waters. Luckily, diving was not much of an option in the BZ waters. The troughs between waves furrowed so deep beneath the waterline that to submerge at all required perfect timing, and with a broken system that would be impossible. James enjoyed the freedom of riding the monster waves across the turbulent seas.

Their debriefing was on hold while they waited to hear from the Federation command. After making it far enough away from the BZ's landmass, Rhia had sent a message via an untraceable tunnel communications system, and although incomprehensible to James, he knew Jon would be able to decipher the message. She had embedded a digital signature into the communication so Jon could pinpoint their network for a future response. Their techie warned it was a risky way to send a message if they wanted a response, but there was no doubt in her mind the Federation team would get it.

Waiting only delayed James's inevitable confession and sent him deep inside his own head, terrorizing his thoughts with every waking moment.

His team noticed his odd behavior but with varying degrees of concern. Liam, Teresa, and Rhia were nonplused by his quiet. They understood it to be the same as losing anyone in battle. Clint did not notice. Heather suspected something, but James knew she would not press him. Deck was a wreck.

As far as losing Bob, they all reacted differently. Clint dealt with Bob's loss the same as he did anything that bothered him and spent hours in the engine room. He took to sleeping there overnight with Kady bringing him meals from the mess hall. Deck behaved as if he'd been in the engine room with Bob. He walked the halls muttering about death with a depressed and horrified expression on his face. In truth, Deck had been the hero of the day. The third explosion was entirely his idea and played double duty by distracting the crew of the *Odyssey* and giving Liam time to seal the BZ troops inside the ship with corrosive wiring. Their thought had been if anything happened to James, at least they played a small part in making life difficult for the entirety of the BZ military.

Still, Deck walked around in more of a stupor than James. It reached a point where Wally asked Deck to stay in his room because he was depressing the other members of the ship who were happy to be alive. The scout promised to lighten his mood and transitioned to wearing black in mourning as often as his limited attire would allow.

Even with Deck's self-induced depression, James could not bring himself to tell the team what had happened. He tried. The first night in their bunks he talked to Heather, but couldn't form the words. What should he say? *I killed Bob?* It felt wrong. It didn't tell the whole story, but who cared? The truth was and forever would be that James killed Bob. That was his life. That was his story. But he made up his mind. He would tell the first person he saw the next day. No matter who it was. He needed to say something. He needed them to know.

Wind dumped a fresh wave of water into the glass with a *THUD*. Surprised by the sudden noise, James stepped back from the ship's window.

"Aggressive, huh?" Wally walked into the annex and stood at James's side.

The tall, lean sailor folded his long arms across his chest. They watched the ocean in silence for a few moments.

Fields of waves stretched into the distance, blending in a spray of foam and froth.

"What're you doing up here?" Wally asked. He wasn't deliberately digging but given what James had promised himself it felt different.

*Come on, man, say something.*

"Good place to think, I guess," James replied. This was not an easy conversation to start. *Saying, "Oh, by the way, I strangled our friend Bob and haven't been able to say anything until now" is a dumb way to do it,* James thought.

Wally chuckled. "I always think of this as the worst place to think. So much going on up here. Not right *here*, I guess," Wally said, glancing at their empty area separated from the bustling command room, "but in general. Very stressful for me."

"I guess that's true. Did make it through a contained nuclear blast though, so it's kind of comforting."

"Good point, mate. It beats a bomb."

James grinned. "Beats a bomb."

Silence returned, and the waves continued their cycle. Wind wailed in the background and the ship moved over mountains of water.

"It's remarkable to think you guys actually blew that fucking thing up. I mean…We've been doing this for years. Years! Hell, our f'in' captain invented taking on the Roll and found those caves. But you all went in with only three weeks to work and only lost one guy." Wally shook his head. "Amazing."

James was quiet. This was it.

"I mean, hell, I could never do that," Wally continued.

"You could. If you had to. And we lost someone, so not a complete success in our book. One life doesn't get omitted because you saved thousands. A statistic doesn't replace a person."

"I know, I'm not being flippant about that, mate. I'm sorry if it sounded like it!" Wally's hands went up in apology and blush in his cheeks matched the red in his shirt.

"No, none taken. I mean it. It's just…the ship was different than…" The words caught in James's throat, and he forced his teeth together, grinding through the words in his head.

"What's that?" Wally's apologetic tone turned to concern. James sensed eyes fixed on the side of his head.

"On the ship. Those signals that Bob responded to. The BZ messed with his head. He reacted."

"Of course he did. But that doesn't change any—"

"Wait…" James held up a hand interrupting Wally who politely backed off. James took a breath and continued. "On the ship I heard one of the BZ commanders. He spoke to me. He flipped Bob while he was in the ship. He…"

A shift under James's feet distracted him. Waves crested and fell into one another, but something was not right.

"James?" Wally asked, concern edging his voice.

"Do you hear that?" James asked. The wind died and the spray abated.

"What?" Wally asked, turning his ears to the glass.

"The wind… It's…slower." James counted heartbeats between the gusts.

Wally crunched his face in concentration as he listened. Water lapped against the side of the boat, but their pitch through waves lessened, flattening as if they were off the shore of the Federation. By James's calculations they had a month of travel left before they reached the edge of the BZ's loom range. Wally's face morphed from concentration into concern, and he picked up on what was happening.

"Fuck." The tall sailor turned and flipped the alert for the ship. Red lights flooded the space. Sirens whined in the background. The sailor grabbed the intercom speaker and shouted into the receiver, "Mothership detected. Repeat. Mothership detected."

Cold fear formed in James's stomach. Activity on the bridge increased. James followed his sailor friend into the adjoining room.

Janus strolled confidently through the doors as James and Wally entered from the annex. The captain's face remained inscrutable as he assumed his position, listening to the report from his crew.

"What are we working with?"

"Winds lapsed within the last three minutes trailing off to nearly twenty knots below average for loom waters. Significant decrease in height and velocity of waves leading to a flatter, calmer surface."

"Anything on the horizon?"

"Nothing visible yet, sir."

"I've got visuals!" The yell from a woman with dark curly hair drew the room's attention. Anticipation mounted, culminating in a mass of muscle tension in James's core. Janus left his post and walked to the woman. James followed, standing behind the captain.

A high-resolution picture from the HOLO could not compete with the natural obscurity provided by the violent ocean waters, but when his eyes adjusted there was no mistaking what lay ahead. The top of a mothership floated above the water's surface. Artificially heightened waves from the BZ's looms could not hide the presence of the mothership towering over the water's edge.

"How are the repairs coming on our dive fins?"

"Another day until they're ready," Janus's bridge chief replied.

Janus stared through the thick glass separating them from the sea. James glanced at the door as Heather ducked into the room followed by the rest of his team minus Clint.

Having made up his mind, Janus clicked on the intercom. "Kady."

"Yes, Captain," the engineer's voice crackled back over the speaker system.

"Bring us up to full speed."

"Aye, Captain."

To the rest of the crew Janus spoke, "Load up all the remaining torpedoes and activate them in the launch tubes. Prepare escape pods and ready evacuation."

Crew members moved to follow his orders. Wally grabbed James's arm and pulled him from the room. "With me, team. Let's get out of here."

"What's going on? What's Janus doing?" James asked, running through the last few minutes in his head.

"He's going to hit the mothership head on with our explosives primed."

"This doesn't seem like a good idea," Deck said, trailing them.

"Got a better idea?" Wally asked.

"No, but we're talking about a ship that can impact the looms on a mass scale. This won't work, Wally," Teresa said, jogging behind the swift-moving sailor.

"It's the only shot we have. Turn ourselves into the weapon. We'll get you off, don't worry," Wally said over his shoulder. He stopped in the hallway and opened a door to an unfamiliar part of the ship. Lights flipped on, revealing a set of pods running in parallel lines along the walls. Steel frames gleamed in the artificial brightness and noise from the alarms clanged across their metallic surfaces.

"Here's the exit. Let's get you all packed up, and we're off."

"Wait... We—"

Wally cut James off with his hand. "Nope. You get in those pods and get the hell out of here. That's the order from the captain. Pack up. I'll help you ship off. You've got two minutes."

Wally walked swiftly from the room without giving them a chance to respond. The team stood surrounded by the blare of sirens and red lights. Anguish and helplessness washed over James.

"Let's go, I guess..." Deck said. The question in his voice was unmistakable. Running away did not mesh with how they approached this war. This mission had not gone the way they planned, and mounting adrenaline forced its way into James's head. He stared at the pods, indecision spreading through his brain, tainting his thoughts.

"What're we doing, James?" Deck asked. James turned to his friend, his blank look signaling a sense of helplessness enveloping his entire psyche.

"Hey, Kady sent me up here," Clint's voice came through as he walked into the room. "What did I miss?" Clint asked, joining the team's circle.

"We were given the order to abandon ship. They're going to torpedo themselves at the mothership," Deck replied, catching the mechanic up.

"Fuck. What's the call, James?"

Heartbeats flooded James's ears. Every moment of the last month collided into one. The failed first mission, the Sentinel teams, the caves, the Resistance, Raspin's voice, Bob's limp body. It coalesced into a whirling scene of horror, flooding James's mind. He bit his tongue, tasting iron.

*BEEEP!*

One of Rhia's rotating HOLOs let out an alert and flashed in bright colors from her bag.

The slim techie whipped out the device, and a HOLO screen expanded over their heads. Rhia's fingers flew across the keyboard shining off her chipped fingernails until the HOLO went blank, and a familiar face appeared in front of them.

"Hi guys," Stacie said with a smirk. Her hair was pulled back in its usual tight ponytail, and a fresh set of bandages covered one of her temples. "Welcome back. Would you mind asking the captain to slow down?"

# Chapter Twenty-Three

Gusts of wind and watery mist whipped at the crew of the *Kaleidoscope* standing atop the Federation's new mothership, the *Imperator*. Federation and NOLA soldiers surrounded the warrior sailors blocking them from the elements, but the sea would not be denied its due and washed the deck with fury. Janus performed the ceremony amidst the driving winds, which was carried out after every run through the BZ.

The ritual comprised of a bottle of whiskey and blowtorch. Scores of marks etched into the skin of the ship were placed under the windows of the bridge. Prior to the ceremony, Janus cut six more lines into the metal, one for each person lost during the voyage. The bottle of whiskey bled its perfumed aroma into the air when he popped its cork and poured a shot glass for each. The shots were thrown into the wind, spraying the malty liquid in a tan mist across the bow of the ship. Afterwards, the bottle was passed sailor to sailor until its contents were drained.

James waited his turn and took a deep swig of the dark liquid. Warmth spread to his fingers and he relished the bite clawing the back of his throat. Momentary distractions helped him cope with his secret about Bob, stashed inside his psyche.

Clint took the bottle next. Staring aimlessly in the distance, he drank from the glass container, wiping his mouth and handing it to the next person. "See you later Bob," the mechanic whispered. He left the group, no doubt returning to the engine room.

Federation soldiers parted, creating an aisle for the bulky mechanic who ducked into the dim light of the *Imperator*'s entryway. Guilt ate at James's stomach, combating the temporary relief provided by the whiskey.

"I'm gonna duck out," James whispered to Heather. She squeezed his hand, and he followed Clint's path into the massive ship.

While on the *Odyssey*, James had no time to appreciate the feat of human genius it took to create one of these ships, but the *Imperator* gave him a new opportunity. He jogged down a set of staircases to a random floor and pushed open the hatch. While the ship was technically brand new, it had a nearly identical layout to the *Odyssey*. Long, wide hallways designed less like a battleship and more like a floating city meant to haul legions of humans from one side of the world to the other. Different functions and weapons systems were stationed throughout each part of the ship, leaving James in awe of its immense scope. Today, he found himself on the transport ship deck. He followed signs on the walls indicating a hangar until he ended in a massive room.

Towering ceilings contained the hulking ships the BZ used to carry their troops ashore. Each was set on rollers, poised next to a garage-style door with ramps installed on both sides for troops to fill for assault.

Size failed to make sense in the enclosed space. All the battleships fit comfortably next to each other. The fact that there were three more rooms filled with the same number of ships throughout the *Imperator* baffled James's mind.

"Son of a bitch," a bodiless voice cursed, echoing in the vast space. James turned the corner around the final ship's bow to find his sister, Mar, shaking her hand as she rode her platform to the ground.

"Goddamn clamps. Always get stuck. Gotta ask Turk about that," she murmured, unaware of her brother's presence.

"Gotta be careful with that. Liable to lose a finger," James said, leaning against the ship.

Mar's eyes jumped in surprise but calmed when she recognized her visitor. She gave him a casual middle finger, blood dripping freely from the cuticle. "Screw you. I'm fine, by the way. Senseless bastard." She gripped her finger to stem the bleeding.

James pulled Bob's med kit from his pocket. "Here, let me see that." She held out her finger. He covered the torn skin with gauze and wrapped it with tape, leaving blood stains running down the back of her hand.

“That should do the trick.”

His sister inspected his handiwork. “Thanks.”

“Anytime. What are you doing anyway? No funeral ceremony?”

Mar shook her head. “This thing’s new to us still. Stacie asked me to finish running inspections on all the transports. These ships are so massive though they’re taking forever. I have to do it all alone since my partner gets seasick too easily.” Mar rolled her eyes. “Why the hell he decided to come on this mission beats the crap out of me. Can barely keep his breakfast down.”

“I know the type,” James said, recalling the voluminous amounts of vomit Deck produced on most of their trips. “Tell him to find Deck. He might have the answer.”

“Good. Stacie’ll have my head if I don’t finish these,” Mar said, looking the length of the room and checking off boxes on her HOLO. “Better than the general though.”

“I’d hope so,” James said. He was aware of Croyton’s lack of patience when it came to simple tasks and did not envy her place under his command. *Maybe I’m under it now too?* he thought briefly, realizing he didn’t care and moved on.

“I’m sorry about your friend Bob. I only met him that one time at Mom’s place in Deerfield, but he seemed like a good person.” Mar stashed her HOLO in her pack and led the way towards the garage doors blocking the sea.

“Thanks.” James did not want to talk about it. They had been on the ship for less than a day, but the guilt made it seem like a week. His place in Bob’s death entered his thoughts whenever the moment struck, but he kept pushing it down. *The time will come to tell them.* Leaving it for another moment was easy, but with trouble sleeping and no appetite affecting his everyday life, James knew it was not long before the pain would eat him alive.

“He was so calm and ate like nothing I’ve ever seen in my life. He downed nine tacos in six minutes! Kev told me that was normal though,” Mar continued, marveling at Bob’s appetite. “When he wasn’t eating, he told me about the stuff you guys had done. Midway, Rio Negro, early days of NOLA. Sounds like a wild time."

History spun through his mind while his sister spoke. Her words lit into him like a dagger of shame puncturing him with every syllable, but a strange catharsis accompanied her words.

"I told him the story about when you and I were playing rock wars in the driveway, and I threw one at your head. You remember?" she asked, looking at him quizzically.

"Remind me."

"Well, I whipped a rock at your head. It missed and bounced off the gutter on the side of the house. Smashed right through the car window. Mom and Dad heard and ran outside to stop us. They were so mad. New car, broken window, and their kids were throwing rocks at one another for fun. When they started to yell, you spoke up and said you had been the one who had hit the window. They tossed you in your room for two weeks, but the whole time it had been me." Mar looked at James as he relived the situation—the fear, the smell of asphalt, and yells ringing in his ears. He'd known it would be better if he accepted responsibility rather than blaming his younger sister. The decision made sense then. It still did.

"I was so thrown off by that and was for years. Talking to Bob cleared that up for me." Mar stopped at the exit and turned to her brother. "I don't think I ever said thank you for that, so thank you."

"Next time you're taking the blame," James said, grinning.

"Good thing everything on this ship's bulletproof. I'd know—I checked all those windows," Mar said, nodding at the ships.

A *buzz* jingled in James's pocket. Late for another debrief meeting. *Crap.*

"I gotta run, but good seeing you," James said, jogging to the door.

"Feel free to join anytime!" Mar called after him as James sprinted into the hall.

When he arrived, the room was full, and the HOLOs connecting them to the Federation HQ were up and running.

"Sorry I'm late. Got distracted." James said, catching his breath. *This ship's too big.*

"No worries," Dolly's HOLO image spoke from the front. "Anyone else?"

"This is it," Stacie said. James took the seat between Heather and Deck on the far side of the room. Clint and Kevin sat across from them screened on either side by Jon and Rhia who stared at floating HOLOs. Kyle sat next to Stacie, casually leaning back in his chair with his arm slung over the backrest. He waved from across the room.

"Okay, first order of business is debrief. Who's up?" Dolly's transparent face inspected the room, searching for a volunteer.

"I'll go." James did not realize he had said the words or raised his hand, but when he did, it was too late to stop moving. Finally, he was in front of the room.

"Floor is yours, James." Stacie stepped aside and patted his shoulder.

Saliva pooled under James's tongue, evaporating the second he tried to speak. Salt and steam filled his nostrils bringing him back to the engine room. He forced himself to settle, counting his heartbeats as the eyes in the room watched him.

*One.*

*Two.*

*Three.*

*Four.*

"James, if you—"

"We were caught in heavy fire when we reached the last engine room," James interrupted Stacie, gathering himself and beginning his story. "Bob held the fort while I worked on hooking our breaching cord to the door. I had the same idea as Liam, but in reverse—needed to keep everything out. We managed to get the doors shut and melded together. We didn't have much time and were behind schedule. The unexpected bomb from Deck had already gone off and the remote detonation would only work if those last bombs were hooked up. Sure, the other engines might blow, but to ensure complete destruction all engines had to go out at once. Overload their safety mechanisms and cause catastrophic failure.”

“Understood, James, thank you. What happened after you closed the doors?” Dolly asked, gently pushing James along.

“Right. Well, I hooked up the initial trigger mechanism and started to set up the remote detonator connection when one of the signals began.”

Quiet filled the room, and James focused on the back wall. He dug his fingernails into his palms. “Raspin’s voice came over the intercom. He started talking to us… Bob began to act differently. When the signal ended…he wasn’t Bob anymore.”

The air in the room stilled. Eyes bore into him with a range of emotions James could not decipher. Their gazes tore into his unprotected body in the middle of the room.

“Raspin made Bob attack me. I planned on letting us fight it out while the explosions continued. Hoped it would knock Bob out of his trance and we’d get off the ship or die trying. Either way, we’d deliver some sort of damage, but…Raspin told me he would enjoy using Bob’s memories. He could retrace all Bob’s steps to rip apart the Federation, the Resistance, neuter our attack on the ship, and win the war. He would flip our friend’s memories against us and destroy the Federation once and for all. I knew what I had to do at that point…”

James lifted his head and looked at his friends who stared at him with grief-ridden expressions. “I killed him. I killed Bob. Or what was Bob. I…I’m sorry I didn’t say it earlier.” Hot tears streaked down his face. “I didn’t want to. I would have died there with him, but it was my only choice. I…I’m sorry.”

He couldn’t bear to look at the people in the room anymore. Shame and guilt washed over him in waves of crippling anxiety. They’d ask him to leave. Tell him to never return. He’d be cast out from the Federation, an Exil forced to be alone for his life. *I deserve it.*

A hand engulfed his shoulder and pulled him to the side.

"You did the right thing James," Kevin's laconic voice spoke with a hypnotic calmness. He guided James to his chair. "Bob's better for it. We've all seen what the BZ does." The massive man placed James in his seat and knelt before him. "You helped him escape in the only way possible." James made eye contact with the gentle giant who nodded at him with assurance. "We've always got you buddy."

"Well, I feel like a jackass now," Deck said, staring glumly at the ground, "Here I've been carrying on like an idiot and you…sonofabitch, James."

"It was a lot," Liam said. "Quite the lady in mourning."

"You would have been a hit in ancient Egypt though." Teresa pushed Deck's shoulder playfully. "Mourning was a profession."

"Maybe I've found the wrong calling," Deck said, musing to himself.

James laughed. Relief flooded him and the weight of the shame and guilt, embedded in his mind having lost a friend, dulled slightly, knowing the people surrounding him supported his decision.

"James, take a look at this," Stacie's voice broke in, and the group turned to the stationary HOLO screens behind the dais.

An aerial view obscured by plumes of smoke wafted across the screen, growing more definite. The sight astounded James.

"Holy shit," Heather muttered. She was not alone.

A crater filled with gray and black ash-strewn water lay where the *Odyssey had been* docked a week before. Pure devastation ruled the area. The buildings in the vicinity were shells of their former selves or completely destroyed. Half of the city's structures lay in shambles, roofless and falling in on themselves. Fires continued throughout the area, burning with white heat.

"We pulled these from our satellite data this morning. You put more than a dent in the BZ's capital. You may have ruined it forever. As far as we can see, Centria is gone. The population has all but fled, and there's no sign of a military presence anywhere within a hundred-mile radius." Stacie flipped through images showing the reaches of the *Odyssey*'s explosion at the outer borders of the city and into an unfamiliar countryside.

"What's the delay with these?" Teresa asked, standing up to move closer to the projections.

"Two days."

"Two days?! Those fires have been going for almost a week?" Liam asked.

"No sign of stopping." Stacie added, "No one to stop them."

"Have our Resistance friends seen these?" James asked, worried about their reaction.

"Not yet," Dolly interjected. "We'll share with them today."

Claudia would happily give her life to see the BZ destroyed in such a spectacular fashion. He hoped she'd be okay with the world it housed being destroyed too.

"We've dealt the exact blow we wanted to and extinguished their ability to continue attacks on the Federation. At least for now," Dolly said as the images switched to a new ship. James noted her comment "for now" to revisit later. It did not sit well with him, but the lack of scrutiny from the rest of group pushed him to ignore it for the time being.

"As you have seen, Stacie, Kevin, Kyle, and Jon man—"

"We can reorder those names…" Jon chirped snidely, his face awash in HOLO light.

Clint pushed the cocky techie's arm, causing one of the HOLOs to disappear from its rotation. "I missed you."

The mechanic grinned, getting a slitted-eye stare from Jon while he pulled up the HOLO again returning to his work muttering, "Jackass," loud enough for everyone to hear.

"Anyway, the Federation and NOLA joint operation.—hope that works for you, Jon—went better than expected."

"Yeah, how are we on this thing here? Have we not asked that yet?" Deck said, looking about the room perplexed, before whispering to James on the side, "Have we been told and was I ignoring it?"

"No, we haven't said anything. There's been other stuff going on," Stacie said.

"Oh, good. Here I am thinking I missed something big. Let's hear it."

"Not much to tell," Kevin said. "We ran an op onto the ship when it entered the canal, let the Federation squads inside, took out a whole bunch of BZ soldiers. Now we're here. End of story."

Deck stared blankly at the stone-eyed chef with bafflement and annoyance. "That was the lamest story of taking over one of the largest ships in human history I could have imagined. Nothing else?"

"You can read the report we put together. Right now, we need to focus on the next part. Croyton's out in the field with Caitlin and a group of Federation-friendly Exils. They're headed to the western BZ border to contact the Exil's leadership."

"Leadership?" James asked.

"They've banded together out there. Started a series of city states to stop any sort of BZ encroachment and, eventually, fight against reforming the Federation. We'll need them to take on the last mothership though. One of the reasons we captured the *Imperator* was its lack of manpower. All its people are stationed out west or building a troop presence in the east. It was nearly depleted. But the *Societas* is a different story. A majority of the BZ fighting force resides with her. We don't have a shot without the Exils joining our fight. We'll be outmanned, outgunned, overrun."

"Croyton's got an in?" James asked. HOLOs panned over satellite maps of the Exil city states across the western Federation. The maps stopped, zeroing in on a stretch of earth with a wide swath of empty gorge cutting through the middle of red rock formations. River water flowed thousands of feet beneath the rim of the canyon, and the screens ran into a mass of tents stacked on platforms covering the width of the river and traveling past the next bend.

"Part of the Grand Canyon. They built a city into the rock walls and a platform full of tents over the river. It's the Exil HQ. They call it the Park."

"Stupid name. NOLA's ten times better," Deck muttered.

"Agreed, but not the point. We have it on good authority the Exil's leadership is stationed here."

The last part of the sentence made James clench his fists. They were making friends with an untrustworthy group of Exils who would trade the country for their own self-interest.

"Why are we doing this again?" Heather asked, echoing James's thoughts.

"No choice. We need their people. We'll lose if we don't have them."

"Where are we fighting from anyway?" James asked, realizing he had no clue of the goal for this entire charade. "What good is getting an army together if we have nothing to attack or nowhere to fight from?"

"Best question all day!" Dolly said enthusiastically. "Jon, would you please?"

"If everyone were as polite as you," Jon said as the HOLOs changed views again.

"Horse's ass," Clint mumbled, and Jon swung a hand wildly behind his head missing the engineer's smirking face.

"This is where we'll fight," Dolly said, ignoring the momentary outburst. "Federation HQ. Stationed on the lake, we'll funnel them through this channel and attack with everything we've got. The lake will provide its own challenges, given the time of year we expect the mothership to hit, but we'll deal with that when the time comes."

A scenic lake front opened next to a steep hillside filled with green foliage sliding to the waterfront where a brick seawall separated the water's edge from the hulking fortress erected behind it. Parapets jumped out from the architecture every fifty yards alternating with heavy weaponry of every ilk. Soldiers patrolled the wide pathway on top of the wall while drones scaled the sides and floating mines hovered in random flight patterns outside the battlements.

"Now that's a hell of an HQ," Teresa said, nodding.

"There are fifty thousand soldiers lined up behind these walls. The firepower in those cannons is enough to take on a mothership, but the defensive power isn't strong enough on its own without our mothership providing cover. Even still, the blast power from their ship will knock us out, and we'll have to put our numbers against theirs. This is the final battle, and the BZ knows it." Rapid-fire imagery moved across the HQ in a remote tour. "The BZ's going to bring all their troops to the battle which, by our estimates, will be upwards of a million. If the Exil's can spare 500,000, we'll make it a fight."

"When?" James asked, running through everything in his mind.

"Three months. BZ mothership is flying through their channel. Sentinel activity is down, and it appears they're abandoning some of their bases. They're bringing whatever they have left James. This is it."

A stone formed in James's stomach. This was bigger than anything they had done, including their latest mission. He hoped Croyton knew what he was doing.

"Any update from Croyton?" James asked, pushing the gnawing doubts from his mind.

"Our first check-in is scheduled for a week from now. They should be within ten miles of the Park. And we'll be back in NOLA"

"How many are with him?" James asked.

"Ten. Handpicked by the general and Caitlin," Dolly answered.

James's eyes raised in surprise. "Caitlin?"

"She insisted," Kevin grumbled.

"Croyton needed her," Stacie said, eyeing Kevin.

The chef snorted, and Clint patted his shoulder, calming him.

"Either way. Each of you has a download of Croyton's latest intel packet. Read up on them. We'll meet here for the check-in call. Good?" Dolly asked. Her head searched the room, counting the nods.

"Great. Good to have the team back together." Dolly nodded at James who returned the gesture as the NOLA leader's screen went blank.

The team sat in odd silence for a moment before Deck spoke up. "Kevin, I want food. Kyle, I'd like a beer. Jon, I'd like some music. Once I get those three goddamn things taken care of, I'll start this fucking homework, but today's for Bob. I want to eat until I throw up. Because it's what he would have wanted. Am I right, guys?!"

A collective chuckle rippled through the room, and the strum of a guitar came over the speakers as the group of friends celebrated their friend's life.

# Chapter Twenty-Four

Springs under his bunk creaked when he shifted nudging his mind awake.

*Goddammit.* He squeezed his eyelids, pushing his brain back to the dreamless sleep where his thoughts floated moments before, but no luck. A steel gray wall met his line of sight. The moment was over. His day started now.

He sat up, moving with precision to avoid the shifting bed springs, primed to snap and wake Heather with every change in weight. After a successful dismount, James pumped his fist silently and went into the bathroom when *BANG.* Pain erupted in his toe. He clenched his teeth. White knuckles gripped the doorframe, and he stared at the ledge separating the bathroom from the bedroom. He cursed whoever designed boats as the pain subsided and the dull throb from his broken toenail crushed his ego. A glance at the bed told him Heather had not heard a sound, but he didn't care anymore.

Darkening skin already surrounded his big toe and a beautiful collage of color floated to the surface of the nail bed. The door swung shut, and he continued his morning routine.

"Fucking ship design. Moronic," James growled. Cold water on his face helped push the pain from his mind. A HOLO monitor sat on the edge of the sink, and he swiped across its control. Weather, date, and time popped up for him, and he read through the daily report trying to ignore the fact that it was only 0430.

Running shorts and shoes waited next to the door, and watching his footsteps while ignoring his toe, he snaked through the room, kissing Heather on the forehead.

The ship was in a state of slumber, but a military vessel was never fully asleep. Soldiers walked the halls, waving or moving out of the way nonchalantly as James jogged to the top of the ship. He exited to the roof and took off across the open expanse. Groups of patrolling soldiers stationed on lookout waved when he passed. James ran the perimeter, admiring the seas splashing against the gargantuan ship. Wind whipped into him, adding an extra layer of difficulty, but the effects of the looms were not close to their original strength.

Jon, Rhia, and some of the other techies had gained access to the loom's controls and tamped down the effects the machines exerted on the waters. Waves and wind were still stronger than normal, but it was nothing compared to the seas experienced by the *Kaleidoscope* on their original journey. The *Imperator* would have handled those waters much better than the smaller ship. Lessening the loom's effects made it pleasant enough to enjoy the outdoors again without the risk of flying off.

The top deck took up nearly a square mile of space, and after his fourth loop James began pushups and sprints, relieving his pent up energy. He would need a level head later that day when they talked with Croyton. The general had a way of getting under his skin. It was better for everyone if James was calm. Deck suggested chemical alterations too, but a clear head would be key, although the idea of a whiskey or two was tempting.

Sweat dripped down his forehead, leaving a puddle on the ground as he finished the last set of fifty pushups. With a final heave he pushed to his feet. Dull orange glowed on the horizon, and the sun's rays greeted the edge of the day with a spray of saltwater, catching a medley of purples and reds floating in the mist.

He sat to watch the rest of the sunrise when he heard a shout. "Hey there, buddy!"

James turned to see Kyle and Kevin walking his way. The two were equally covered in sweat, and James pointed at the spot on the ground next to him.

"Take a seat. Show started." James pulled the wet T-shirt off his back. Chills ran across his skin, but the mist felt good on his overheated body.

"Exact reason we're up here," Kevin said, sitting on one side of James while Kyle took the other.

"Every day, man, workout and sunrise. Good way to start."

"Living the life," James said, jealous of their routine.

"Take advantage of it when we can," Kyle said.

"Smart men. Where were you guys? I didn't even see you up here."

"Weight room on the top floor. It's quieter there than the ones near the bunks. After that we run the perimeter," Kyle said. He stood and pulled his leg up behind his back.

"You must have missed us," Kevin added. A small bag appeared from his back, and he handed a water bottle to James who chugged deeply.

"I'll remember for tomorrow morning," James said, making a mental note of their schedule.

"Please do. Love to have you join. Can't keep kicking this one's ass up and down the ship," Kyle said with a smirk, finishing his stretch and returning to his seat.

Kevin swiped at his friend's head who ducked, using James for cover.

Sunlight reached halfway over the edge of the world, balancing in the space between the water and sky, reflecting off the ocean's surface.

"Long way from Croyton's camp," James said. Remembering the clouds of breath mingling with the steam from his coffee when he woke. Those early mornings had lodged themselves in his memory. He had changed so much. Twelve years, countless battles, and miles traveled. Time collapsed into  a single instance within James's thoughts, running him through the war that had taken up his life.

"Hard to imagine it," Kyle replied.

"I like NOLA a lot more," Kevin added.

"Agreed," Kyle said.

"Not a hard choice to make," Kevin said, mimicking a scale with his hands. "Mind-numbing months of torturous training with an emotionally deranged sociopath or being in charge of a military base?"

"When you put it like that…" Kyle replied, nodding along.

"Glad we don't need to make the decision. Never really did though," James said. "There has to be a story though. How the fuck did you manage to take all…this?" James waved his hand at the sprawling rooftop.

"Boarded similar to the way you did. But like we told you earlier, there wasn't a whole lot of resistance," Kevin started. "Maybe a few thousand soldiers on board and not a highly trained force. These were the shipbound soldiers. Not their field teams or even Sentinel operators."

"But it must have been difficult," James said, searching his friends' faces for clues.

Kyle shook his head and focused on the horizon. "They barely fought back. We took the ship in under half an hour, maybe less. The reaction wasn't of a group of people fighting for their lives. They were…"

"Accepting." Kevin said, finishing Kyle's thought.

"Yeah, accepting," repeated Kyle, nodding to himself.

"Not many casualties," James said, trying to understand why Kyle and Kevin acted so strangely.

"Not for us," Kevin replied.

"For them…."

The two quieted. Engines hummed in the background.

"It's okay to win, guys," James said. He recognized their guilt and wanted to pull them away from whatever thoughts they were trudging into.

"They didn't make that decision, James. Mindless automatons, set up as sacrificial lambs by their leadership, considered a statistically acceptable loss. Not the open battles like we've had, no matter how little they understood… This…this was slaughter." Kevin spoke carefully, and Kyle stared stone-faced at the distant horizon.

"War will do that," James said, unsure of what to say. "War's evil has a way of forcing horror upon all participants regardless of the choices we want to make."

"I hope it's the right one," Kevin said.

"I get it. With Bob… He wasn't…"

"No need to explain, man," Kevin said, clapping his shoulder.

"No. I think… The thing that I can't get over is that I had to hate my friend in that moment. I had to do what I thought I couldn't. He wasn't Bob at that point. He was one of Raspin's things. One of the monsters I've fought all this time."

"It's how we respond now that matters, James. We have three months to win or lose. There will not be another shot," Kevin said.

"We'll have to end things our way."

They nodded, and the friends sat together, the guilt of their actions plaguing their consciences.

"Come on." James jumped to his feet. They needed a distraction. "Race to mess?"

Kyle glanced at Kevin who grabbed James's legs from under him, slamming him on his back. They jumped to their knees as James tried to trip them, scrambling to the door. They wrestled and sprinted across the top of the ship, enjoying a momentary break from their burdened thoughts.

The group rounded the corner with Kyle leading the way. James gripped the railing to stop himself from flying onto the stairs, and Kevin skidded to a stop before he crashed into James. *That would have hurt.*

"James?" A voice broke through the wind. Claudia sat alone on the edge of the ship's roof.

"I'll meet you guys there," James said to his friends. Kevin left him with a fist bump, and he and Kyle raced down the stairs.

James's hair blew into his eyes when he sat next to Claudia. An hour had passed since he first stepped foot on the roof that morning, but the endless ocean still enthralled him. Awkward silence hung between the two former adversaries and wind howled as the lone voice in their conversation.

"I'm sorry about Centria," James said finally.

The Resistance leader shook her head. "It couldn't have survived. I knew that. It's why we were on the ship to leave. Even if you failed, our Resistance was over."

"Still, I know you wanted a different ending."

"Thank you."

Silence returned to them. A group of gulls flew over the edge of the ship, no doubt confused by the presence of the mountain floating in the ocean. Birds pecked at the metal plating of the *Imperators* roof, hopping confused from leg to leg, trying to make sense of where they landed. Finally, the birds took off into the air, fighting the wind to gain altitude and using its energy to aid their flight back to the water's surface.

"Do you remember the conversation I had with Bob?" the woman asked.

"I do."

"Did he ever tell you about our conversation?"

"Nothing. I never asked though."

"That's a good leader."

James nodded in response.

"Either way, I wanted you to know how that all went."

"Listen, that was between you guys. Obviously Bob did—"

"He wasn't coming back, James," Claudia cut him off. She waited while James processed the information. "He knew what had happened to his brain. He understood it better than anyone. His plan had been to either give himself up for the sake of the mission or to seal you all out during exfil."

"What…? What did you say?"

"Different than what you may think, I tried to convince him to stay. Not go on the mission at all. He wouldn't hear of it though."

Moments during the mission lined up in James's mind that made more sense with Claudia's revelation. Taking on the soldiers in the engine room and blocking James when he welded the doors shut. If he couldn't come out the other side, he would make sure his friends would.

Emotions swarmed James's thoughts, and he clenched his jaw, wishing he had known. "Why didn't he tell us?"

"If he had, would you have let him join?" Claudia asked. She turned to James making eye contact with him. "He went out there knowing he would not return. Knowing it would be to save you. To save what you are fighting for. Remember him for that. Not for a conversation you didn't have. Either way, wanted you to know." The woman stood and walked back towards the steps.

James turned around. "Thank you."

"You're welcome."

Salty air filled his lungs, and James looked out over the ocean, contemplating his friend's sacrifice. Wind tore at his clothes when he stood and smiled at the sky. "Thank you, Bob."

A group of birds swarmed over the edge of the deck, and James headed back to the stairs to join his friends, the memories of Bob playing through his mind.

# Chapter Twenty-Five

James sat alone at the coffee shop a few blocks from NOLA's central HQ.

Spanish moss dangled in thick folds from the trees combining with the hanging baskets of greenery, brightening the overcast winter day. Swirling clouds hung low in the sky, and cold air poured over the southern fortress. The unusual humidity caused James to wonder if a snowstorm might be on the horizon. As rare as they were in this part of the Federation, the phenomenon was not unheard of.

"Someone sitting here?" A familiar voice broke his solitude, and he turned to Cristina's smiling face looking at him over his shoulder. Her blond hair bounced around the edges of her cheekbones, and the effortless happiness the woman exuded filled the space.

"Just the ghosts. All yours now."

"I'm much better company than ghosts," Cristina said, accepting the invitation.

"That depends."

"Depends on what?" Cristina asked. She set a small paper bag on the table next to her mug.

"What do you have in there?" James asked, eyeing the bag.

"A little treat for the rather hungover man sleeping on my couch."

"I feel like I should try some. Just to make sure he can handle it. Don't know if he can stomach anything for a few days after last night," James said, recalling the state their scout had been in. Their reunion with the bar in NOLA was a party for the ages, and James lamented being unable to take part as fully as the rest of his friends. Croyton would not take kindly to an inept group.

"Here." Cristina tore off an edge of the pastry. "For your company. Last from the tray, so it's not like you can get one yourself."

"Thank you, my dear." James took a bite of the doughy bread, savoring the cinnamon mixed with the sweet apple juice nectar. "God, these are the best." He glanced at the counter, wondering if he had time to wait for a new batch of the fritters.

"Not a whole lot of those in the BZ?" Cristina said with a wry smile, sipping her coffee.

"Spinach and eggs. Healthy, not satisfying."

"Sounds gross."

"It was."

The two enjoyed the sudden swell of noise brought on by a group of families who entered. Kids ran to the back booths of the cramped café eliciting smiles or frowns from every table they passed. James chuckled as two frizzy-haired toddlers fought to control their part of the bench.

"What do you think of that?" Cristina asked. Calm purpose etched into her features.

"What? Kids? Love 'em."

"Do you want them? You know. You and Heather?"

"I think so. I mean, I know I do," James answered. Truth was, he never thought he'd live through the war to be able to make that decision. To be this far along and think about something that should have been so close but was on the other side of untested violence—it seemed like tempting fate.

"You'd make a good dad. If anyone can keep an eye on Deck the way you do…"

James laughed. "There's not a single person in the universe who can keep an eye on Deck. Except you maybe."

"You do. That's what I know." Cristina's eyes remained fixed on the children until she turned suddenly to James. "Keep watching him, James. I need you to do that for me."

The unprompted switch in tone threw James and he nodded at her. "Always."

Christina looked him in the eye and nodded, her face relaxed as she smiled again. The behavior confused and disarmed James in a single motion. "Good. I've got to get out of here. Hangovers need grease. At least that's what the

243

man on my couch tells me, and I called in a burger and fries from Tony's."

James glanced at the clock on the wall. 1300. Call was in five minutes. "I'll walk you out."

"HQ?" Christina asked, as James held the door for her.

"Yep." James knew Cristina was aware of exactly what was happening, but the unspoken intel she and Rich were fed by their respective partners was a secret that did not need to be addressed.

"Good luck. Tell her I say hi." Cristina pecked him on the cheek and walked towards Tony's where a group of soldiers sat outside drinking beer, watching the attractive blond make her way inside.

James puzzled over her words while he walked to the HQ. *What's going on with her?* he thought. *Maybe Heather can talk with her.* He had seen these situations play out with NOLA soldiers' wives and girlfriends, but Cristina was different from them. *Not for me to worry about*, he thought, brushing it off for the moment.

Before he knew it, he was outside the doors of the HQ. Gaslit candles flickered in their hurricane lanterns lining the beams of the extended awning. Stacie, Heather, and Kevin stood waiting by the doors.

"You're late," Stacie said. She leaned against the doorway peering at him from the porch.

"What's new?" James asked, kissing Heather and greeting Kevin with a fist bump. "You're early."

"Better than late," Stacie said with a grin, and she led the way into NOLA's central command.

"Where were you?" Heather asked, dropping behind Stacie and Kevin. "She's technically right, you know."

"Ran into Cristina at the Quip. Lost track of time." James shrugged.

"Don't tell Stacie that," Heather whispered.

"I already knew," Stacie chirped.

James looked at the braided bun moving steadily ahead of them.

Kevin turned around and signed: *Witch.*

James rolled his eyes, grinning as they followed Stacie through the first floor of the NOLA HQ.

The familiar bustle of the room that always bled into a nauseating sense of urgency had ebbed since James's most recent visit to the military base's strategy outpost.

"Quieter than I remember," Heather said, reading his mind.

"Yeah, it's reasonable in here," James replied, trying to figure out if it was fewer people, less gear, or something else missing in the space.

"Dolly sent a lot of people north already. They're helping Croyton and his folks prep Tundra," Kevin said over his shoulder.

"Tundra?" James asked, unfamiliar with the word.

"The Federation stronghold we showed you."

"Why's it called Tundra?"

"It's fucking cold," Kevin replied, jogging up the stairs.

"Guess that explains it." Heather looked back at the room. "How many do they need?"

"All of us eventually. Now come on. The general will be on in any minute." Stacie said, yelling over her shoulder. Her patience wore thin, and James skipped a few steps to catch up

James grimaced when he stepped onto the second floor, remembering who they would be communicating with in the next few minutes. Croyton would want to know about them losing Bob. That was a conversation he did not relish.

The calm that always greeted James on the second floor was accompanied by solitude. If the downstairs lacked the fury of a warring machine, the upstairs had turned into a chamber of overwhelming emptiness. The walls, normally covered by blinds due to the secretive operations, were open wide, and the vacant interior reflected the loneliness that inhabited the floor.

"This is weird," Heather mumbled as they strode into the only conference room with its blinds still drawn.

Dolly, Mar, Riley, and Rhia were already inside, working feverishly on their HOLOs. They did not notice as the group entered, and the four visitors waited quietly against the wall while they finished their work. HOLOs ran lines of code, and the tables were set in a rectangular horseshoe.

Mar glanced up and nearly fell back in her chair. "Holy shit!" She held her hand over her heart and panted, composing herself. "You *cannot* sneak up on people like that."

"No one's sneaking up on anyone," Stacie said, "Get your head out of your HOLO."

"Knock first." Mar shook her head and looked back at her machine. The curly-haired woman switched modes, moving on from the exchange with Stacie. "Rhia, where are we?"

"Almost ready. Riley?"

"Platform's steady," Croyton's daughter replied. Her unwavering calm did not surprise James given her family lineage, and he watched as she gracefully moved between screens.

"Turning the tunnel on in three, two, annnd we're on." Mar spoke with finality. James stood while Kevin and Stacie assumed seats on their side of the table. His fingers dug into the backs of his chair while they waited for a connection.

"Come on…" Dolly whispered under her breath, loud enough for the room to hear, her cigarette sending a wreath of smoke into the still air.

*What's going on?* James thought, his nerves heightening by the tense moment and the reactions of the others. Judging by their behavior, this was not expected.

"What if—"

Mar's words were cut off by static from the speakers, and the figures in the room froze.

"Hello?" Dolly asked timidly. "Do we have contact? This is NOLA HQ." The woman waited, her cigarette poised at her lips. "Hello?" she repeated.

*Maybe the static was merely a blip in the device,* James thought when they received a response.

"Hey Dolly, it's Caitlin. How're things going?" The air, stifling moments earlier, lightened and Kevin's shoulders relaxed.

"Caitlin, good to hear your voice. Are you all safe?"

"Roger that, Dolly. Getting our video feed up..."—Caitlin's voice hung in the air until color splashed across the screen transforming into the face of James's sister—"now." She smirked into the camera.

"Good to see you," Mar said.

"You too. How's everything back home? The other team return yet? They see the *Imperator*? Is James jealous?" Caitlin asked.

"They're in the room with us now. Mission was a success." Dolly replied, waving for James to approach. He complied and squeezed between a gap in the tables towards the middle of the room to get closer to the screen.

"Hey there, we're back." He found it strange talking to his sister with her so far away. He was used to being the one reporting in, not the reverse. It did not sit well with him.

"I'm glad. Everyone make it back okay?" Caitlin asked.

James's head dropped. "Bob... He..."

"I heard. I'm sorry, James." Croyton's angular jawline cut into the picture, and the commander of the Federation assumed his position at the center of the lens. "He was a good man."

"What do you mean you heard?" James asked, not sure how to respond to his former commander.

"Claudia sent me a tunnel communication telling me you returned minus one and mission was accomplished. Success in my book," Croyton said, his eyes unwavering.

James's hands balled into fists and his nails dug into his palms. "It's not that simple. He wasn't a st—"

"We don't have time to go over this now James." The general turned to Dolly who sat behind James. "Give me a rundown of what's happened while I've been gone. We have two minutes."

As Dolly spoke, James's anger peaked. Croyton, brushing off the death of one of his own. One of James's best friends, more like a brother, and the general didn't consider it worth his time to learn more. Heat rising in his head, James walked to his place behind Kevin. Heather placed her hand over his.

"Brush it off," she said. James took a deep breath and let the moment sweep away from his mind. By the time he was ready to rejoin the conversation Dolly was almost finished with her report.

"We have three more transports headed north over the next few weeks. Then we're done."

"Good to hear it. NOLA defenses okay?"

"We'll be fine," Dolly replied. James grinned at Dolly's resistance. This wasn't his place.

"Good. We've got to keep moving. Caitlin!" James's sister reappeared over the general's shoulder. "Take this. We need to move."

"On it," Caitlin replied, accepting the device and rolling her eyes.

The room stifled their chuckles as the sound of truck engines emanated in the background.

"Give me a second," Catilin said, holding a finger to the camera.

"Take all the time you need," Dolly replied, waving at her protégé.

The camera went blank, and the team looked around the room restlessly as sounds came over the speakers in muffled bursts of bangs and shuffling gear. Finally, two more truck engines roared to life, doors slammed shut, and the camera came back on.

The HOLO's angle had changed to the center of their truck console's dashboard. Croyton drove next to Caitlin.

"Can you guys see everything okay?"

"We've got you," Kevin spoke up from his spot in the room. Caitlin smiled, giving him a thumbs-up. James glanced at the giant chef who returned the gesture with a grin.

"We're thirty miles out from the Park. We'll hit the Park's border in the next five minutes or so. I talked to our contact. Said we shouldn't have a problem coming through the front door," Croyton said.

"That's good news," Dolly replied.

"Surprising even," Stacie said. Her brow furrowed, and she looked over the intel packets that Croyton had sent over. "Who is this guy? Seb?"

"Their leadership. Came out of the Western Federation. I knew of him, but he worked in a different part of the military. My source tells me he's a good guy but hates the Federation."

James snorted, loud enough for a glare from Dolly, a grin from Kevin, and a poke from Heather.

"Sentiment aside, he's managed to do the impossible here and bring the entire Exil force under a single banner. We didn't ever expect that to happen. We need them as much as they need us though. The BZ put up a stone wall on their borders running massive Sentinel defenses along the Western Front."

Thousands of the spectral soldiers entered James's mind, and he could only imagine what an entire border of Sentinels could look like.

"They're consolidating manpower elsewhere," Heather said.

"You got it. They know we're ready to take on their Sentinels, so why not leave them here?" Croyton pulled the wheel sharply to the side, and Caitlin grabbed the HOLO emitter to stop its sliding.

"Exils haven't figured it out yet."

"They have. Don't have the infrastructure to fight like us though. Tents and lean-tos aren't the same as full blown cities," Croyton replied as the car steadied again. "Either way. We can be an asset to them and vice versa."

"They send us soldiers, and we give them the ability to destroy the Sentinels?" James asked.

"That's right. But more importantly we end the war."

"Don't the Exils want a different world than us?" Heather asked, echoing James's thoughts.

"Who gives a shit what they want? This is the only option. If the—"

*BOOM!*

The camera shook. Waves of static coursed through the images of Croyton and Caitlin.

Jumbled yells and shattering glass tumbled out of the speakers accompanied by the familiar sounds of gunshots and large explosions.

"Caitlin?!" Kevin yelled from his seat. The chef towered over everyone in the room and stared at the screen as smoke passed over the camera lens. Shadowy figures moved in the background and the grunts of a physical struggle blasted through the room. Fighting bounced off the walls. Unable to do anything, James's gripped the back of his chair in horror, hoping his sister was still alive.

*Pop pop pop.*

Gunshots continued, waves of apprehension poured down James's spine. Without warning, a hand fell limply in front of the lens. The lone appendage was dragged away leaving a blank, cracked screen and whisps of smoke.

The camera on the HOLO shook and was freed from its place on the console. Daylight shone through facing the frozen ground and its liberator turned the camera around.

A bald man with a shadowy dark beard stared at them. His eyes were ringed with exhaustion, but held the same maniacal look as Croyton's. The eyes of a man who lived with any decision, good or bad, the same way.

He glared at the faces staring at him through the HOLO, and James tasted blood from his cheek.

"Now we know you'll negotiate for real," the man said, a commanding drawl accompanied his voice. "Be here in a week." With that the camera turned off, and silence engulfed the room.

Kevin left the room and James followed him, skipping down the stairs. He did not need to look behind to know Stacie and Heather were on his heels.

This was it. They had a war to win.

# Glossary

**Asian Republic** – otherwise known as the BlankZone (BZ). The part of the world East of Europe that stopped responding to any interaction with the rest of the world after the Melt.

**Bio-Medicine** – devices and remedies that utilize advanced DNA synthesis to speed up and aid in the healing process.

**Centria** – capital city of the BlankZone.

**Combat Suit** – tactical uniform that is designed for use in battlefield situations. Multiple versions of combat suits exist with the newest versions containing highly elaborate camouflaging technology.

**Deerfield** – an independent city-state that operates entirely in isolation.

**Emitter** – a device used to support the display of a HOLO.

**Exil** – outlaw member of society found in the Federation. While there are some larger groups of Exils in the Federation most are independent bands of former Federation soldiers who survive by any means possible.

**Federation of the Americas** – the continental government organization comprised of every nation state in North and South America. Formed as a response to the Melt.

**Forgotten World** - an independent, pseudo-terrorist organization that is believed to have taken over the BlankZone.

**HOLO** – an acronym standing for Highly Operable Light Object. HOLOs have a wide range of capabilities and are used in telecommunications, visual representations, and have uses far beyond their current known abilities.

**Ionic Weaponry** – anti-Sentinel devices used by the Federation and NOLA soldiers.

**Loom** – terraforming devices created by the BlankZone to reshape the world to meet their needs.

**Mag Key** – a device that uses magnetic fields to lock objects.

**The Melt** – an event of unknown origin that separated the world and created a rift between the East and the West during a heightened period of global interaction.

**Midway** – newly formed city after the Melt that can be found along the East Coast of the Northern Federation in the Mid-Atlantic region.

**NOLA** – a semi-centralized fighting force based in New Orleans. Home base for many Federation soldiers who did not want to become Exils after the fall of the Federation. Many of the former recruits with James joined up and hunt Sentinels or are rented out to independent city-states for protection from the BlankZone.

**Nomad** – citizen members of the Federation who travel the land rather than attach themselves to a group.

**Pulse Pillar** – large ionic weapons erected in most Federation cities as defensive measures against Sentinel attacks.

**Republic of New World Order** – The official name of the BlankZone's nation.

**The Roll** – the action taken by Federation, NOLA, and independent ship captains when they are breaking through the BZ's seabound defenses.

**Río Negro** – town in the Southern Federation near the BlankZone border.

**Roach** – a small, automated video drone used for surveillance activities.

**Sentinel** – a defensive tool used by the BlankZone to protect its borders.

**The Wall** – a self-sustaining tidal wave that runs as protection for the BZ's home waters.

# Acknowledgements

As always I have to give a tremendous amount of thanks to every single person involved in this book. I've said this in every single acknowledgment that I write, but it is absolutely due to the people I have surrounded myself with that make my writing worth it. When I started out, I edited by myself, thought of the story by myself, and put everything together by myself. The result sucked. Having the people around me to assist and push themselves to make my dream a reality is humbling and pushes me to do better.

To my first editor, my mom, thank you for pushing so hard to meet the deadlines I set. I know that I can ask a lot, but the fact that you were able to make it happen means the world to me. To Hannah, my copy editor, it is always after I read your work that the book stops being a manuscript and becomes something publishable. To Daniel, my cover editor, thank you again for putting together such a great illustration of the character. And finally, to Alexa, my wife, marketer and the chief reason why I do *any* of this, thank you. For everything.

Wrapping up the fourth book in the series I realized the thing I like the most about writing is creating connections between the characters. Building relationships whether they are familial, platonic, or romantic is what makes characters interesting at the end of a story. No one sits there and remembers what a character did in a vacuum, but how they interacted with the world around them. I think that started for me at a young age, getting to know my sisters: Kathleen, Margaret and Maryclare. You three laid the foundation for how I communicate and work with the rest of society and that goes directly into my books. Whether it's writing the beginnings of a friendship or figuring out how to word a challenging piece of dialogue I always have my first friends to think back on and use as reference material. Thank you for giving me that.

Finally, I do want to thank you, the reader. Over the last five years and four books you have stuck with me.

Living through the publishing errors, long story lines, the (hopefully) tragic endings to some of your favorite characters; thank you. This is the penultimate book in the Crafting Humanity series and, if I'm being honest, a story that was never in the cards when I first planned the series, but I was so excited to write it. I loved exploring the world of the BZ and I really hope you all did too. As I write this, I am nearing the end of Book Five and it is the strangest thing in the world to me. I set out to write one book 13 years ago and ended up here, finishing the fifth book in the series, two more than I ever planned, and am already looking ahead to more stories in the future. By the time I'm writing the acknowledgement for the next book I hope I can give you more news on that front, but for now I'll keep it at thank you. Thank you so much for taking the time out of your day to read my book. It is an honor to be chosen by you.